Multiple Exposure

A Novel

Shana Thornton

Thorncraft Publishing
Clarksville, Tennessee

This novel is a work of fiction. Names, characters, incidences, and places are the products of the author's imagination or used fictitiously. Any resemblance to actual individual people, living or dead, places, or events is completely coincidental.

ISBN-13: 978-0-615-65508-6
ISBN-10: 0615655084

Library of Congress Control Number: 2012941646

Thorncraft Publishing
P.O. Box 31121
Clarksville, TN 37040
thorncraftpublishing@gmail.com

Printed in the United States of America

10 9 8 7 6 5 4 3 2 1

For Terry,
who is a wonderful husband and father,
and who continues to believe in me.

CONTENTS

ACKNOWLEDGMENTS

My gratitude goes to those people who helped me to create this novel by reading, editing, and donating your time and services.
Terry, I appreciate your confidence and your words, "Listen to me. Trust me," especially when I was full of doubt. Thank you for bringing sushi, wine, coffee, and nourishment to me during all of the late nights you learned to enjoy. Thank you for supporting me and pushing me to take the time to tell this story.

Kitty Madden and Beverly Fisher, This novel wouldn't be the same without your edits and questions. You were essential to this creation, and I thank you for giving your time and editing skills. You are valuable friends, readers, and editors.

Bill Ferguson, Thank you for your corrections and expertise. Your advice made this a much better book.

Melissa Corliss DeLorenzo, Working with you has been an inspiration. Thank you for your honesty and for going through the book line-by-line.

Stacy Leiser, I feel lucky to have received your edits and suggestions just in time.

Christy O'Brien, Your intuitive guidance has been unmatched. Thank you for communicating the confidence you have in my abilities and for everything you've given to this project.

Mitzi Cross, I am so grateful for our long walks and talks, for the times when we sweated together, both literally and metaphorically, and for your praise.

Mom and Dad, Thank you both for a lifetime of encouragement and support.

To those who read the book in all of its many drafts and offered feedback, criticism and encouragement—my Mom, Rachel Barrett, Deb Burdin, Amanda Thornton, and Rita Yerrington. I am so blessed and thankful to have you in my life.

i

1 EXISTING LIGHT

The cave was dark in the night and all the day. The cave was hollowed out with moans and whirling whispers, and birthed darkness into the light, allowing her self to be used by the water and limestone, the bear, the tribes and visitors. They torched the walls to create a guide, but only the bear could nestle, could soothe and settle the milk in her breasts. Those paws scratching out a low dip for a bed. Palm of the earth cupped for their hairy grunt and slumber. The bears didn't know anything about graffiti, the stuff I spray-painted when the boys held my feet in the palms of their hands. They didn't know those feet kicking the columns, pounding, pounding, pounding repetitions to topple the innards of the interior. Another sweaty boy's running will—his full might to kick a column in the cave formed by a patient drip. Hacking to sever the crack at the base of a stalagmite. Those bears didn't see it. They already left and didn't allow the invisible to consume them. The bears took those hefty strides. They followed a path out of here, to a range that jutted onto higher elevations. Their mother led the passage and they had been gone for so long that we almost forgot this place belonged to them. People had forgotten too much about the cave and its inhabitants, and out of what was left, we wove the lies with our own history.

*****

Memories filter in and drift out again, and it's easier for me to remember other people's histories, and facts about their lives, rather than my own youth. I do remember the first plum I ever ate, probably because my dad died that year, and everything changed for me. I can't recall when the hallucinations began, but around this time they started to take shape. The star Sirius was somewhere in the sky overhead illuminating the hot breath of the Big Dog constellation. The Dog Days of summer baked the grass in the field where my cousins and I drank the juice from plums. I was seven and the only girl. My cousin Jordan was a year older and naturally curious about spiders and anatomy. He had three younger brothers, each a year apart. My older brother Tyler was twelve, and too sophisticated to be curious about anything. I was submerged in the ways of boys who wanted to be men—their world of searching, tracking, tagging, and classifying.

Aunt Darcy gave us red waxy plums from the family trees used for making brandy. The plum trees my family cloned over and over swelled with virgin juice that was called "almost too good to be fermented" since they produced good eating *and* drinking fruit, or so I had heard. Even though I was offered plums all my life, the puckering look on someone's face created my easy refusal to bite into one until then. That summer day I don't recall any reluctance. My teeth simply tore into the skin, puncturing the taut dark exterior that gave way to the soft, sweet flesh inside. I slid a piece of plum into the corners of my mouth to chew. Just below the ear, my jaw caught and jumped with the sharp ripple of waxy sweetness that escaped from the skin of the fruit. My nose squished itself into full lips with a hard pucker. My eyes shut and fluttered and opened wide. I quickly took another bite and held the juice from the skin in the dip of my tongue. The plum contained the perfect tartness. No other fruit, or even candy, could match it.

Aunt Darcy sat on the shaded patio connected to the greenhouse, where trees had been grafted. She called with one echoing shout that pitched itself on the end of my name. "Ell—LEN!" Then she flicked her fingernails into the sun above her head, waving me toward her. I was barefoot. The juice of the plum ran down my arm and chin and streaked across my feet. As I approached the patio, I picked up my shirt again to wipe away the stickiness.

"Don't show your navel to the boys," Aunt Darcy whispered as she put up a flat hand with cinnamon-colored nails as a sign that the boys should not come any closer. They trailed behind me and were closing in quickly. I was confused.

"Your belly button," she said. "Don't show it to the boys."

I didn't understand. I looked down at my stomach and expected to see something suddenly different about my belly button—perhaps an extra oozing body part, a sign that said NO boys allowed, a black hole into outer space. But there was only a wrinkly little indention as if a balloon had been tied off and floated far away somewhere. That's how I began to imagine it sometimes once Aunt Darcy brought it to my attention—that it was a secretive area of the body.

Aunt Darcy continued, "You're growing into a pretty girl and you shouldn't show the boys your navel. That's private." She whispered even though they couldn't hear us.

"I didn't show it to them."

"I know you didn't mean to, but when you wipe your mouth, they can see it. Boys are curious. Here's a towel so you can wipe your mouth. Just be careful and don't raise up your shirt in front of the boys!"

I kept tugging at the bottom of my shirt the rest of the day. My cousins and brother walked in the crispy golden grass, combing it for spiders and other bugs. Jordan kept aquariums that housed black widows that we found around Granna's garden. Knobby and loud, Granna was an atypical grandma, and I created her name when I was a baby with fat legs and no memory retention. Granna wouldn't spray insecticide to kill the spiders no matter how many we found. Jordan had found a black widow in a web underneath a G.I. Joe Jeep. Another was under the lip of the concrete stairs leading to the basement. A brown recluse lived in the retaining wall on the outside of the basement.

Jordan wanted to know what his mother had told me.

"Nothing," I said and moved my head so that a clump of my blonde hair fell over my eyes. I turned away behind my shoulder. That was my defense against my cousins. It was a defense that didn't work later in my life too often, but at least Jordan respected that simple gesture.

At seven years old, I was taller than Jordan and his brothers. Actually, I was almost level with Tyler and he was five years older, almost a teenager. My pale shoulders sagged as I strolled across the field, away from the pack of boys. I've learned that this posture signals weakness and invites others who are stronger to follow unless they have more promising prospects for play, so I've tried to correct my spooned-over shoulders, among other things.

"Come on, tell us," Jordan pestered me and followed, which made the other boys follow too, even my brother. If

I had confidently marched across the field, they might have left me alone. But I sneaked a sulking glance over my shoulder.

Jordan begged to know what his mother had said. He trailed after me, repeating, "Come on and tell us." When I felt far enough away from Darcy so that the swell of the field obscured the looks on their faces, I revealed that my navel was supposed to be a secret. Jordan asked to see it in order to make sure nothing was wrong with it. He excitedly thought that I might have a deformity of some sort.

"A colored navel or one that oozes green liquid," he said laughing. "Oh, or a teeny baby might be stuffed in there and if we close one eye and squint, we might be able to see it swimming inside of Ellen's private parts."

He wanted to see it, and so did his little brothers who nodded their heads in unison. I glanced toward the greenhouse but could only see the top points of glass reflecting the sun. I took a deep breath and lifted my shirt and turned my head to the side with my eyes closed. The boys were quiet. I waited for a few seconds but they were too quiet. I opened my eyes and looked at my navel, then at the boys. They had lifted their shirts and were staring at one another's navels. Jordan lifted up his shirt too. "Looks the same as mine," he said. He stared over at Tyler who squatted to the side of them. "What about yours?" Jordan asked.

"Forget it, gay-wads."

"What's a gay-wad?" Jordan asked.

Tyler stood and strolled back toward the house. "Stupid little kids," he muttered.

"He's weird," Jordan said and glanced quickly at me. "Sorry, Ellen." He let his shirt fall down.

That afternoon we found a scorpion in the grass. Tyler almost stepped on it with his bare feet. We blinked with full-moon eyes. None of Jordan's field guides mentioned that scorpions should live here.

The scorpion was then housed in its own special aquarium. About a week later, it killed one of the black widows and the brown recluse when my cousins decided to have a fighting competition with the arachnids and insects they had collected. Jordan wanted to know if a spider would eat a scorpion. I couldn't watch the fights. I saw two minutes of the scorpion versus the black widow. The scorpion unrolled its stinger with a sudden sharp arch that seemed to vibrate repeatedly for an instant then recoiled. I was mesmerized in that moment, but walked away, imagining the terror they both felt.

That was the summer Aunt Darcy decided that I couldn't shower with the boys or change clothes in the same room anymore, either. I could hear them laughing in an adjoining room. I could hear them arguing in the shower. Another rule came that night when I could no longer sleep in the same room. That's when I suddenly knew too much without being able to name it. Maybe I tried to forget the disconnection from my family by drinking at such a young age. Maybe my dad's death and drinking caused the hallucinations of the boy and the Native tribe, or maybe I drank to forget my real life and imagined another one around the cave.

MULTIPLE EXPOSURE

*****

Cumberland Cave had smooth teeth carved into the limestone. Eighty years ago, they were precisely polished stone steps that swayed along the cliffs with deep curves. They welcomed big brass bands performing on riverboats that docked in the city. Musicians from Benny Goodman's band left the riverside and the city; they cruised out of town and carried trumpets and drums, the clarinet, into the twilight area of Cumberland Cave where they danced audiences into the kingdom of swing.

Under the moonlight, people were pushed by the humidity, smothered toward the cave, where cool air currents gushed out of the darkness. In the white-gloved hands of ladies, fans fluttered beside the delicate moths of dusk. Helen Ward's voice serenaded across the salty, sparkling limestone. In the pockets of men, you could smell flasks, shots of Tennessee brandy made by my family. Even during the prohibition, the Masters family continued making their traditional plum brandy and bribed the local authorities. Granna said that most of the farmers were caught up in making applejack, brandy from apple trees, but the Masters focused on plums. "Smart decision since those temperance ladies waged war on the apple tree cause of the Jack's trading it and cut them down. Plums made it through." She smiled. The Masters family always "turned the tables" and my Granna was fond of playing Benny Goodman's song. Since the mid-1800s, the plum trees had been cloned and cultivated with care about a mile from Cumberland Cave. Masters Brandy quenched the thirsts of the cave's visitors for generations and those stories grasped my attention since I could prop my head up to listen and skin my knees on the trails surrounding the park.

The afternoon I found the turtle, I had sneaked and tried my first sips of the family brandy. After the hot flush of swiping the brandy and running away, my young mind didn't think about which direction, just away, I found myself perched on a short bluff close to Cumberland Cave. Then, I wandered the trails until the heat blurred my vision and dragged my shoulders down, until I stumbled and scraped my palms, elbows, and kneecaps. Tiny rocks and dust embedded into the skin and got trapped in the blood. Anticipation quickened my pace as I approached the cool entrance to the cave, longing to sit in the cold shade and place my hands on the stones to stop the stinging sensation that pulsed across my limbs. I was thinking about the stage and what it must have been like to hear the big bands. In our house, Granna had pointed to a photograph of Helen Ward, her name signed with a red pen across the bottom. One of Edythe Wright in a thin dress and Tommy Dorsey with a trombone. All signed to The Masters Family. The music, "You Must Have Been a Beautiful Baby," an elusive sunny side of the street, filled my childhood with nostalgia for something I had never experienced.

On the trails, I imagined that Edythe Wright removed her high heels while she walked around the lake toward the cave. I wanted to envision where she stood on the stage. My sweaty hair clung to my face and shoulders and caused a constant irritation. I climbed the ramp to the cave and stopped while I twisted my hair swiftly into a knot on the top of my head and wound a band around it tightly. It fell forward and perched itself like a horn on the front of my head. That's when I saw the turtle sitting in the center of the platform. Its eyes closed slowly as if absorbing me. Then, it looked as if it had been awaiting my arrival. I could feel its focus on me in the emerging silence. "Turtle?" I said aloud. Turtles stretched their necks, poised on the toppled dead trees along the edge of the lake, but I had never seen one on the platform.

As I walked closer to the turtle, the smile slipped from my face. I saw the slick, wet pulse oozing with yellow running tissue and dark pieces of jagged shell crushed into the tender, exposed flesh. Part of the shell splintered into the turtle's back right foot. The turtle moved its head in and out of the shell with sleepy old eyes. The shell looked like it had been smashed. My head was hot, and I felt trapped as I looked around, enraged, searching for the boys responsible for the cruelty.

No people were in sight. There was silence except for the cicadas, chirps from cardinals, squirrels bouncing through leaves. The turtle retreated in and out of its splintered and broken shell, stretching its neck toward me, in a constant rocking motion, as if at some point when it retreated, the darkness would be there waiting for her, the home that she had always known would cover her safely once again. I searched at the turtle's foot, followed the bloody trail twenty yards to a small pool of blood that shined in a circle of sunlight filtering through the trees.

I looked up and found myself standing underneath the bluff that hangs over the cave's mouth. My head pounded at the temples as my hands trembled. Above me, a rock ledge was lush with ferns, small cedar and oak, violets, stones, and leaves. The turtle had fallen onto the concrete in an effort to reach water. It crashed onto the pavement. Dropped, probably flipped back feet overhead at least once, just like in one of those lazy cartoons. Only in real life, the turtle fell from the rocky, rugged overhang where vines and tiny rocks and water dripped onto the concrete platform that was poured into the mouth of Cumberland Cave.

I quickly ran back to the turtle and knelt in front of it. As I glanced through my hair that had fallen into my face, I saw a boy, dark with black hair falling down his back. He carried a fishing pole made from river cane and glanced over his shoulder in my direction, but continued forward. "Hey!" I shouted, thinking maybe he could help me know what to do. I shouted again, closing my eyes in the middle of the shout, and when I opened them, he was gone. Gone. I looked behind me, and nowhere did I see him. The turtle pushed its head into my hovering hand. I was astonished by the turtle's determination to reach the water—the continued journey after the tragedy of its fall. After the shocking smack of concrete, the turtle had dragged itself toward the water, bits of shell falling along the way, slivers of flesh, a deep wet stripe of blood that didn't completely fade for months. I returned daily and could mark the spot years later, even if I couldn't really see it anymore but had only memorized the location from my reverence to the turtle.

I didn't know what to do, except kneel there in front of it, my hand stretched out, hovering over the dark, scrabble skin of the turtle's legs and neck. Its smooth shell screamed and swooned and pierced its wet, fragile body. I stood there without any ideas about how to stop the pain. *The turtle wanted to go to the water*, I thought, *but it didn't make it.* And suddenly, I couldn't deal with discovering more pain, more death. I trembled and turned away from the turtle and started down the ramp again, looking for the boy. I stopped. My shoulders sagged and swayed, and sweat slid around my face and tickled my skin and ears. That irritated me. I couldn't get the image of the turtle's eyes out of my mind, and the way it stretched its neck out to me, and just as abruptly, I turned and quickly scooped up the turtle. I didn't know what made me do it, but I had to. The wet blood stuck to my palms. I bobbled the flesh in my hands thinking that I didn't want to add to the turtle's pain while it tried to retreat into its home. Small, quick streams of blood wrapped swiftly around my wrists and dripped to the ground as I turned the corner. At the shoreline, I closed my eyes as tightly as possible, and whispered, "Please forgive me turtle. I want to take away your pain," and placed the turtle in the water. It sank with blood catching the clouds of mud and algae in the water. The feet tried a frenzied run, a quick thrash and let go. I saw its legs fan limply against the mud before the water was too clouded to see any more details.

As I hurried around the lake and crossed the creek, I noticed the boy staring from the bank with his fishing pole in hand. His dark skin had blended into the trees that stood on that edge of the lake, where old trunks spilled over and started the stream running to the river. That same stream passed Aunt Darcy's house. I stopped and faced the boy. His eyes were fixed on mine and his mouth was a straight line, as if he knew what I was doing, that I had killed the turtle. I wondered what I would do if he said something to me about it, but he looked down at the end of his fishing pole where a shiny fish flopped in shattered glints on the end of the line. Then, he glanced at me through the corner of one eye as he tilted his head with a smile. His black hair suddenly arched away from his back and his body thrust itself as his arms shook in the air, in imitation of the fish. He laughed and pointed at me and flopped his arms again. A car horn blared in my ears suddenly and I looked down at the pavement, the street, the Cadillac and the man waving his arm and beeping. I moved to the side of the street, bewildered by how I was there, and looked back to the shoreline, but didn't see the boy. The man rolled down the window, "You alright? You lost?"

I pointed ahead of me, into the sun, "I live just up there. Sorry, I thought I saw someone, and I didn't see you there."

"Try to pay attention. You could get ran over."

I was walking by this time. "Sorry," I interrupted.

"Hey, have you been—" The driver began to ask but another car was behind him, horn beeping, driver throwing up a hand. "Hurry home, kid," he said and muttered, "Masters family… always…" as he rolled up his window and flipped his sun visor down.

2 DEPTH OF FIELD

I fell in love with David amid all the books and his photographs of every corner. Falling in love helped me remain disconnected from my thoughts. You might think that since he was a photographer and we built a small darkroom in the basement of the house we rented that I'd have all kinds of darkroom intensity and passion to talk about, but I don't. The truth is, the darkroom cloaked us, and when we were in the same space with all those chemicals, I couldn't smell our sweat and heat and saliva. I liked that, to be alone with our smells and know they combined to make something different. Too much covered it as the years passed. I always wanted light, to be able to see what was going on. I didn't close my eyes when I made love to David, not then anyway.

We met in college. David was originally from Montana, but his dad was in the Army and moved the family all over the Southeast. Just before he retired, he ended up in this town. After David started college, his parents moved back to the mountains. David called them by their proper names then. Phil and Linda were back where they could drive around with a shotgun mounted to the window of the truck, back where people had sense enough to turn on their headlights every time they got into the car to drive, back where you didn't need a gun permit to carry. David had mimicked them in college, even making fun of them sometimes, as if he were so much more laid back and refined. After getting back to their home state, they couldn't manage a visit even once a year. I didn't know them and didn't know what to say for conversation. I took a double take at the airport just to be certain I was picking up the right people. And Linda talked about how much better Montana was, while Phil dropped in statistics about his home state.

I inherited our first home, much to their chagrin, since they wanted David to come back home with them and raise his family there. But our home was my grandparent's property across from the cave, and we were moving into real life. I took a job at the University, while David started his own business. We were on the brink of dreams coming together, but the images didn't take. You can't get a roll of film back once it has been exposed to the light. And, David was bored, complained that he was begging people to take photos of their kids and their families—he had to entertain a crying sixteen-month-old and get a perfect shot of the baby, sitting in the grass on a hot Fourth of July.

"It doesn't mean anything," he said to me, slumped on the couch. "I've tried to get jobs in journalism, and there's nothing around here."

I didn't want to take the bait, didn't want to move, give up my career, a position I just started at the University with the possibility of tenure. I couldn't change—I was so stuck and attached to my home, to my family's history, the town where my dad died. For my PhD, I drove three days a week, two hours each way, in order to stay in place. I chose the closest university with a program and committed to four years, nothing else, until a position opened at the University here. I published enough papers, drove to presentations and flew to conferences, but I couldn't think about moving. Leaving my Granna before she died was inconceivable, and just considering a move away from the farm after I inherited it felt like a betrayal.

But David was frustrated, stifled here. Living in a military town, an event like 9/11 isn't a cliché to consider life changing. Everyone knows retaliation is coming and that our community will be required to make sacrifices. Benefits will emerge, as they always do, but the hollow places prevail. Vacancy takes over. David took our move into real life to a new level by saying that he wanted to join the military. I argued, "How could you walk into a life that you've always complained about?"

Some men took an oath, touched their toes, scanned shadows and landscapes due to their natural instincts as warriors. They were born to hunt. It was essential to the survival of the species. Sometimes, I thought that David was only an imitator, absorbing instruction without needing verbal commands. He was a keen observer who could take sharp, precise photographs that were copies of other people's work. I blamed him, thinking that David lacked the self-discipline and originality to become a photojournalist for a major network or publication. After college, he had lingered in the nameless places with ezines that deteriorated within months. His talents dissipated in the framing shop and in the lines of film run through C41 processors at a drugstore. Weddings, babies and puppies, family portraits in matching shirts and pajamas, christenings, bar mitzvahs, rock performances by local bands at the local dive...that was the ragged run of paycheck-to-paycheck, scheduled twenty-four hours a day, self-employment in the photography business for David just after college. So, when the military suggested officer status and plenty of photo ops, David took the deal with his handshake and signatures, a quick bus ride to basic training and Officer Candidate School. His photographs became stunning, but they were secondary to his service in Iraq and Afghanistan. Taking photographs became something he did to distract himself. For his actions in combat, he won awards, stories he didn't want to share, and rows of ribbons.

"I could go to officer training almost right away," he said. I knew that this meant he would get the status that his dad never had. His parents hopped on the first plane when he told them about his decision. I was still trying to talk him out of it, but Phil wanted to hear the deal from the recruitment office himself. He wanted to be with his son.

"Only you can decide," Phil said, removing his ball cap and wiping the sweat from his bald head with a handkerchief. David and his dad fished at the lake, while Linda and I sat in lawn chairs and stared at the stagnant water. "You're the one who has to live it," Phil said. Linda held the fishing rod until Phil replaced the handkerchief in his back pocket. David stood beside his dad. They had the same stance, their weight placed on the left leg. David's shaggy, black curls flipped out of his ball cap. I noticed that David looked tired behind the stubble, like the decision weighed him down. Phil must have noticed as well. He said, "Will you be okay with losing all that hair?" Phil laughed.

"Last thing I'm concerned about," David said and shrugged.

"You might as well enjoy having longer hair while you can," Linda said. She ate potato chips and licked the salt from her fingers. I slapped at mosquitoes on my shins. The flies buzzed around my head. "I always envied your hair color," Linda said while tapping her fingernails against the plastic on the armrest. "Don't you, Ellen?" I nodded.

David asked his mom, "What do you really think?"

"About the Army?" she asked and kept right on talking without waiting for an answer. "Your dad would have given anything for this opportunity. I mean, I don't think you'll have any problem getting into the candidate school and making officer. Just decide if you want to do it."

"I don't know what else to do," he said and turned the reel on his fishing rod. "I can't continue developing pictures of birthday parties, and nothing, just nothing important."

Phil watched the dragonflies' shadows moving below us and turned to try and find the owners of the shadows behind our heads. He laughed a little when two of the dragonflies flicked their iridescent wings and shimmery bodies against one another. "David," he said, glancing in my direction from the corner of his eye, "do you remember how we used to fish here sometimes when you were in high school? To think, Ellen lived just over our shoulders the whole time."

I swatted a mosquito on my arm, smeared its body into my sweat and scratched at the red bump it created. I waved my hands around my face to chase away the gnats.

"Hmm," David murmured and nodded, looking out over the lake.

David's initial motivation to join the Army was boredom, and that night before we fell asleep, I accused him of seeking change in the wrong way.

"I want a purpose," he said. We lay in bed, facing one another. His voice was soft but earnest. "To believe I can

19

be different," he said. "Please, don't think I'm stupid, but this is a higher purpose for me. I need to know that I could help change the world somehow."

"What about being a life-flight photographer for a hospital or something like that, like we talked about before?" I asked, my heart jumping up and down in my throat with the feeling that I wouldn't change his mind no matter what occupations I suggested.

"That's a nursing degree," he said. "And, I have a photography degree. Besides, the Army will pay me during the training. They'll pay for any further education I need, and I'll be working, doing something more than standing behind a counter in a drug store."

The next day, he signed and quit the drugstore. He would take a bus away from me and we didn't know where it would lead.

In the midst of all that training, he became branded by that role in his life. He had a mission that he believed in, even if I didn't always have sharp clues as to what that might be. He tried to capture the truth from different ways of life with his camera—he said, "Defense is crucial to survival," and closed his eyes, inhaled, waited and added after opening his eyes, "Sometimes defense means advancement, making a move." He compared it to buying a home and then protecting it, having the right to defend it. When I considered our child living in that home, or someone else's child, then I understood how he looked through a window.

David was gone to train here and there, lived in another state to train for a Special Forces unit. I didn't know all of his moves, and maybe I was always in that fog since birth. I sensed that other academics were as well, so that's why I remained safe in the confines of the classroom, where I didn't always have to speak. I could write or move phantom-like through doorways and down stairways on campus, show up for some committee meetings, take notes, lecture, and publish a little paper at a regional conference—enough for me. Before his first deployment, I got pregnant with Maggie, and we made the choice to provide stability to her by staying put in a town that was familiar to me, in a town that contained my history. This place retained more than I often wanted to remember, but I learned to claim it. Is stability about the people or the place or both? David and I asked ourselves that several times.

We chose to create a home base and provide that to David whenever possible. He was often assigned to a post in another state. David said, "My answer may not be ordinary but neither is my job. Since my job is high-risk, you should maintain a home for you and Maggie that could outlive me."

After a few weeks at home again, he traveled the desert in Iraq and climbed cliffs in Afghanistan with one hundred pound rucksacks on his back and shot photographs of the tribal ways of life that had endured in that country. Sixty pounds of baby weight stuck to my hips, thighs, biceps, and stomach as I climbed the stairs of my childhood home with my arms full of boxes. I swore to distract myself from worrying about David and the war by sorting my grandmother's collections from her eighty years on the planet. She died suddenly, in her sleep. Her body was just worn out, and I was at peace when I found her motionless in her bed. Relief settled into me easily like I had been worn down slowly by a smooth river. Everything was too simple, the funeral washed on by.

You might say, the business in my head kept going. After David was deployed, I broke the monotony of teaching and sorting by walking the trails on our property and across the street at Cumberland Cave with Maggie curled into a sling as a newborn, then a front pack, and finally a backpack. Loaded with Maggie while climbing those hills, I caught eerie glimpses of my childhood doppelganger.

I ended up in the military life even though it had been one of my greatest fears. I was always traveling after the ghost of my dad, trying to capture something more significant than his death. It's a shattered memory—sharp fragments that solidify more in my dreams. I was six years old and had just returned home from school when I found my dad. He was blue, strained, and unconscious. Those are my best adult words to describe that particular breath in my life. The electric energy was sharp but silent. Something rattled my teeth. I screamed repeatedly. The only thing Mother had ever said about that afternoon was that I shrieked and trembled, and had to be given oxygen since a panic attack ensued. Dad was wearing his uniform when I found him in the basement. A light was shining down from a shelf. I can only guess that he was repairing something, but I could never begin to guess what it might have been. Sometimes, I pretended it was a toy, other times a bike, part of a car, maybe he was cleaning a gun, or simply organizing his tools. I never knew him in the way someone wants to know her father.

My flimsy limited memories of him are Number One, of a day when I cried for Mother until Dad was so angry that he threatened to spank me. I ran away from him, around and around the bed, then under the bed, and he went from side to side trying to catch me until he began to laugh and gave up on the spanking. Number Two, he took me to my first day at kindergarten, and he wore his uniform. Nothing else was significant about the day. I don't recall any words of wisdom that he passed down or any moment of rescue. A few simple moments are all that I remember. Number

Three, he made me eat scrambled eggs one morning for breakfast and I vomited on the floor beside the table. Number Four, he sang Roy Orbison songs with me, and we danced in the kitchen while Mother cooked. Maybe this happened one time only, but I like to imagine that it was more frequent. Number Five, he often fell asleep in our backyard tent and stayed there all night. At Granna's house, everyone joked that Dad stayed the night in the tent and cooked breakfast on the campfire the next morning, while the boys walked back to the house in pairs during the night to find a bed in Aunt Darcy's house. At least, that's how my cousin Jordan tells the story when he reminisces about my dad. For me, Dad's death and all that transpired because of it replaced most of my memories.

After his death, Mother and my brother, Tyler, became stronger, certain and assertive. Their survival was aggressive. A wedge began to develop between the three of us. I was the loner, the sensitive and obscure one. We didn't talk about Dad or his death after the initial shock and social wave had dissipated. Mother was in school to become an aesthetician at the time and she finished, often leaving us with Granna and Aunt Darcy. I didn't mind since they were our connection to Dad, and Granna succeeded in providing distractions that kept me busy. She told me stories about the Masters family, about how to distill brandy, about the animals and their patterns, how to track something through the woods and find the patterns of the sky. I was so busy that I filtered out their gossip about Mother and her lack of mourning. Sometime within the next year at a conference, Mother met Darryl, a young dermatologist who was constantly in motion—shaking hands and making deals.

My brother was like his dog, following around at Darryl's side, taking mental notes, emulating, and happy to have a role model. Who could blame him? Dad had been tough on

Tyler, trying to make him more of an outdoorsman. Tyler liked pressed white shirtsleeves and cufflinks, the neat Mercedes, and the polished floors in Darryl's world. It was different and that was magnetic at such a crucial time in Tyler's life. Darryl lured Mother and my brother away, even though his actions weren't deliberate, but I didn't conform to Darryl's life, I couldn't escape the memories of my dad and his family, even if they were filmy. I wanted to hold on to my dad's fading hand as tightly as possible, while Mother and Tyler adjusted swiftly to Darryl as their savior. They were all on a zip line and dragging me along a year later to Georgia where Darryl moved his dermatology practice, away from Granna and my cousins, from the city where the only memories of Dad I possessed could be maintained.

*****

Maggie learned to sing when I rocked her at night in the white wicker chair that faced a window draped by a purple sheet. We watched the clouds bloom into sunset through the sheet that grew lighter with each sunrise. Eventually, it faded into the sky except for the bright, wilted sides that tried to slip to the floor. The street lights obscured most of the stars. I had lost the knack for identifying them.

Granna taught me the patterns in the sky, tricky dots with unbridled mythologies and histories, bearing down on people and leaving us breathless in reaching for explanations. When Aunt Darcy had shamed me about showing the boys my navel that summer, Granna laughed wildly, "Hon, that's your sugar bowl." Before I was a year old, Granna had proudly taught me to show off my sugar bowl to relatives and friends.

"Where's your sugar bowl?" Granna would ask and wink at her friend. My sticky kid fingers would grasp the hem of my dress and pull it up to reveal my navel. Granna said that I often fell over trying to get a look at it myself. Granna laughed until she coughed. She told me that story over and over as I grew up. Since I couldn't adapt to their way of life, Mother and Darryl had sent me to live with Granna. I was such a loner, anti-social with a book covering my face, lost somewhere in the woods. After a month of trying to push me toward the bus stop, Granna gave up and home-schooled. It was easier than tracking me down after receiving a phone call from the school secretary that informed her of another day when I skipped. I could be counted on to read and study when left alone and that was enough for her. For years, I rarely left the property, except to explore Cumberland Cave and the park.

Granna rested her thick hands on my shoulders. She dug her thumbs along my spine, following my hair up to my neck. I tensed but waited to move away, slinking as the star Vega does along the horizon during the summer. Granna could be described in the way that she described her land, as a hard-tanned farm. The limestone creek that bordered the prehistoric glacial shelf plumped the rugged character of Granna's hundred and fifty acres, which contained my Aunt Darcy's home, where she and my cousins lived until I was fifteen, when Darcy married a man assigned to a military post in Alaska, where they went to live.

Like Granna, I had developed the habit of talking to myself, especially at night while searching for the stars. I audibly reasoned and questioned the possibilities. The vast is tricky and needs the defining points repeated sometimes. I wasn't surprised when anyone talked to themselves, muttered grocery lists under their breaths in the store, tilted their heads and counted on their fingers when thinking about errands, or laughed aloud when recalling a conversation with a friend. Yet it did startle me to discover Maggie lying on her back and talking to herself in the middle of the night. I had been jostled out of bed by a dream—I was standing on a street corner in the desert, meeting some men and carrying a baby in a baseball bag. I bent down, unzipped the bag a little, and tapped the baby on the nose. It smiled at me. Then, I was running with the baby down the street, panicked. I could hear the pounding of my feet and the heavy breath from my mouth. My ear grazed hot concrete when I turned the corner.

When I sat up in bed, awake, I heard Maggie from the other room. At first, I thought that I was still dreaming, and then assumed that Maggie was crying. I hurried into the bedroom and realized in the doorway that Maggie was trying to sing, Twinkle, twinkle, little star. Maggie said, "Light. Light. Moon," and laughed. I noticed that the purple sheet had fallen from the window to reveal a large full moon. Maggie continued talking, "Cookie. Shoes. Sugar bowl. Knees. Toes. Eyes. Teeth. Cookie. Moon..." Practicing all of the words that she had learned and chuckling every so often.

Maggie was making a list, just like I did with everything, just like I had learned from Granna. Little scraps of paper would fall out of Granna's pockets, even the tiny pockets. Lists would linger in the bottom of her purse until they were worn, some words creased so deeply that they had faded in the center and lost their purpose, some lists contained the unchecked items from previous lists, lists of lists. Some items on a list might arrive and depart in the same day. I could swiftly draw a line across a word's neck. The words trailed down a post-it, a bank statement, and the back of a receipt, even a candy wrapper, and the jagged paper ripped from a notebook. Some words were flanked with stars and exclamation points, a date behind it. Dates.

They eerily coincided in ways the stars should not reveal in order for me to make facts of history.

Granna kept lists of her personal history. Dates and important events from the past, along with a list of dates for birthdays both dead and living, and the shorter list of anniversary dates. Dead birthdays, as she called them, were written in blue, while living ones were written in red. All other date lists were written in black ink. Granna kept a book of lists that named the containers of her beads and stones, titles of novels that stood on cedar shelves and wrapped the walls of her cedar home—the one built by Papa's grandfather from trees on the property.

Papa's family renovated the old house three times and created a distillery for making plum brandy. The Masters family story is that Papa's great-great-grandfather brought the Chickasaw plum trees from a valley along the Cumberland Plateau, where some tribes had lived in the caves and continued to cultivate the trees. The great-great-grandfather brought a load of trees back with a horse and wagon and everyone thought he was a loon to plant them on the one field of farmland on his property that stretched toward the river. He crossed those trees "with a Slavic variety," Granna said. I didn't know what that meant as a child, but later came to realize that he had created his own particular variety of plum. I've often wondered where he came across a Slavic variety of plum trees, but there are some mysteries that history can never recover.

After serving in World War II and later, being wounded by falling off the back of an Army Jeep, my grandfather Papa was paralyzed, but he distilled brandy for his entire life. I never knew him in person, just through the legacy of his work I could see in his home. Papa died shortly after a head-on collision the year before I was born. Granna was a carpenter and landscape artist who had made her rounds out West. She fired special tiles and used unique stones to create a garden dedicated to Papa. Then, after my dad died, Granna never made brandy again. She had never been ripened to the fruits of that labor, but had only continued because it was my grandfather's family legacy.

"Sometimes, we keep up a task for the history of preservation," she said when we were in the distillery, looking around for the last reserves. "I'm ashamed that I let your Papa down in that way." She stared at the barrels, balled her fists. "It was too much for me after Jake..." I wanted to hear more about my dad, but she stopped short, not bringing up his death. "Let's take a walk," she said with a sudden high ring in her voice.

The memorial garden she created for Papa wound through a cedar grove with reindeer moss and guardian stones that Granna hauled on her back from the limestone creek. The garden paths forked so that one ended at the plum orchard and the other stopped in the cemetery where Dad and Papa were buried along with a long line of Masters family members. We often ate lunch in the cedar grove. During the summer, we might have slivers of crunchy, biting jalapeños with onions and tomatoes drinking vinegar, scooping garlic from the bottom corners with the edge of chewy bread. Granna slipped avocados in half adding twisted limes and dusty cumin. She smelled like a vinegar-stewed cherry. The trees that Papa planted on the edge of the hillside sang out in shrill, little tart cherries every spring. Granna and I fought the birds into the highest branches and ate too many before we were out of the tree. We carried the few that remained in our basket up the hillside to the house and they went into the oven as a cobbler. A couple of months later, we chanted, "Blackberries whip our shins next to the blackberry flies with blueberry eyes and red raspberry guts inside." Granna and I made up sayings under the sun.

My cousins said our sayings were weird, and they told ghost stories as we walked a path down to the cemetery on the other side of the property. Darcy swept the dust and twigs away from the headstones, and we left our offerings: wildflowers, a dead butterfly, a matchbox car, a compass and a collection of rocks.

Aunt Darcy walked ahead of us and, on the way back when the whippoorwill started to announce the arrival of spirits with the lightning bugs and crickets, Aunt Darcy hid behind the trees and waited for us to pass with hurried steps. Then, she sneaked along beside us behind the ridges of rhododendron, the hovering May apples, and the fringe of ferns. Bluebells snuffed their soft lights. Owls whipped around the wind in a bold shriek that made us dash quickly ahead of Jordan who walked along as if the pace of the rest of the world was ridiculous and silly until Darcy pounced on him with a roar of victory that caused him to pee his pants. He cried out with what seemed to be terror, but was only embarrassment. That instant contained a color and form and all of the boldness of sunlight, as if the scene were vivid instead of shrouded in the gray pitch of evening. He ran away, so quickly through the woods that we weren't able to follow him.

During the winters, Granna and I ate early evening dinners. We sat on large stone benches and cupped a basket loaded with hot bread, bowls of soup, boiling cinnamon milk, and black tea. We drank our meals on the edge of a small opening among the cedars before the tulip poplars rose along a steep hillside. Pansies were often frozen beneath our feet. Sometimes, I sat in the snow or on the cold ground of soggy February since the benches might send an ache along my spine and into my head.

I imagined Granna's bones as those stones and her temperature could be regulated with ease. She never expressed discomfort with the seasons. Her hips and fingers were hard and solid. Her arms and collarbone were smoothly tumbled moonstones. She had polished agate legs, a marble head, a howlite spine, jasper kidneys, apache tear lungs, and brown tourmaline feet. The rest of her was pottery, parts chipped and broken, worn by fingers and arms, cracked on the side, faded paint around the edges, adorned with a gem or two.

"I brought this stone from Central America before I knew any better," Granna said once while I imagined her jawbones swirled with creamy browns and dark flakes of gray.

"What do you mean?"

"Before I knew anything about disturbing native environments. Same as all of that coral I brought from off the coast of Brazil. It's selfish and trouble to take something from its home."

*****

When I hiked the Cumberland trails, spiders created viscid doorways across the paths. If I caught the first line of web without seeing the spiral, I knew that the hike would become long whether I intended it or not. Pulling the first line away from its sticky post dragged the whole web in a filmy cluster across my hair, clinging to my skin, and all caught up in the fibers of my shorts and t-shirt. A spider frenzied itself with spinning new lines across the path. The spider suspended its web between trees, sewing invisible threads over the head of a jogger, then a man training with a fifty pound backpack, two kids, two G.I.s jogging, an old man walking his dog, a woman in a sweat suit though it was ninety degrees. I often wondered why some people walked as if they were wrestlers trying to lose pounds by sweating through winter clothes in the humid summertime.

When I walked through at ten a.m. after grading papers at dawn, chasing Maggie, and cleaning up splatters of oatmeal, the water bottle in my backpack carrier sloshed back and forth between Maggie's feet. I stopped and watched the people.

Some of them believed this place had healing properties. Maggie's shoes tapped against the metal frame of the carrier as if hidden drummers danced just over the rocks, or behind the ridge of cedar trees—when I walked along the trail after all those joggers and speed hikers and dog walkers, with Maggie's drumming pack, I inevitably pulled the spider's main thread and took the web as far as it wanted to go along on my journey. How could it have spun so quickly? Sometimes I felt a full web and wondered how the person in front of me had avoided the tapestry.

The trails rolled with loose rocks, geodes gathered in wedges worn by water rushing across the forest and trickling into the cave, where the feet of trees waded in the darkness of Cumberland Cave's hair. I climbed the hills and navigated the culverts beside the paths every day, sometimes twice a day.

I had chosen to study history in order to stay away from present day events. I wasn't current and didn't want to be, but my husband was in a war. I considered myself an antique—lean, pale, and big-eyed. I dressed in solid, plain lines. History also beckoned from the shadows of street corners and the precipices of churches, from the iron railing of a factory to the crumbled wood boards of an outhouse. I saw images in my mind like double exposures of film.

"Multiple exposures," David said when I explained it to him. "Those can be wild photos."

Yes, I saw life in multiple exposures. Shadowy figures from the past lived along every sidewalk. Flickering holograms in the bright light. Some days they seemed to be existing transparencies that were comfortable. I saw the present avenue with cars pulsing under the lights as well as the past, one-lane dusty outpost with horsetails flapping through a deepening dusk. I ignored them as vivid imaginings. They were random lives that shifted like a vitascope if you could only tilt your perception. Like pre-Civil war trunks buried deep in the forest, on the edge of a hemlock cluster, and nothing to mark it but a dead man's feet until bulldozers tear open fields for a neighborhood. What has been is always there...just waiting to tell its story. Sometimes, what has been is easier to see than what will be or even what is in the present, though every moment wants to tell its stories. From the corner of my eye, I saw the double image, and as a child, I ran, straight for it, I'd catch that elusive window and dive through it, arms encircling the ancient tribe on the other side.

I spent my days walking, re-walking, and marking off the minutes of never-ending time in the layers of imprints. I couldn't ignore the multiple exposures from my past anymore. Even when I hiked the trails around the cave, I could recall how the voices of a tribe had formed until their faces took shape in the foliage. Their stories soon followed, echoing into my mind like turning pages from a picture book, like an ancient viewmaster. I looked into their faces, hidden underneath a fountain of hair, observing from the limestone bluffs, peering over the fallen, mossy trees. When I stopped on the trail and squinted into the forest, their faces had dissolved and vanished into memory. Those pictures formed every time I walked the trails, even on the days when I was preoccupied with thoughts of David, the war, my parents, students, or something as ordinary as a television program. No matter what topic captured my thoughts at the beginning of the hike, I couldn't distract myself from remembering that in my childhood, the tribe was vivid. They had materialized and showed their forms to me.

Their lean bodies quietly watched me at first. Then, they parted the dusty hair from their eyes and pulled the vines away. They began to move toward me, no longer content to watch from the bluffs. Their hands reached for grapevine. They floated on May apples and buckeye trees into the present. I could almost hear them breathing, digging up the bloodroot, scouting out the dry land fish in the springtime among the old fall leaves under the tulip poplars. Then, I saw the visions of their life at Cumberland park. Young boys running into the hollows, hiding from one another, creating trip vines, racing through trees, blending into boulders, crouching into tree trunks, and playing other hunting games. They learned to hide and cower and shift positions without snapping sticks or rustling leaves. They learned to imitate birds, squirrels, bobcat, deer, and bear with their voices and their bodies. Their voices floated through the forests with codes, directions, and other bits of information. The first time I saw the braves moving, talking, pointing at me, I became so frightened that I ran. The fear flushed me out of the trails. My heels scooted downhill underneath legs that tried to find a pace until I reached the smoother path, closer to the tree trunks. I remembered stumbling along above the gullies and hollow. I maintained a frazzled, rattling trot until tears blended into my sweat. The path was quiet. No birds sang or whipped their tail feathers up from the wild flowers. No wind shook the trees. No dogs barked in the distance. I looked over my shoulder often and almost tripped again and again. What if someone was watching me? What if someone tried to jump out from behind the tree?

As an adult, these fears resurfaced and I imagined myself in a skirmish with a man, his knife reflecting the sun, his gun hidden underneath a sweatshirt. I would scream repeatedly and run, just keep running, just keep running. I grew agitated and anxious in my fear, panting and jogging faster as I imagined trying to run from the attacker with Maggie bouncing in the backpack. These weren't Natives that I imagined, but men from my time and place, and I feared that I wouldn't make it far if I actually had to run from someone. *He could grab the baby out of the carrier. He could kill Maggie with ease if he was a soldier. What if he was a former soldier who had become crazy? Why would I imagine a soldier? It could be anyone. What's wrong with me? Do I fear the gun, the uniform? Do I fear or am I just pre-programmed to assume they'll go mad? He'll have residual effects from this. He will. He'll leave me for a woman soldier. He'll find someone with similar interests. She'll be tough and fit. She'll understand what it means to be a military wife.* I turned suddenly in a circle, recalling the imaginary killer in the forest, my mind whirling, ever vigilant, I continued the possibilities—a sniper camouflaged by the forest with a silencer that allowed him to take out women who hiked the trails. My mind flung itself further into fear until the phantoms of the past resurfaced in my vision.

The sight of a body in the ditch startled me. I shook my head side-to-side. The bodies were still there, like a hologram flickering in the ditch. Wide eyes vacantly stared at the bellies of flies. I hadn't heard the flies until then. The trail was muddied with blood. I looked back to see the barefoot prints. Black hair fanned away from one of the faces. Fallen tree trunks shifted into legs and twisted arms. Stumps of heads. Vines of hair. Skin with bloody handprints on their arms, their legs. Dismembered anger swelled inside me and swarmed around my head. I wanted to cry out and was about to scream when a man in running shorts darted past, "Nice day," he said and continued running. The dead men were gone. No dark bodies in the ditches, like I had imagined as a child.

Maggie gave a little kick. I shook my head, felt a tear slide back toward my ear. Walking away from the hollow, rising along the ridges of fern-trimmed stones, a doe and fawn crossed my path. I was sick and just wanted to return home. I felt crazy with how vivid the images from my childhood had become.

Eventually, I learned to walk with the hills. Some people tried to climb and conquer to reach the summit. Not me. I knew how to ride along the ridges of hills as if the hills themselves were moving my body from one side to the other, from the low places to the high. One step at a time allowed me to glide. I might be flying low over the paths to a passerby. Some hills enjoyed running and pushed me quickly. Others ambled precisely toward the center of the forest. Some were heavy joggers. There were light sprinters or flying squirrels, moving by great leaps and bounds to secret, rocky enclosures as if the tree canopy was a giant spider web suspended over the top of the forest.

I was having a hard time not admitting that my heart was breaking. David was on his third deployment at that point, first one in Afghanistan, then one in Iraq, and back to Afghanistan again. I didn't even know that four more were coming. I heard from him less and less since Maggie was born. He was in Baghdad during the birth. Two weeks later, he arrived home for eighteen days of leave. We didn't talk about the war or the distance, and I just didn't know if we could communicate about anything. During his last leave, he rejected pleasure in almost every form. I tried to bribe him with alcohol, but it was no use. He was rigid. He ran, biked, jumped rope, watched television, ate, ran, jumped rope, and watched television in a never-ending cycle. It was as if he was punishing himself for something. I sensed his secrets. What amazed me was our inability to speak about the mundane, about our general interests in movies, books, friends, weird facts, and even food. He had no opinions or suggestions or desires. David answered if questions were asked and otherwise, avoided contact.

I jumped and stomped my feet suddenly one evening while preparing dinner, "David, what the hell is going on?" I waited in the pause. "I can't do this!" I said. "I just can't do this. Please, talk to me. Say anything." He stood frozen in silence. His face was completely blank as if he might be looking out over the forest or standing on the shore of the ocean.

I waited and expected, but nothing happened. I flicked my fingers anxiously. I shifted my weight and put my hands on my hips. "Are you serious?" I rolled my eyes, everything to try to provoke him. "You can't even say one word. Not even, 'I'm sorry Ellen. I just need some time. It's not you.'" I waited.

He didn't even clear his throat. He stood there, blank and curious.

Then, I felt like he was provoking me with the silence, his refusal to interact with me as his wife, friend, co-inhabitor of our home for the next fifteen days, or whatever the hell it was, but then it wasn't going fast enough for me. "So, is it me?" I asked.

He stared, swallowed, and shifted his weight. He shook his head side-to-side and looked defeated. His eyes looked at the floor, as if he was searching into a hole, deep down into somewhere I couldn't see.

"What is going on in your head?" I asked loudly as if he might be deaf. "Da-vid," I said very slowly when he didn't answer again, "Seriously, you need to get some help. Please, talk to someone if you can't talk to me, because this is ridiculous and insane and…" I was frustrated and on the verge of tears, shaking my hands, staring at him intensely, maintaining eye contact, threatening, menacing, "…dysfunctional. Do you understand that you need to be present in life?"

"I am present," he said and cleared his throat. He sort of chuckled at the end of his sentence. I imagined that he thought himself to be far superior to me in his self-control, when in retrospect, that laugh probably meant that he was hiding his emotions, trying to keep them at bay. I could sense what he thought—that I was a spoiled professor who had all of the comforts and ease of life—and I said as much.

"That's not what I think," he said. "Don't assume that you know what I think." His lip curled up toward his nose in a little smirk.

"Do you get some sort of thrill out of this?" I asked. "You know that's really screwed up, David, that you can smirk about this. You act like I'm your entertainment. I'm available for you to mess with my head. Don't you see what you're doing? Let me answer my own question since you're incapable of communicating with me. You're distracting away from the point so that you don't have to admit that something is wrong with you, that you have some kind of weird issue if you can't even talk to your wife about anything at all."

"I talk," he said. "I just don't talk as much as you want me to or as much as you do. I talk. You have no idea what it's like over there, the daily struggle, the need to be constantly focused, no idea. You have absolutely no idea. You're spoiled."

"I have no idea because you don't tell me anything and hello! I'm not living there. I live here. All I can know is what people tell me, what's on the news. That's why I want to talk to you in person when you're here and on the phone, the Skype, when you're there. That's what I'm trying to do, talk to you." I started crying and that was the end of the conversation. If I had gained any ground, it was lost when the tears fell. "Don't you see? I'm just trying to connect with you." I sobbed and leaned against the kitchen counter.

David took a few steps and hugged me, but then I felt that he held me without bending his waist. His arms were wrapped precisely around my sides with his hands resting on my lower back. He held his posture and his breath during the embrace. I tried to kiss his neck, wiped my tears on the collar of his shirt, kissed his neck again with extra gentleness so that he wouldn't walk away from my sudden need to devour him, to sweat against his skin, and to sleep beside him. But I moved too suddenly. If I had waited thirty more seconds before touching him, it wouldn't have seemed so needy and deliberate. David rolled away from me, clearing his throat, saying he needed something to drink, giving me a small peck on the lips and pat on the back.

When he left for Afghanistan again, the loneliness swelled with the pressure of silence and irritable sighs when we spoke on the telephone. Expressions of our longing had drained our energies during the first deployment and again when he was in Iraq, until they finally felt repetitious, even boring. I was giving up and starting again daily.

When David returned home, he felt like an intruder, a stranger. He grumbled. He jumped at every sound in the dark. He scowled at Maggie and me sometimes. Our comfort was an irritation to him. When we played in the living room and he could smell food simmering from the kitchen and hear a distant television echoing from the bathroom upstairs, dogs barking, and the geese honking from the lake in the distance, that's when David seemed the most uneasy, like he had entered a fake world, some place where everything seems nice but isn't. I imagined he was convinced that terrorists might be lurking in the shadows, just around the corner, stalking across a swift ocean. After he drank a few beers one night, he admitted that all he could sense was the underlying instability.

Linda called from Montana every time he was recognized or someone nodded their head in his direction, but otherwise, she said, "Oh hon, I have no idea what he's doing on his latest assignment. He hasn't called Sarge lately." I shuddered. I couldn't imagine calling David by his rank. I had a fleeting thought sometimes that Mother may have called my dad, "Captain." But that only put me in a rage toward Linda and her boasting phone calls. She didn't ask, "Should I come down and help you out? Do you need some company?" Instead, she had said, "David has promised that y'all will visit as soon as he comes home from his next deployment."

"Visit where?" I asked.

"Us. Here," she said brightly.

"I don't know about that," I said.

They had visited once during David's leave just after Maggie was born. We had arranged it all. The timing was crucial, and we all trembled with anxiety when she showed up early, requiring a cesarean. David's commander made sure his leave coincided with his parents' visit. It felt like someone waved a magic wand and they were all gone again and I was at home with a different life and a baby. My existence did not seem the same. It was as if body snatchers had parachuted into the night, hooked chords up to our brains, and switched everything. The quiet sounds invaded after David and Phil's loud shouting at the television and Linda's bragging voice over the phone to her church friends and David's siblings.

But, when she called, she never asked about my loneliness or my sabbatical, or my job once I started teaching again. You'd think that since she was an Army wife herself that she would have intuitive wisdom, but she seemed clueless. Maybe she had been so engrossed in her children while Phil was in Vietnam that she never felt lonely. After that, Phil wasn't deployed repeatedly, just out in the field or sent to training, but those were brief stints, nothing as long-term and secretive as David's job. Though David had brief deployments compared to some troops, he had more of them and when he wasn't deployed, he was often training and that was mostly in another state, and I think he took extra side jobs as well, but I've never known that for a fact. It wasn't the same as most military families. We didn't move when he was assigned to a Special Forces unit. He made the long drive and stayed there alone, so we were apart more frequently than most military families.

Linda did ask about Maggie, "What's she eating now? Is she a fussy baby? Does she sleep through the night?" I liked those questions from her, but I was still greedy for attention and craved it from someone. I was stingy with answers to her. "She doesn't eat many solid foods yet."

"Well, what kind has she tried?"

"I don't know, just a few."

"Does she like vegetables? David liked sweet potatoes. You should try those. What about fruit? Have you mashed a banana and given it to her?"

"She tried a fruit, I think. Well, Linda, I hear her crying from upstairs. I better go. I'll talk to you later. Bye."

Once, she made Phil return the call, but I let it go to the answering machine that was, ironically enough, on the computer. "Hello, Ellen. I know we don't have all that fancy computer stuff for keeping in touch," he said through the speaker, "and it might be annoying to take twenty minutes to talk on the phone the old fashioned way, but I'd appreciate it if you'd try sometimes. We just want to hear how Maggie's growing and how you're getting along."

I didn't know them, and I couldn't imagine their interest in us. They had two other children, a daughter and a son, both older than David and living in Montana. David and his siblings had treasured their childhood time with their grandparents in Montana, and had made a pact with their parents to return there once Phil retired and the kids were grown. Everyone kept their end of the deal, except David. They saw me as the reason why David and his family weren't with them.

Maggie didn't really know David, and I had decided that she might not ever know him. I could sense that David felt sick when he thought about his previous self, before images of war contained a smell beyond photographic paper. After all of that training, he wouldn't talk about the past at all with me anymore. There were no hand-in-hand strolls down memory lane.

David had been highly sensitive to smells since he was a kid. Broken glass had a smell just as strong as copper pennies in a sweaty palm to him. I tried to close my eyes and imagine what David could smell. Most soldiers' wives might be horrified by the idea of trying to know what happened during battles and ambushes, but I knew that combat contained the scent of melting skin, burning hair and pants and shoes, oily guns, powdery concrete, acidic air, sulfur water, animal dung, sweat from stained armpits, crap in someone's pants, piss in the corner, incense burning on a table, curry from a kitchen, cigarette smoke, liquor, waxy cards, flint and lighter fluid, leather, aftershave, hot plastic, and often a sudden, misplaced fragrance. Like once at a checkpoint after a suicide bomber's body had detonated and scattered, David and his fellow soldiers smelled oranges, as if they might be swimming in a glass of orange juice with thick bits of pulp. He told me this story only because a reporter had interviewed them about this incident. They received medals, but David didn't like to talk about it unless he had a few beers in him. Bragging rights didn't interest him as much as they did me. I needed the stories to justify why he wasn't with us.

Afghanistan, on the side of the cliff. Several rounds slammed into the helmet of a captain. They had decided to rest in an area that they thought was secure. David was firing off shots from his camera of the valley. His cover was secure while other men in his unit tried to rescue the captain, whose leg had been struck just after his helmet was hit. A group of terrorists fired across a rocky embankment. David and his group were dangerously close to a drop-off. David told me that he could smell the film in the camera. And the clarity of that awareness caused him to move, to drop the camera that was then struck by bullets in midair. He was running, scrambling, moving toward rocks and rolling along their surface until he reached another soldier who had been hit. David smelled the sweat of enemies across the rocks. People didn't smell the same. Their diet leaked into the air through their pores.

Sometimes, the blood smelled the same. He knew for certain. His comrades called him the Bloodhound. His ability to find food when necessary and to smell other men approaching had saved their asses a few times, even during field exercises. He could smell a deer over the next hillside in the forest, not to mention sheep or dogs.

That's all I really knew about David's job. He carried digital cameras most of the time, and when I had asked about the film, he said, "You learn a trade but you never give up the traditional method. You never know when you might need it." I certainly didn't understand how old-fashioned film cameras could be above trouble and considered valuable in the twenty-first century. He laughed at my trust in contemporary technology, "If something happens to that digital camera, every photo is gone. Something happens to a film camera, and I may still have the film in another pocket. It's good to have both," he said. He had always been secretive to some extent and I expected it, but when he went to Iraq and witnessed the debris from suicide bombers, he stopped talking about it altogether.

He told me about one suicide bomber after he came back from Iraq. The bomber at the checkpoint had been a woman. He wondered if she had been wearing perfume that smelled like honeysuckle. The scent was trapped in David's nostrils, hairs, sinuses, and ear canal. Did she have some of the flowers with her, wound into the bomb material? David couldn't be certain he smelled the honeysuckle or if he just imagined the scent. He asked another soldier they called Bacon, "Do you smell that?"

"Yeah, it fucking stinks, as usual, as always, man."

"Do you smell perfume?" David asked. Bacon stared at him like he had lost his mind. David looked at him hopefully. "It's sort of fading now?"

"No, man, I don't smell perfume unless charred flesh is the new fragrance that's being promoted," Bacon said. "I guess it is." Bacon pointed across the road where people walked by. "A dead man rotted there in the ditch after we shot him for aiming his fucking machine gun over here," Bacon said. "Seemed like we could smell his dead body forever. He just laid there rotting for weeks. This place stinks, man."

When he told that story, it was the last time he softened for years. He sat on the edge of the hammock in the backyard. I lay beside him. He said that the perfume smell had reminded him of me. He said, "I hadn't wanted to think about a man rotting in the ditch, so I tried to find an image of you. I just wanted to smell your skin and hair and know that I was good..." He seemed confused and shook his head like that wasn't the right way to describe what he had felt at the checkpoint. He turned in the hammock slightly. The back of his neck was exposed to the sun and his collar was soaked. He wrapped his hand around it so that his elbow crossed over his eyes while he cried without shaking, sniffling, or sobbing. When I moved closer to him after a few minutes, he allowed me to make love to him and I wanted to keep him in that trust with me.

3 LIGHT SENSITIVITY

In the early morning, sirens cried through the fog shrouding a dim glow of emergency personnel in the parking area to Cumberland Cave. I started to cross the street when two cops stopped me and asked if I happened to hear any commotion at the park during the night. I asked what was going on, trying to peer into the fog. They asked if I lived alone and if I'd seen any strange people or heard loud noises lately. I laughed saying that there's not much more to hear than owls, tree frogs, and crickets. An occasional howling dog. I live too far from the neighborhood and the park to hear conversations or even loud music and laughter. Sometimes, I can hear traffic on the highway, especially when they're building neighborhoods beyond the by-pass and heavy construction equipment passes through. We're located just outside the city limits, but wildlife still dominates my property.

The north side of my grandparents' property bordered Cumberland Cave. On the southern bluff of our property, there's a separate entrance to the cave, but it's about seven miles or more underground, and some of it is crawl space.

That space connects to the main entrance of the cave, where the park is located. The cave lingers down there with its own lives, coiling underneath Granna's house and under my feet as I run along the trails; the cave undulates cool stalactites into points.

Jordan is my closest neighbor. He lives in Aunt Darcy's house and has renovated it and cares for her portion of the property she inherited after Granna died. Darcy still lives in Alaska, but keeps the house, "just in case," Jordan said, waving his hand. "Whatever that implies," he mumbled. His house is sealed away from the road in a low gully filled with ferns. Green reflections glow onto the white house so that it looks mossy until you get close enough to see it's actually the reflection. Jordan added tall glass windows, so there's an odd depth and optical illusion that materializes as Maggie and I walk down the hill to his house, as if the house were split in two and the forest kept right on going straight through. I'd like that, living in the forest. I do as well, but I'm on the high point of the property and Granna's house is a cabin that dwells among the trees, standing as tall as possible with them. Granna's house is narrow and earthy and blends into the environment in a different way than Jordan's. He's folded into the land and must strain to hear the traffic.

Across the street, facing the parking area of Cumberland Cave, there's a subdivision of about twenty homes that blend into a few other neighborhoods until they crowd into the city and lean together downtown. Our downtown isn't particularly urban, but it does have a fair share of warehouses lining the riverfront and a city square that hosts the courthouse, law offices, city hall, the police station, post office, along with boutiques, shops, and a few restaurants filtering out of the city. It was a typical, Southern university town with coffee shops, a diner, a handful of thrift stores and bars.

That morning, after the fog parted, I stood on the edge of the road and watched police officers talking to people in the driveways of the homes on the border of the neighborhood across from the park. The park and cave were closed for a week and then people kept driving by. News reports didn't reveal too much since no one had been charged with the murders yet. I didn't know much more, but I knew three students from the University had been murdered. A junior and two sophomores. I didn't know them. Both girls were nursing majors. The boy was undecided. Students wrote memorials on the sidewalks on campus, filled the parking area at Cumberland Cave with candles, flowers, and mementos. All three of the students worked at The Grille, a favorite old-style diner across from the campus. The University held prayer vigils and counseling sessions. I paced in my house as the mania of the town whirred. Storeowners sold out of ammunition, and gun sales hit record highs, the news broadcasters announced after confirming there were still no solid leads in the case. Around campus, I heard songs about killers from more than one dorm window and car stereo, almost as if they were inspired by the potential of a murderer among them.

The tribal people had named the river The Warioto, and the water from the cave and the lake flowed into the Warioto. I wondered about the murders while Maggie and I stood on the bank and watched a blue heron poised on a tree trunk that was collapsed into the water. The park had reopened after a week and people visited relentlessly. Students kept leaving flowers, candles, cards, and photographs. I didn't know how long a murder investigation scene should be closed. A week seemed short. Two weeks since the murders, and Maggie and I were silent and alone with the bird who kept one eye on the stillness beneath the water's surface and one eye on the movement along the bank where we stood. I was surprised no other people were around. Not even a lone fisherman, and there was always someone fishing. Just the heron on a cool, sunny day the first week of May.

The lack of witnesses to the murders flashed into my mind. I wondered how someone could commit a violent crime in such a well-traveled area. When I began reading about the case, I discovered that people had been lingering around all of the locations used by the victims and the murderer on the night of the crime. People saw similar but different images that night. Like variations in an inkblot, witnesses saw flashing lights, yellow cars, gold cars, stop signs, closed gates, shadows in the lights, high beams, low beams, no lights, and parked cars. These were the details in the news. I wondered how so many people could be so confused and have different interpretations. Was there an interpretation for the truth, for facts, or was there no such thing as a solid fact? Maybe all murder investigations were full of coincidences, ironic twists, the confusion and inability to recall one's own past recollections.

I stared at the heron as if it might have the answer or know the secret. Maggie shifted her weight in the backpack carrier. The heron tilted its head slightly, sizing us up or focusing on a fish. I couldn't be sure. As I walked away toward the cave entrance and platform, two fishermen, and then a woman walking a dog passed.

Suddenly, an image of the bloody, drowning turtle that had fallen off the cliff and onto the concrete platform tumbled into thought. I rounded the mouth of the lake and would reach the platform soon. The platform was a hard stage. A thick brown smack in the middle of nature, fringed with wildlife. If no stage had ever been built, no concrete smoothed by the arms of men in front of the mouth of the cave, no steel saws used to cut a diamond edge into stone, the turtle would have tumbled into the tops of dogwood, red maples, redbuds, maybe slid down a branch with a buoyant rumble to an undergrowth of Indian paintbrush and woodland fern fronds, happy to roll out a leaf mold cushion of tangled, damp ground. Little pools of muddy water may have formed around the edges of the cave's mouth. Soggy dimples. Instead, the illusion of the lake lingered along the horizon for the turtle who saw herself stepping onto the bank, entering the water to swim out toward a tree trunk and climb toward the sun to stretch out her neck.

I walked the top of the bluff to find the turtle's original path. The ledge over the cave, from where the turtle had fallen, created the illusion of a shoreline on the lake. The lake didn't seem far below at all. It appeared to be there, higher, another lake on top to meet the bluff. I had to rub my own eyes to keep from believing it. A person could walk into another reality there. A turtle could do the same.

I read the basics of the case again. The Grille closed at midnight, and the three had worked the last shift together. They were murdered close to the lake sometime before dawn. Supposedly, all were robbed, and their identifications were missing. Jordan told me the detectives said that all three were stabbed repeatedly and nearly decapitated.

I couldn't believe it happened across from my home. On the television, images from Iraq showed prisoners of war being decapitated, weapons that looked no bigger than a pocketknife stretching through the sinews of a soldier's neck. I was haunted by those hooded men, then the hollow eyes of men begging for their lives—of those men who could be my husband. I was enraged at the filming, at the foreign website for broadcasting, for showing the struggling images of Daniel Pearl, at my students who seemed so disconnected and blank, as if the deployed women and men weren't people living in their community, as if the reporters weren't our citizens.

I reserved the computer lab and gave my students an assignment to research war tactics, since the Geneva Convention and rules of torture were recently re-opened to debate. I expected them to use the database to access journals. We would then discuss their views on torture and war crimes in class. I wanted them to give a presentation as well. They were to choose an event in history along with a contemporary example, find some similarities and then add that to a general discussion on torture. They worked in the computer lab for a week when I first had to tell the guys in the middle row to remain quiet and that while they may find content worth discussing immediately, they should refrain until the presentation two weeks later. The following week I left the students in the lab with the attendant and went to find some videos at the library. I told the students to maintain the same rules, and hold their questions until I returned halfway through the class. When I returned, almost everyone in the lab was gathered in the middle row, including the attendant, watching two computers simultaneously. "What's going on?" I asked.

They quickly dispersed and one of the students said, "We just found some interesting information about torture."

"All of you are reading it?"

"It's a video," another student interjected.

"I found one of the concentration camps from World War II," the first student interrupted, "and we all just started watching it."

That wasn't a lie exactly, but I was humiliated when Dr. Hamilton, chair of my department, said that my students had accessed inappropriate materials during the times that I had reserved the computer lab. Among others, they had been watching the video of Pearl and some other beheadings and other torture videos created by terrorists, and Dr. Hamilton added, "just after students have been violently murdered and no one's found the murderer." He felt, like so many other colleagues, that the students had "disconnected from their community, from the war, from tangible reality, but they're viewing their time in history like it's a movie, or worse, a video game." While I was shaken and frightened by the murders, I had no idea, no premonition, of how much they were going to become a part of my life in a few short months.

*****

Jordan grew up and joined the Army, served a swift four years, and got out. He had been caring for Darcy's place, which is exactly half a mile from mine. In between the two homes is a part of the property that we named No Faces, when we were children. When one of us disappeared for a few hours, we always said that we had been to the No Faces to think. The No Faces stood along our property on Bert Road, an old country farm road where the town folk artist once lived. He erected a small parade of concrete statues by shaping pounds of concrete. The ten-foot-tall farmer in overalls rode a horse alongside more farmers. Two soldiers shook hands. They lined the roadside with a bull and goat. He had made a tribute to the Shawnee, Andrew Jackson, and a couple of governors, to name a few. Granna said that the artist, whom everyone called Guthrie even though his real name was completely different, something like Edmond Dotson, had lived in a tree house. Some locals started a rumor that money was hidden inside Guthrie's statues. He created forms, mixed the cement, painted it, climbed the trees, pointed a sword, and lingered in the fog before daylight watching each pierce of light upon the haystacks.

One night, when I first came to live with Granna permanently, the moon was covered in clouds and no rain fell but the humidity blanketed the fields with irritation and boredom. A group of boys with baseball bats and bricks faced the statues and busted off their heads, or so Granna guessed after finding them headless the next day. One horn from the bull statue swung limply beside its face. Now, those statues in overalls and blue trousers stand as headless Greek Gods in our countryside.

All of it was depressing if combined, so I avoided the place and argued with Jordan about who would keep it up since the high school boys had started a tradition of throwing beer bottles at the statues on some drunken nights. When I was only fifteen, Granna had stooped under the No Faces and picked up broken glass and made me promise not to sell, saying, "No extra land is being manufactured these days." She wasn't sick and didn't die for years, but maybe she needed to settle it early on.

After the murders, I was nervous about walking the trails at Cumberland Cave alone. I asked Jordan if he would go with me. He needed an extra push for an upcoming race and agreed to meet me. Jordan had grown into a muscular, competitive marathon runner who also worked as a high school counselor. He received constant attention from the high school cross-country runners who had begun summer training camp on the Cumberland trails. Soon, they all knew his name and he gave them pointers. By the end of the summer, he was an assistant coach for the team. The following year, he was the head coach. Jordan didn't miss details. He knew when I had nightmares, just by the tension in my stride.

He was perceptive; maybe that's why the cops questioned him. Luckily, the police and the private investigator left me alone. Jordan said, "Evidently, the private investigator is from Colorado. Can you imagine having to pay for some guy to scour the city for information about your daughter's murder?"

I knew that he didn't mean that literally, but then again, he was trying to imagine what it must be like for the parents. I took offense to the idea of my child being murdered. "Damn it, Jordan! This is really getting to me. Why are they even questioning you? And why can't they find the murderer? And what if they allow guns in here, Jordan? They're probably going to pass that bill now. Can you imagine that?" Some politicians in the state government had decided to try and push a bill through that would allow gun permit holders to carry inside state parks. They were also discussing another bill that would permit university professors to carry guns in the classroom and on campus. Students ranted, pointing out that some of them were also permit-holding adults who should have the right to protect themselves and not rely on professors. Looking into my classroom, I wondered how many concealed weapons might be shoved down their pants.

Jordan and I talked and moved swiftly along the trails and the noon hour had browned us earlier in the spring than expected. I panted and stopped on the hill, smearing sweat across my brow with my palm and patting my pockets for a handkerchief.

"First of all, they're questioning me because I live across from the park," Jordan said. I must have fired a glare at him, as I wiped the sweat away from my face with the hem of my shirt. He gave a bothered glance toward the fleshy roll beneath my navel and quickly turned away and continued, "You do, as well, but way over there, and there's not a parking area almost directly across from your section of the property. They're questioning the people in the neighborhood, too."

Jordan and I lived on a parallel line, but his house was on the side closest to the parking area. "As far as the gun bill," he continued, "it's for those with permits who carry already and we're trained, Ellen. Permit holders aren't the people opening fire at a school or a supermarket. You know this, Ellen." These thoughts accumulated with the unexpected ninety-degree weather, and I wheezed and tried to take a few deep breaths, but my chest pinched itself underneath my breasts. I coughed and sputtered and couldn't take a breath in. My knees buckled a little, as I tried to gasp and gulp the empty air.

"Raise your arms," Jordan said.

I shook my head side to side, got in little lines of air thin as a strip of pencil lead. "Why?" I tried to ask irritably, and my face only bulged with hot pulsing vibrations.

"Relax," Jordan said. "Droop, droop! Feel your body droop!"

Then, he whispered softly, "Imagine that it's cold." I wilted and imagined a fall wind whipping me away as if it could lift me and I drew in breaths. I don't know how many had gushed clearly into my nose as I sat beside Jordan on the hill. He cupped my knee and smiled, "You okay now? Just stay relaxed and let's drift along," he said standing and reaching his hand down to me.

I dreamt often about the tribe and my childhood vision. As a child, I imagined the members of the tribe overtaken in an attack by warriors from another tribe hidden among the stones. They fired poisoned darts and arrows down into the training rituals of her tribe. They killed her husband—the woman, in my dream, who discovered the bodies. She and her son were returning from gathering supplies. A tribal celebration was planned to honor their newly trained braves and the warriors who trained them. Her son had been wrapped in a crude sling that rubbed a blister underneath her breasts. Her hands felt for it. She carried another bag of fish, stones, and canes. She was chewing something like a sweet piece of grass when she discovered the men. The sun reflected her face in the pool of her husband's blood. She vomited. She was scared that the men from the other tribe were still lurking in her area so she crept into a ravine and followed it along a ridge until she saw the mouth of the cave and the lake. For two days, she watched the area and ate the supplies that were intended for the celebration.

Before the bodies began to smell, she dragged her hair through their blood and across their bodies. Then, she grabbed their ankles and dragged them away, her husband first. For two days, she dragged their bodies over the hill and smoothed ferns to the edge of a meadow. Her son rode in the sling and nursed from her breast even while she rested the ankles of dead braves on her hips. The vultures swam in the sky, dipping lower and lower as the days passed. That's when the full tribe materialized on the other side of the field. Several old women sang as they surfaced, as if being beached below her burial mound. They had seen the vultures over the cave area and followed them. The tribe helped her bury their warriors and then they left the area. She would not go with them. When they departed, she returned to the cave for the first time since her discovery of the slaughter.

She knew why the tribe had departed so quickly, but she would not avoid it and carried a torch forward into the cave. She had no expectations, but found the shaman floating face down in the river just after entering. The shaman's gray hair undulated in tiny coils as if she had birthed baby snakes in every direction. A large piece of wood pinned the shaman's body against the wall so that she couldn't be released to the waters of the Warioto. She sat the baby in the center of a ring of dead wood that was cushioned by vines and moss gathered from outside and used to create a mat for sitting on the cave floor. Then, she ran into the water and pulled the shaman up the slick muddy bank and onto the cave floor. Both of their bodies were painted with gray mud. She left the shaman lying horizontal on the bank. She backed away toward the cave wall, crouched low, and ran toward the shaman. She pushed the body with all of her force and dug her shoulder underneath the shaman until the old woman's body started to roll quickly down the muddy bank and into the river with a splash. She rolled down and into the water herself and shot straight up and pushed the shaman's body again and again until the slow current of the water picked up and forced the body out of the cave. She watched the shaman's feet disappear and struggled up the bank inside the cave. She wanted to stay in the cave and snuff out the light, forever lost in their underworld, but she couldn't punish the baby. She scooped him into the sling again and walked into the light. The shaman's body was slowly drifting in the center of the river and would flow on until reaching the big Warioto.

In my childhood, I couldn't sleep at night once I began to explore the visions. They increased. When I explored the trails, I saw braves camouflaged with leaves and vines. I saw tree bark wrapped around a mother's shins as she nestled into wild hydrangeas on the hillside. The plant, known as seven barks by the settlers, bloomed white disks like the moon. She lifted the roots and ground them, heated them, and the men could urinate again without pain. But they were gone and no one's pain needed to be alleviated. The woman waved her soft hand to move the gnats away from her ear and transformed into a doe resting in the cool ravine along the trails. At night, dark shadows might hover near my pillow, tap my shoulder, approach the side of the bed with the smell of sweat and salt and smoke wafting around the walls, lingering in the hallway during the morning.

Then, two more murders were reported at a national park a hundred miles away. Located in our state, the media was camped out in another town, pressing the realization of a serial killer in action.

I copied David's habit of cavernous listening, when suddenly I turned everything off and stopped. Braced. Just listening to the quiet and trying to calm my own breath, my heartbeat thudding in my ears, pumping over and over so loudly that I couldn't hear anything else—waiting for it to quiet, the fear had become so audible. Wait. And finally, hear the crickets, hear a moth flap against the screen, hear a dog bark, hear creaking closer to home, avoid developing the wide-eyed alertness that unravels the night into an endlessly poised moment of wait and jump— I'm perched.

Those childhood imaginings became my adult nightmares. I woke for nothing except knowing the fear of darkened stooping figures, forms in shadowy dance, wearing dark clothes like those who might glide by with bombs underneath. There were nights when I might be startled wide awake, exceptionally alert, as if David were in the house, and had nudged me to listen for the phantom sounds he heard in the night, a burglar, spies, terrorists, all sorts of crazy people who might hurt us. I could hear his breath on those nights, steady, but unlike the breathing of his previous self, of the guy I met in college, the panting of the dark room, the concentrated push while jogging a trail, the appreciative exhale during a good meal, the restful sigh beside me in bed—those breaths had been overtaken by the precise, controlled ear of hollow listening, empty of true form. I tucked my knees under my breasts and sobbed into that hollow breath that lingered in our bedroom. I peered through the lines of fabric in my sheet and covered my head in fear. I wrapped my legs around the blankets and embraced the pillows with my tears until I was exhausted into sleep, probably giving in to those emotions with a frequency that alleviated the light, weighing it with my pitch black panting, my groping fears.

I wanted to shake and cry myself to sleep the night of July Fourth, but Maggie's temperature soared to one hundred and four degrees and tried to climb higher. In the bath, Maggie screamed and shook, covered in chills. In the car, she cried constantly and whined for me to take her out of the seat. In the grocery store, she wailed for medicine before I uncapped the bottle.

Then, the fireworks began on the drive home. A couple of units of soldiers were home from deployment, so roman candles, black cats, bottle rockets, and poppers smoldered for days. In the neighborhood across from the cave, loud shots fired and screamed and popped. Maggie shook and cried, trembled and tried to bury her face into my breasts. Her crying became uncontrollable. I had never seen a child have an anxiety attack. I tried to soothe her, to reassure her, to explain. None of my calming methods worked. I rocked and sang through Maggie's fading tears. The medication finally tamed her fever, and her body twitched and kicked as if fighting off invisible enemies. Her eyes dropped. Then, a firework screamed ahead of a trail of smoke. More POP, POP, POPPOP POPPOP, POP, POP! Maggie's eyes opened wide, as she trembled. I continued singing and cracked one eye open to peek at Maggie.

More and more fireworks screamed and popped in the distance. Maggie kept the blanket wrapped around her ears. One of her palms was pressed into her own cheek. That was David's gesture, a way that he comforted himself when he was engrossed in thoughts. In the middle of the night, that gesture often accompanied his hollow breaths. I thought of him leaned against a wall, stooping, crouched behind a concrete post or truck, tuning his breath and his ear to the emptiness, to anticipated sounds of gunshots, bombs exploding in a war zone, approaching footsteps. Or, I imagined that he wasn't listening at all, and then was at a loss for a picture of him, wanting to know with certainty what was in his mind. I reached my mind out there to the corners, and I wanted it to travel far, stretch those thoughts until I felt his in the abyss, until I knew that we had connected across all of that space and time and darkness. I had to tell myself, yes, he is still alive. He will come home. He still loves me.

I wished that David were at home. We could go downtown and watch the fireworks together. The previous year, he had been here. He was on leave. When the cannon fired the first big shot of the evening, I remembered how uneasy and edgy David had been. Maybe Maggie and I were best alone. David had been sarcastic and jaded about the celebrations. "Civilians are so spoiled," he said. "You all have no idea how lucky you have it."

Jordan went with us to watch the fireworks, and David made him feel so uncomfortable that he walked home that night, six miles. Jordan and I had been complaining about the rising gas prices or the poisoned produce and many other current events, even celebrity gossip. In retrospect, I can imagine how annoying it must have been for David. Daily life was about death and permeated by another culture, mounted in religion and warfare, concepts completely foreign to me. I could hear a million stories, but I hadn't breathed it. I hadn't lived away from not only family and friends, but my country and culture with no chance of returning for months, no afternoon walks, no plans for the beach, no night at the movies, no pancake houses, no parks or theaters, no ice cream stores and libraries.

But, David wasn't at home for that Fourth of July. I imagined him in Iraq, playing video games, drinking with other men and women who missed their families, and lifting weights to pass a lot of time. That was one of the early deployments, so I imagined he was having a good time. How could I be relieved by David's participation in a war so that I didn't have to suffer his discomfort with civilian life? Guilt invaded me with every cannon blast and streaming rocket that I heard. But I went back and forth…thinking that I was relieved that he wasn't at home so that I didn't have to feel uneasy around him, and wishing that he were at home with us. I craved his presence in our house and the feeling of being next to my physical body.

My thoughts moved on to believing that he was probably having an affair and who could blame him? He was in a war zone. I cried for wanting to have an affair myself. Other men looked appealing, but I knew that my imagination was probably better than the reality would be. After so many deployments and so much training, he was wired for combat. But I didn't trust anyone to hold me like David had when we were in love. I didn't trust a stranger to give me the comfort of one familiar touch and wanting to know me.

In spite of the repeated cannon blasts, Maggie's cries dropped to a low whine and faded to a snore by the time I placed her in the little bed. I looked at Maggie for a long time. Her black hair curled around her ear like David's hair in his baby pictures. I really missed David with a horrifying loneliness. I recall thinking that he might already be dead while I worried over imagined affairs. Symbolically, though, the person I married definitely seemed dead to me at the time, separated from his emotional pain, as if he stepped aside and let another entity take over his body so that he could survive. My mind ran away with that notion as I imagined David talking with other soldiers, buying porn and trade videos or magazines, hiring a prostitute or trying for a shot with the slut in another battalion who gave blowjobs to all the guys. My anger fired on ideas about David's participation in raids and ambushes. Did he hurt women, children, boys, fellow men? Did he treat them like they were all criminals? Had he become a secret barbarian who abused bodies? Did he poke and prod and shout and point his finger, his gun, his inner firing squad?

The horror of my husband, my lover, becoming a stranger caused me to collapse against the doorframe. This madness was overtaking us. I didn't know how to stop it from becoming Maggie's life. How could I protect Maggie from what David had become when I didn't know David anymore? I went back and forth between bad David and good David, visualizing both, allowing him to be both men. He could be a mentor to soldiers, encouraging them to stay focused, and helping them to cope by being reliable, working out, and training them to be prepared. Something bad might happen to David. He could be abducted, beaten, abused, and decapitated with a dull knife. I punished myself by visualizing David's head in place of John the Baptist's. I softened it to survive and cope; I horrified it out of guilt and real sickening. Is this really happening? Is this really my life? Fear. Every day, we were at war, blood pooling, a body goes stiff. I experienced limp limbs from the heft of carrying the telephone on some days. I forgot about war sometimes. I laughed at jokes about terrorists. We were sometimes invincible, forged-with-metal tough, made out of skin that can't be up-armored if the walls melted through. Of the many fights in my head, I knew the gut punch to vomit, soft tissue prevailed and I was mostly weary and wanting. Kneading my hands over and out, fumbling for a phone with his voice, tossing aside all agendas when it was time to pick him up. I favored recovery even when he was my adversary, and I wanted to beg him to make me his battle, to turn back, care about produce, learn to pour concrete. He could be a wild-eyed folk artist or a fast-food manager. He could be walking the hallways of a hospital, taking a patient's blood pressure, telling her that the doctor will be in as soon as possible. The seat behind the wheel of a bus might not be the most comfortable after hours, but it seemed safer than wherever David was. I raced ahead and considered a car accident, a plane crash, an accidental shooting here, all in the paper this week. My thoughts moved with the pace and spark of sirening bottle rockets and pulsed in my temples.

The sickness overtook me by the time I reached the bathroom. I was losing it. I couldn't escape the sound of explosions and lay in the darkened bathroom. I could see the night sky through the window. One firework might shoot out against the sky suddenly. Another struggled above a distant treetop as if it had been trying to ignite itself all night.

*****

The ringing of the telephone through the computer speakers and David's voice woke me. I saw his face flash onto the computer screen. "Are you there?" he asked.

I hesitated and looked toward my bedroom.

"Ellen?" he called. "It says you're online. You there?"

I turned on the webcam and smiled with a tired expression. "I fell asleep here," I answered and rubbed my forehead. "Maggie's asleep." I thought about the dream of the shaman and wanted to stand underneath a shower, then open the door and walk, walk far out into the night.

"How are things going?" he asked in a loud voice.

"It's okay, David. I can hear you. You don't have to shout."

"Yeah, it's just kind of loud in here," he said and turned the camera to show the soldiers camped out in his room with video game controllers in their hands. Two guys shouted, but the others glanced from the corners of their eyes while talking amongst themselves. It was weird, him calling me like that. Privacy was important all of the time, but especially during deployments. He also usually maintained some distance from his men's free time.

"Looks like you guys are doing well?" I pulled a smile across my face to alter my questioning statement. "At least, you have a moment to chill out and relax. That's good." I tried to cover my apprehension.

"Yeah, we've a got a little time. Just a little," he said. One guy chuckled and rose up on his toes a little, glanced at a buddy from the corner of his eye. Both of them grinned as if at an inside joke. I couldn't help but wonder if David was making an ass out of me, then thought that one of them must have said something at the same time as David. "Look, I saw a news report that they're still looking for the murderer or whoever's responsible for killing those students," he said. "You doing okay?"

"Yeah," I said. Too much activity in the background drew my attention. It's easy to overanalyze when you don't see your husband very often, when he's deployed more months in the year than at home.

"Have they stopped by to tell you anything about it?"

"Why would they?"

"I don't know," he said. "It's practically the back yard."

"It's not that close," I said. "Ask one of the developers. They could pack at least ten homes between here and the cave."

"Close enough," he said.

"For what?"

"For concern, Ellen. You know where the guns are and don't hesitate to wear one around the house, to leave them within arm's reach. Maggie can't even walk yet."

"She—" I stopped short of telling him that she could walk and run, and that he was really far behind in years. I also wanted to say that I wouldn't wear a gun in my own home. A few were loaded and placed strategically around the house. Three guns were evenly spaced in safe locations designed by my grandfather and that was enough for me. I had a shotgun in a wall closet beside the big windows on the upstairs landing, a pistol in a box mounted to the kitchen sink, and an AK 47 in a trapdoor under the bed. It may have seemed extreme until you considered all of the other gun hideaways that I didn't use, but that they had created during the Prohibition. Then, you can understand why they wanted their arms to be extensions of the literal ones.

"So, did you go?" David asked as if I had missed part of the conversation.

"Sorry, I'm just tired. Go where?"

"To the FRG meeting," he said. The guy who had stood on his tiptoes earlier glanced blankly toward the camera.

"Oh," I said. "No."

I thought of FRGs as competitive, like the combination of a sewing circle and a locker room. Family Readiness Groups were the military's answer to people who asked what they did to help foster the growth and togetherness of the family and the community, to create a communications and support network for families when their loved one is proudly serving the country. I tried it once.

Most of the women were younger than I by ten years with three to five children and maybe more on the way, who called one another and gossiped about which husbands had hooked up with a slut from another unit or who spent all of his money on steroids or was an alcoholic or whose wife was seen dancing at the clubs and leaving with someone cute or whose wife has been sleeping with his best friend or whose wife just left and went to her parents' house and may not come back at all or whose son doesn't know him.

At the one meeting I attended, the commander's wife shared updates. They had tried to rope me into the groups until I told them that I'm anti-social. They tried it with all the officers' wives. During the meeting I attended, the commander's wife fit the role and advised not letting the Army life get to you and being tough. She pounded her little fist with plum colored fingernails, then arranged her hair. Creamy brown waves framed her face, in spite of her age. Her shirt was a heavy cream silk that revealed her slender neckline and distinctly engraved collarbones. Her body draped itself down to the floor in heavy, dark chocolate pressed pants, her feet splaying out like a dancer's into her brown leather heels adorned with a small leather bow on either side.

"Listen, ladies," the commander's wife said with her neck slightly wavering back and forth like a small green snake rising into a higher branch cautiously but confidently. She smirked, "You've always got to take care of yourself." She waved a hand above her head, in front of her face, and around her chest, stomach, and hips for emphasis. "Take care of yourself. Don't forget it when you're worried about everyone else. This is my best advice. I want to tell you this and have you remember it. Take care of yourself, and you'll be an example to the rest of your family." I hadn't imagined she would say that. She looked straight at me and smiled confidently as if her head finally came to rest on the highest limb.

Other friendly wives, sure to be helpful, spread food across the tables. They could sink their smiles into croissants, their compliments licked with icing from the cake, their encouragement captured by the fork and twined until the noodles fit neatly between slightly parted teeth. Dabs of olive oil and vanilla whipped crème lingered around the edges of their mouths: one side savory, the other chilled. But, to be fair, I never gave those women a chance as a way of protecting myself with a hard, judging shell.

I did the same thing with Linda and Phil. And who could blame them for not planning to visit while David was deployed? They would skip visiting their granddaughter since I wasn't going to interact, but instead remained sullen and afraid, which seemed critical and withdrawn. Linda called repetitiously to check on us just after the murders, but I clammed up, didn't share my thoughts, didn't reach out to her or any women, women who could understand because they too knew the way I lived loneliness. I was too conscious of my loneliness to let it go and it grew out from me, pushing people away by its darkness.

4 PRIME LENS

Granna said, "You're demonstrating how not to consume the experience," when I used to insist on sulking before Mother and Darryl visited for a weekend or were brave enough to take me to their home. When I visited them a few times, we played pretend while sunning poolside, shopping, lunching, and then they took calls for medical emergencies, during which time I sat in front of a television and awaited the gifts they gave to me out of guilt. I piled many of the gifts in a spare bedroom at Granna's house. Finally, Mother and Darryl spent the night in the spare bedroom, where they were forced to confront all of the dolls, snow globes, nail polish, purses, bracelets, necklaces, and other cheap plastic they had given to me. After stumbling upon the years of linen sundresses, gumball colored tank tops, cropped cotton t-shirts, tailored pants and shorts hanging neatly in the closet, I heard my mother searching frantically, opening drawers to discover a stack of birthday cards and

Christmas cards with folded, crisp bills, tens, twenties, fifties, even some hundreds. A check never cashed in a random card that Darryl hadn't even bothered to sign.

In another drawer, photos of the four of us when we were Dad's family, when Tyler had fat legs and I was growing in the womb, when Tyler and I chased one another after a tickling match and pillow fight and then without Dad in the photos and a few during visits without Tyler in the photos. Just a couple in which I looked sad and Mother and Darryl looked irritated and uncomfortable. I stood in the hallway and listened. I heard her telling Darryl that she didn't even recognize herself in those old photos. The mother in those earlier photographs wore a strapless, red terrycloth sundress and a broad sunhat beside two longhaired children on the beach. That young mother smiled above her brown, wide feet and would have never imagined being the estranged woman who wore a white starched shirt with only the top button opened and the tight smile stitched beside her daughter's solid stare into the camera lens. In that photo, they visited for a "graduation" party, and Mother had made air quotation marks with her fingers every time she said the word graduation to anyone.

Even though it had been my graduation from high school, a small celebration that Granna had prepared with extra care paid to details, Mother picked at her plate of food and discussed Darryl's dermatology practice as well as the latest conferences in Italy and Greece, where even she was a guest speaker. She leaned confidently against one of the mahogany side tables, into which Granna had carved vines with birds. The tables flanked the sunroom filled with gifts, mostly from Granna and a small group of Granna's friends.

After eating a few bites of frosting from her slice of cake and spooning her résumé into every conversation, my

Mother retreated to her cell phone, until declaring that Darryl needed to meet immediately with the Director of Nursing at their dermatology office. She kissed me hastily, fanned Darryl's business cards to everyone in the room and clunked down the driveway in their Mercedes without waving, smiling, or even honking the horn. When the passenger window rolled down, I thought that Darryl was going to tip his hand to me or offer a last remark. Instead, he tilted a cup and allowed old brown coffee to splash along the gravel on the driveway. I knew that they were already engrossed in analyzing everyone from the graduation party and how bleak the prospects were for me in the future. Their words would lick up one another's shame, an opportunity to assuage and blame chance for a daughter that just didn't fit in with their lifestyle.

When I lived with Mother and Darryl, she used to say, "We don't want no whipped pups around here." Her face would be hard and serious; then she smiled and laughed, rubbing my hair. "News flash!" she would ring out with a sudden, clear voice. "Ellen Masters is a champ!" Eventually, she only threatened me with the phrase "we don't want no whipped pups around here" in a growling tone that didn't offer a news flash or a confident statement of victory. She grew tired of my melancholy, the telephone calls from the school about my inability to interact and my tendency to withdraw. Panic attacks, a shrink that couldn't get me to say a word, until I finally allowed the sentence to tumble out, "I want to live with my Granna," as tears streamed down my face. After he spoke with Mother and Darryl, the deal was in motion. Granna became my legal guardian, while Mother and Darryl made travel plans. Sometimes, I wonder, what did Tyler really think? We were just so different, from the very beginning. He never wanted a sister. Mother told me that in the car on the move to Granna's house, when I asked why he didn't care about me. She followed it with, "He's just an obsessively focused individual."

"Focused on what?"

"Studying," she said. "You know that." She smiled proudly, "He has to work out that energy and keep going. He's a go-getter. You're just different, that's all. And, I'm nothing like anyone in my family either, thank God."

I didn't know anything about her family. Did she see them? Who were they? She waved every question away and changed the subject, so I learned early not to ask about them. So much so, that I forgot about them, just as I had left my own brother behind, in present life and memory.

*****

As the wife of a soldier, I became quick to catch the news flashes on CNN and FOX, but that FRG woman I tried to befriend always had more information. And, she reported news about my husband's suspicious behavior and his failures with a ring to her voice, as if it were a personal victory. I took it as such, as if she was proud that there was distance in our relationship, that our marriage seemed to be falling apart, and that I didn't understand the ins and outs, the details and endless acronyms of military life and deployments.

She called to check on me, asking if I had protection.

"Excuse me?" Her tone was so soft and private sounding that I thought about condoms when she asked..

"With a murderer out there and our husbands are gone, we need to be safe," she said. "I don't want to scare you unnecessarily, but I hope that you have a big dog or an alarm system at least." I knew that she meant, "at the most you have extra male relatives, guns and old ladies who are regularly at your home." I automatically started locking all of the deadbolts on the doors and checking the latches of the windows and caught myself on the landing upstairs. On the phone, she confided that another marriage was breaking up in the unit. I looked out the window, the clouds ruffling on the horizon. Hummingbirds darted underneath the trees, watching their own reflections take shape and disappear in the shifting light. She gave the details of the soldiers' locations. Then, she casually mentioned that most of the men had been edgy the last time they were at home. Some of them were angry and abusive toward strangers and their wives. "You know," she said, "that there's a big problem with steroid use over there, but they aren't going to really do anything about it."

"Steroids?" I asked. I heard a sudden thump on the window glass, but didn't see anything. I walked downstairs.

"One guy spent thousands before his wife noticed," she said. "And they have three kids."

"Where do they get steroids?" I unlocked the door and peeked out. I didn't see a stunned bird. Sometimes they fell onto the ground beneath the windows.

"Oh, I don't know the details," she said. "Just that it's a problem. Are you worried about it or something?"

"I don't know. Should I be?" I locked the door again and went back up the stairs.

"Oh, hon," she said. "You'd know it if he was taking the juice. He would have mood swings, no desire to be intimate, acne on his back, and irrational anger."

Later, I realized that the conversation seemed staged, as if the woman didn't want to say bluntly, "We think your husband has a drug problem." I crossed the landing and stood in front of the window. The bird was lying on the window frame. Its colors were flat in the shadow. When I opened the window, I tilted it the wrong way and flipped the bird down into the trees and bushes. I searched for an hour and never found it.

David had all of those side effects the last time he was at home. His complexion had always been better than mine, but I rationalized the changes in his complexion and mood as a reaction to dry climate, different food, and stress.

*****

I couldn't eat, started dropping the pounds quickly. My body didn't react well and my appetite slowed. I forced in a few bites of oatmeal every morning. Some days, I ate only oatmeal throughout the day. At least it was healthy and nothing else was appealing. I was nauseated by the smell and texture of most foods.

The dog wandered into the open after two days of loitering in the woods and sneaking forward for harried picks at the scraps I left out for him when I tried to cook for myself. He was medium sized and I had no idea what breed. A mixed together chocolate-caramel-swirled, shaggy-haired drifter with shy eyes. He wouldn't look at me directly for a week. I named him Nuance, and didn't know why. It sounded nice. He looked that way, nuanced, and whatever metaphor that implied. We staggered the same area for three days when Nuance finally stood beside me like he was my dog and had always been. He followed me and whined when he needed to go outside, and demanded to be let outside just before it was completely dark.

"I thought you were supposed to be afraid of the coyotes, not choosing to go run with them?" I said to him while scratching a pointed ear. His tail thumped. Nuance followed me over to the trails. Even though signs were posted that said to keep pets on a leash, I couldn't bring myself to think of Nuance as a pet who required a leash. He had freely wandered since I met him. How could I decide to leash him when he was timid and had walked beside me all around my place and followed me over to Cumberland? Nuance bounced deeper into the forest briefly to inspect the squirrels or to chase deer, but he returned with little bounds back to my side again. He wasn't interested in fighting other dogs, and he definitely avoided other people, even disappearing from the trail when I passed a person, and reappearing later on the trail again.

He delighted Maggie, except for his refusal to sleep next to her. He couldn't be pinned, and sensed anything close to that feeling, especially the encircling arm of a child on a comfortable bed in a peaceful bedroom. Nuance knew that domesticity was the trap to losing his freedom, the kind where a being roamed the wilderness without answering to the scheduled call.

*****

Jordan called to tell me that he ran into the police detective investigating the murders. "He looked exhausted," Jordan said over the phone. "They may have a local suspect. Can you believe that? So many people think it was just someone passing through."

"Did he give you an indication of who it might be?" I asked.

"I have an idea," Jordan ignored my question and said over the phone, "I hope you don't take this the wrong way." I closed my eyes and sighed. These were never good words.

"I want to walk with Maggie while you run," Jordan continued. "I can be your trainer. You've said that you want to run, but you don't have anyone to watch Maggie. I know how protective you are, so Maggie and I could walk around the lake while you run, and you won't have to worry."

I blinked. My head was stretched away from my shoulders by a neck taut with anxiety and the expectation of shocking words. "I thought you were about to tell me something terrible," I said relieved. "But what about the murder investigation?"

"Let's start today," Jordan said over my question again. A couple of helicopters flew over the house and drowned out the phone line. I couldn't hear Jordan for a moment.

"What?" I asked.

"What are your plans for right now?" he asked.

"Answer the question," I said flatly. "And stop ignoring me."

"They have a suspect, I think," he said.

"You said that already. Just one?"

"I think so," he said.

"Well, what did he say?"

"Not much. I don't really know." He sighed. "I don't care that much about it. I was just telling you. I don't know why. Enough of this, just meet me over there."

I darted away as soon as Maggie held onto Jordan's hand. My legs glided along the path. My toes gripped into the sliding rocks and rode the hill until the summit turned me underneath the arch of a living grove of cedars and plunged into the limestone boulders of the hollow. I could hear the tribe as they encouraged my run with their calls of the flute, their imitations of birds, and the panting of their conditioned breath. They had watched warriors perform the challenges from along the bluff, and then leapt along the back trails that connected to the path farther ahead, where they could see the runners finish the obstacle courses. My first run at Cumberland felt like a performance. That mile when my legs were awakened to the discovery of miles and miles to come, and I relived my childhood fantasy that Cumberland Cave had been the training ground for the warriors of a tribe long ago. I saw them blended into the rotted tree trunks, covered in a sinkhole by leaves, and twisted up in the grapevine thickets. They were magicians of shadow and light, of bending the shape and color to match their own disguises.

I had always been addicted to the flight of my mind, but running shifted my vision of history with a greater intensity. It was as if my motion opened a doorway, a past story that allowed me to see the home of an ancient society and their way of life. After the runs, I was more open and told Jordan about my childhood visions. He coached me into training for a half marathon.

My ideas about the tribe encouraged me even more and distracted me from my loneliness. I could sense how fast to run, where to jump, how to lengthen my stride up the hills, how to ride my breath through my nose and deep into my lungs and out of my mouth. I allowed the land to carve me into a fluid being with limbs that respected the trails but weren't afraid to ride them. I didn't use headphones to listen to music, so my runs were accompanied by the rhythm of my breath and my feet, of the trees rocking and creaking, the barred owl chanting beside woodpeckers and the sudden pounding of hooves when a herd of deer dropped down a bank and disappeared.

Four months of nervous humming hysteria in the state ended when police arrested Philip Jefferson for the murders at the park. He was a tall muscular twenty-five-year old with prior arrests and convictions for armed robbery at a park in Georgia. His blonde hair was close cut. On the news broadcast, he was clean-shaven and well dressed. Everyone expected a wild-looking savage or a group of drugged-out crazy people. The more I stared at his image, the more shock I felt. When dialing Jordan's phone number, I trembled with disbelief. "He was in my class," I said with a shaky voice.

"What?" Jordan asked.

"Jefferson was a student in my class when the murders happened."

"What a coincidence," he said.

"Why haven't the police talked to me?"

"Maybe they haven't realized the connection."

I searched my memories. One glance and something looked bizarre in his eyes, in his demeanor, but I couldn't say what it might be. A direct gaze that sent the message, "I am flat. I cannot alter." It was as if his mind had been sealed, broken and glazed over, and there was no way of glimpsing through the surface of that. On the other hand, his well-groomed appearance evoked a gaze affixed only to that surface so that many could have overlooked what was lurking in his mind. My home was so close to the murder location and I reeled with thoughts that he could have followed me home, could have watched me pick up Maggie from the University daycare, and watched our habits. I recalled the incident in the computer lab, trying to recollect his involvement in watching the videos when students were researching the rules of torture. He had been present but not an instigator, and he skipped the day of the presentations and received a zero. He didn't attend the final week of class that semester, so I thought very little about him and assigned the grade of FA, failure to attend, that he earned.

On the heels of my remembrances, I phoned Dr. Hamilton who said the police had collected information from the University already. There was no reason to alarm me or to draw undue attention to me, especially when I was already burdened by my husband's deployment and my home's close proximity to the park.

The police had told Dr. Hamilton that they didn't believe Jefferson was aware of that fact and they'd never mentioned it to him.

Jordan was at my house by the time I finished the call with Dr. Hamilton. "Shouldn't someone have made me aware? Have questioned me about his demeanor in class?" I asked Jordan.

"Did he act strange in class?"

"No," I said. "That's not the point. I would think that would be an odd coincidence, to be in my class and to commit the murders so close to my home. Why wouldn't they look into that?"

"For what? It does seem like a coincidence," Jordan said. "I just think Dr. Hamilton should have forewarned you so that you wouldn't have been so shocked when you heard the news."

"He apologized," I said shrugging. I wanted to grab hold of Jordan and hug him, but I seldom showed affection anymore.

"Good," he said and patted my back, "Don't worry. Hopefully, they've got the right person and we can start putting this behind us."

5 TIME EXPOSURE

"I watched Fahrenheit 9/11 and it made me so angry at the soldiers," one of my students said. Her face was pink and deepened into her shaking hands. "They were so aggressive and rude about intruding into the homes of those poor people. I know that they're following orders but do they have to listen to music about killing people and chant and dance around about it?"

I tried to control my tendency to defense. My mind rattled in hatred for the military and David for choosing it and my mind also caged-in to protect him and so many other soldiers when attacked by other people.

"It's disgusting that they participate," she said, spitting out the words. Other students nodded in agreement. A few put their heads in their hands or stared into their laps where they were texting or using the internet with their phones.

"Participate?" I asked.

"It is a volunteer Army," she said. "What do you think makes them so revved up and ready to kill?"

"I don't think that they're revved up and ready to kill," I said. "It's their job. It's either kill or be killed."

"We don't need to be in that war in the first place. Saddam didn't have weapons of mass destruction, so we chose to go in and kill those people."

"Those soldiers didn't choose to go to war," I said. "They chose to join the military, and our government, which is elected by the people, chose to send them to war. And, we're not only in Iraq."

"Did you see them listening to that music and raiding those poor people's houses?" she asked, looking around at the other students while nodding her head, as if she were trying to rally them.

I rubbed my forehead and strained under the pressure. My mind whirled. I pressed my palms down the front of my shirt and tugged at the hemline.

"Those soldiers were preparing themselves for battle," I said. "Roman soldiers used to bang their helmets together and stomp. The chest bump isn't just a twentieth century sports creation. The war cry isn't a cheerleading term for football games. Warriors and braves from all cultures have pumped themselves up in order to prepare for battle. It's like stoking a fire. It removes fear and increases the flow of adrenaline," I said. "Same as runners who listen to music for a race."

"Except runners don't have automatic weapons," she said.

My face flushed and I wanted to shout. They didn't know that my husband was deployed. They didn't know about the way Jefferson's murder investigation was causing insomnia for me. They were freshmen and I wasn't teaching on post. This classroom was located on the main campus of the University, where students protested the war in the Free Speech zone. I thought they should have been protesting the free speech zone that the administration had enforced, since railing against soldiers wasn't really a war protest and wouldn't help protect their first amendment rights.

After class, I decided to leave Maggie at the day care on campus for an extra hour or two. Normally, I picked her up right away, but I needed to think, yearned for the space, wanted to cry without her watching me sob and shake. Jordan said that he would pick her up, so I went to Cumberland Cave and ran with Nuance alongside me. We bounded on top of the first fallen leaves that spattered bright red beneath the oaks and maples. Then, long golden flakes floated down over the paths along with the apricot-colored and bright green wedges, until they all faded to plum, sand, and toast. Small snakes shook the leaves in a rattle beneath the wind and the hurried steps of chipmunks and squirrels.

I thought I saw Jordan running in front of me at the crossroads and assumed he must be chasing Maggie. Nuance barked and leapt into the piles of leaves toward them. I sped up in order to catch them, but when I passed through the tangle of trails that met before a sharp turn and downhill, zigzagging path, I could only glimpse the top of Jordan's head. I didn't see the dog, either. No barks, no crunching leaves. I sped up, thinking that Maggie had turned into a jackalope for certain. I pursued Jordan around the twists and turns downhill, and then I couldn't catch them. It was obvious that I wouldn't when I no longer saw the top of his head. I was winded and sprinted down to the lake path and turned a circle, scanning all along the trail. There was nowhere else to go. I even thought that they must be hiding from me in the fall foliage, but when I arrived in the parking area, they were in the car, sitting behind the rolled-down windows, laughing after returning from the mall. Shopping bags filled the passenger seat. Maggie played with the hem of her dress that was caught in the car seat buckle and drank lemonade from a restaurant in the mall.

I shrugged it all off and ran through the mists of October and November, and into the holidays. After that, I continued my own training, reaching twelve miles, while Jordan and Maggie shopped for Christmas presents and cold crystals formed over the path and ice began to crunch underfoot.

The loss of vegetation during the winter months made Cumberland seem smaller. I could see far ahead on the path and around the curves toward the next mile. Summer gave the park more depth. At the beginning of winter, I felt exposed as I ran through the cold stillness and was happy to have Nuance as a partner on the lonely trails. Maggie spent her mornings at the University daycare, singing songs and playing tug of war over juice cups with other toddlers. I dropped her off at six a.m., then ran the trails while they were clouded by fog. For a month, I didn't see another human being on the trails during my early morning runs.

Then, I woke on a Thursday in January, waved bye to Maggie, and felt peculiar as I neared the park. Nuance began barking and running in little harried circles. He was barking at me and blocking my path, turning a circle. I felt some aggression from him, almost as if he might bite me if he felt pressed to do so but he didn't want to, though it was apparent that I wasn't listening to something he was trying to tell me. I sensed that he wanted to stop me from going to the park. I thought, *if I see crows around the visitor's center, then I shouldn't run today.* I didn't regularly see crows in Cumberland and hadn't seen one at all that morning. I felt crazy in spite of that awareness. Again the warnings in my head echoed, *The Natives will tell me in the form of crows if I shouldn't run in the park this morning. It could be dangerous.* I scolded myself for such imaginings. *David home again home again jiggity jig, then to market to market, when would market ever be done.* My head recited nonsense, and I felt like I was going mad. Nuance barked, pushed the top of his head into my leg and nearly caused me to fall down. I yelled at him and he ran ahead of me and disappeared into the trees.

Almost a month had passed and I hadn't heard from Jordan. He went to Alaska, to visit Aunt Darcy, and I missed him terribly. Maggie asked for him every day, even Nuance whined toward the path that led to Jordan's house when we passed it on our way to Cumberland. As I moved closer to the tree canopy and onto the rocky path, it dawned on me that Jordan was my best friend. A true first, other than Granna and David. The crows cawed above the tree canopy. I ignored them as I passed a picnic table where a man sat reading a creased newspaper. He wore a gray coat and hat, and even the pallor of his skin was ashen. My mind swarmed with activity like the rotten apples lying underneath a tree in July, and the man looked at me with an intense stare. I smiled and slowed my stride as I ran down the first hill. The man in gray wore gloves with the fingertips cut out of them. I had the most peculiar feeling that he was from some other time and place.

I was afraid to turn around and terrified to continue. The crows landed in a tree on top of the next hill. One bobbed his head. I watched him while I climbed the hill, trying to steady my breath. I heard something else. The pounding was like hooves, so I sped up to see the deer over the hill and caught sight and sound of a small group of soldiers instead. They passed under the crow and it looked toward me, then lifted its wings and soared ahead on the path and cawed as it went. I jogged in place while the men ran through a small clearing on the path and continued ahead of me up a steep hill with a half mile incline. I didn't cross the clearing until I heard the crow about a half a mile away at the first crossroads in the path. I climbed the hill with quick but weak legs. And Nuance showed up again, barking so suddenly that I jumped and shrieked. Hot prickling covered my skin. I felt that I was defying the message I had asked for earlier—I was going against the warning of the crow, but I hadn't technically been beside the visitor's center when the crows showed up. My mind pictured images of being abducted, a crime scene, blood from my body splattered on the winter ground somewhere. I hastily bit a fingernail and spat it onto the trail. Nuance whined from behind me, nipped on my heels until I scolded him again, "Go away!" The park wouldn't be open for a few hours, and no one would even try to look for me since Jordan was out of town. David called twice, maybe three times a week. Only the daycare would try to find me, sometime in the afternoon.

I was frightening myself in more ways than one by thinking, *Maybe I'm just some bored lady with nothing better to do except imagine my own death*. Nuance ran into the woods and stood in front of me again. He whined and turned a circle. I slowed my pace halfway up the hill, trying to catch my breath. His growling broke through the pounding of my heart in my ears. "Nuance!" I scolded and clapped my hands at him, trying to shoo him away, thinking he was growling at me until I noticed that his gaze was fixed on something behind me. I didn't want to turn around and my knees wobbled as I felt the energy simultaneously drain from my upper body and the adrenaline surge through my blood. I tried to free myself from thinking and enjoy the run, concentrate on training and my research when I heard the crow at the crossroads again. *If the Natives are really trying to tell me not to run this morning, if I should have listened to that crow and I should turn around, then let me see at least two deer before I reach the turn at the top of the hill.* I took about five more strides when I heard galloping and pounding that startled me and sped through the forest up the side of the hill. I counted at least ten deer and felt certain that a horn had sounded and I was witnessing Odin's wild hunt in progress. Nuance shot out of the trees, leaping across the path on the heels of the deer in a fury of growls and barks.

Before the herd was out of sight, I pivoted and sprinted along the trail and across the clearing, stumbling downhill, almost falling, and panted by the empty picnic table. The man was gone and his newspaper lay folded on top. I nearly ran out in front of a car in my haste to reach the other side of the street where my property began. When I finally looked over my shoulder at the park, the lake was smoothed by a low cloud and the cave's mouth shrouded in the far bank. The crow flew in my direction from the other side of the forest and kept going away from the cave into the distance.

After that, my runs at Cumberland took on an added dimension. I was certain that the Natives were manifesting their training procedures, as vines lay propped on sticks like the braves placed a tripwire across the paths. In February, ice bent the trees and wove a shiny, slippery obstacle course.

That's when I tripped on a turtle shell beside a muddy water hole about three feet deep. The shell was empty, scratched clean with the deep impressions of claw marks. I closed my eyes when I picked it up and imagined the masked raccoon face peering through the opening of the shell. All the bones were intact. Some of the brown crackling shell pieces peeled away from the main sand-colored fortress. I stopped running to carry it out of the forest. The sunlight stretched between the gray-ringed tree trunks. The knobs on the trees looked like eyes and seemed to have shifted into hundreds of raccoon masks. I saw the Natives, painted and blended with clay and mud, hiding from the settlers in the winter like raccoons, shifting into that image through the cold season. Using the trees as shields, a banded army could cross the bare woodlands striped with the shadows of sunlight on snow.

My eyes started to play tricks on me when I rounded the lake one afternoon and thought I saw David standing on the platform to the cave's entrance. I increased my pace convinced that his mannerisms were David's, that his stance was an exact match and he was looking right at me with a smile on his face. I had even pinched myself over the one-tenth of a mile stretch as I approached the entrance. Within a distance of fifty feet, I thought it was David and was about to start speaking when I saw in the next blink that I would have been speaking to a tree. I felt like a jinn was playing a joke. Whoever the spirit was who could see inside my head, they could stop. I sprinted past the tree and around the trail again, pushing and pushing myself until I vomited. When I crossed the street to my neighborhood, I scolded myself, *How could you be so stupid? I'm such a problem.*

I had been on analysis overload, looking under all of the beds in my house and in the closets every night. I was infested with a fear of murder, since too many coincidences had happened regarding Cumberland Cave and the surrounding property. My mind spun threads and connected them but so far a pattern hadn't grown into either a flowered embroidery or a lace shroud, and I was wilted by the tangles.

*****

Philip Jefferson was charged with five counts of first-degree murder in two different cases. He had written out his life story on college-ruled notebook paper with a black ink pen shortly after his arrest. The DA was pushing for the death penalty and looking forward to an execution date. Experts questioned Jefferson's sanity. Since everyone in our city had been watching the media coverage, the jury would have to be brought in from another side of the state. After arriving at my office on campus one morning in March, I opened the door and nearly tripped over a large yellow envelope that contained a copy of Jefferson's written statement and photocopies of some of the court documents. I had no idea who left the papers. The History Department didn't have surveillance cameras, so there was no way to discover who had left the package or why they had chosen me as the recipient. On the copy of Jefferson's written statement, someone had written in large upper case letters, SHRED IMMEDIATELY! This handwriting was not photocopied, but was written directly across the photocopied papers like a predisposed curse. Jefferson was a couple hundred miles away from Cumberland Cave. He was being transferred for psychiatric evaluations.

In deeply imprinted cursive penmanship, Jefferson declared his innocence. In the case of the Cumberland murders, Jefferson appeared particularly horrified by the violence of the crime. In the other case, Jefferson was accused of robbing the students, then shooting them execution style. At Cumberland, the crime was slightly different. The story went that Jefferson arrived at the diner after it closed. The last customers to leave said that they never saw Jefferson in the store or the parking area. Some customers said that they didn't see a yellow car like his, then changed their stories a few months later. Others were positive that they had seen a car like Jefferson's at The Grille around the time of closing, but also admitted that they didn't contact police until after seeing a news report about the case on television.

Supposedly, the DA would argue that Jefferson followed the three students to Cumberland. This never made a lot of sense to some people in town who thought it seemed more probable that he was lurking somewhere close to the park, but what did they know? Clearly, I was the last to know anything about the case, and I couldn't begin to reason with a written statement scooted under my office door. The three students were Kate, who was twenty years old and the manager of The Grille, Leslie who was also twenty, and Jay, who was twenty-one. Kate, Leslie, and Jay were never declared missing by anyone. As college students, no one had realized that they were missing all night. They didn't know Jefferson at all. In fact, not many students knew him. Around campus, students were saying that he was a loner, sort of odd and wanted to talk about working out all of the time or how he was going to win the lottery. They also said he had a fascination with conspiracy theories, which had been his research paper topic in my course. He failed to attend most classes, and the paper seemed haphazardly thrown together.

I searched for the original news reports again. Didn't one of them cry out or scream? Did anyone make a report about strange noises? I had to question myself—would I have called the police if I heard one scream at two a.m.? What was the time of death anyway? I had never heard a loud noise that night, but I was too far away to hear anything except machinery, firearms and fireworks.

The news reports immediately following the murders and then following Jefferson's arrest were shadowy, scant, and mostly focused on Jefferson's life and mental incompetency. They interviewed students who repeated his isolation from peers due to his repeated theories about government conspiracy, telepathy, staged murders, stabbings, and plots by the government to take him out. Indeed, he covered all of those topics in his written statement, as he was convinced that the murders never actually happened. They were merely a staged event created by military-government officials to test him. Those ideas didn't seem that special. I had met plenty of conspiracy theorists in all walks of life, from enlisted guys and vets of at least three wars to published and respected academics and professors, artists, students, and doctors. The conspiracy theory believer didn't equal a serial killer.

I looked at a photograph of Jefferson. His blonde hair cut close to his face but with enough length to brush a wave over to one side. His smile was similar, a carefree wave, but it contained a slight sneer sometimes. I recalled Jefferson being tall, but his arms and neck were wide. The density was sickening.

It didn't make sense that a man stabbed them repeatedly in a well-traveled area, and that no one heard anything or saw anything until the bodies were discovered the following morning. In the newspapers, every report switched gears immediately to Jefferson. The news stories that were printed prior to Jefferson's arrest didn't contain many details since the investigation was in progress. Initially, I didn't even know if the students had been murdered at Cumberland Cave or if their bodies had been dumped at the location.

I avoided it for a year, but the placement of the manuscript pushed me to find out more. I asked a ranger, who was walking on the trails one day, about the discovery of the bodies. She and I chatted about the beauty of watching the seasons pass and change on the trails, of revisiting year after year and meeting people who reminisce about their time as a child, swimming in the old pool, playing checkers at the mouth of the cave, listening to a brass band; their wrinkled eyes falling back into a faraway photograph, a sometimes dim black and white with the ink faded into a ghostly gray. That reminder of death propelled me into a discussion of the murders, asking her how the employees had been feeling since the arrest and what it was like to work through the murder case. She told me that a woman walking with two dogs around seven o'clock in the morning had discovered the bodies, first one on the trail, then two close to the cave.

At home that evening, I flipped pages, looked for more answers, rubbed my tired eyes, and glanced at the calendar and my notes. After midnight, I couldn't sleep and decided to read Jefferson's manuscript. I needed to find anything in there that offered clues about these uneasy feelings. Why would someone leave it under my door? He was telling his entire life story and like most people who tell a story about their lives, he was egotistical about his accomplishments and appearance. I flipped toward the back to find his statements about Cumberland Cave, since he also commented on the other charges at the other park. I read a few sentences. He was going over the timeline, saying that it wasn't possible for him to commit the murders since he was working a night shift at a department store, restocking shelves and didn't get off work until 11:30. Jefferson wrote that he clocked out at 11:30 and that meant he couldn't have kidnapped the students from the shop at midnight. I was puzzled by this piece of information. Did Jefferson, in fact, have an alibi for April seventh?

And then, I suddenly couldn't focus. I read it again, April seventh. I shuddered. The hair on my head pulsed. I flicked my hands and pushed myself suddenly away from the table. April seventh was the date of the murders. And this night was April seventh, for me as well, at that moment, one year later. Another feeling washed over my head, as if someone had turned on water above me, the sensation poured down my spine and over my skin until the tremors traveled across the hair follicles. What was guiding me? Was someone telling me a secret, telling me a story that hadn't been revealed?

I felt the presence of victims wronged and robbed of their lives, of missing pieces that wanted modes of expression. But what pushed me into a state of terror was the knowledge that my story had just crossed into the deaths of others. I saw the shadow moving around the doorframes, at the end of the bed, in the closets, and through the garden just after dusk. After I awoke with a startling fright in the middle of the night, I saw the image of a cloaked figure leaning over my bed and called out in the night, yelled for my husband, "David!" and slid over to his side of the bed, to his empty pillows and felt his warm body there, pushed myself into the curve of his legs, and rested my nose between his shoulder blades, cradled my face into his back. I closed my eyes tightly, refused to open them and fell asleep.

I awoke the following morning and smelled David, heard him downstairs with Maggie, smelled the coffee. I stretched and smiled, rolled over and fell asleep again. At eleven a.m., I awoke to sounds of Maggie wailing beside my bed, snot was draining from her nose. My baby was pale and shivering, calling repeatedly for "Mommy!"

I questioned my consciousness, *Did I black out? How? What was happening to me?*

Later in the day, I went to the bank for a safety deposit box and left the manuscript there as if it were a confidential poison.

6 TRACKING FOCUS

I stood at the edge of sleep, in the smoky realm when dreams take shape but you haven't committed to one. In my dream state, I saw myself on the shoreline of the lake after running the trails at Cumberland. I stared at the dead tree that went from the bank to the middle of the lake and seemed to be lying on its side with arms stretched overhead. One brown arm was bent as a pillow to cushion the tree's face. In the water, something dark glided toward me from the opposite bank. Swiftly, it waved under the green moss until it reached the bank next to my feet and then it suddenly flew out of the water without a splash or a spare droplet and looked like a woman with long streaming, black seaweed hair who stared, with her nose inches from my lips.

I screamed and sat up in bed, sweating.

The following day, Maggie and I met David at the airport. He was returning from his fifth deployment. I was turning. You know, to the other side of the bed, where you meet yourself in the dark, and you realize, oh yeah, I only dreamt that bit, but did I do that? Did that really happen?

The internal raconteur trembling with all those memories
and stories, the ones I made up to tell my Granna so I
could sneak away and sip reserves of brandy until she
caught me wandering around all that time. I might have
been a young alcoholic, so perhaps that's how I stayed
forgetful.

You don't know these memories unless you slow down.
But you don't dare do that. You keep going in a blur,
especially if your love is in Afghanistan. Some excuse,
some other distance, some entity, it has taken over to move
and roam and feed the dog... but then the dog has run
away, and you feed the baby, the growing child. You think
*I'm too skinny. What's he gonna think when he gets back
and sees me like this? He'll think I'm not eating. How's he
not falling apart? How's he so intact?* There's a
temptation from a terrible consideration, the one not to let
in—is he intact?

Move on to something else. Did I remember to lock the
doors? Wringing of the dishrag in my hands for occupation
on some days. Other times the air blows through my
fingers out the car windows, days when it billows and I
soak it through my pulse with music and beats. The lyrics
move over my lips, and I'm the one with the bulletproof
family. I must tell myself that we can be invincible if we
have to... to make it through this. We'll rely on a device to
keep moving, push on, and search out distractions for us,
just like anyone else; TiVo, movies, Wii fit are all short-
lived and I sweat in the sheets most nights. Wait. That's
the gnaw, waiting. Ten minutes until the arrival. Where is
he? Where is he, his face in those patches of brown?
Modern warfare pointillism. Instead of a park, we're at the
airport. Eye him down and move in. Pulling Maggie's
hand among the crowd . Cookie dropped and left behind.
Clapping shouts for God erupt from a family, relieved
fears sliding out a wet stripe down their faces, kids with

those big nervous eyes smiling the funny distance of uncertain familiarity. Scent of recognition, there's his stride, the detailed parts of him that I've memorized... Wait, where? Poster board signs in the way.

"There?" Maggie points. No, no, that's not him.

There, there now. Wandering. Where to now?

Soothing.

I hear myself ask, "Hey, you hungry?" and that's my first question after not seeing his face in eight months.

*****

The first two weeks after he returned, David remained hidden and isolated. He worked on the computer or in the basement. We barely spoke. I was too afraid to ask him about the war. His answers were quick when I questioned him about dinner or a television program. I continued to do everything for Maggie and maintained the house by paying the bills, shopping for groceries, washing laundry, mowing the yard, and cleaning. He had no responsibilities except to work and fill his car with gas, but he moved my tennis shoes every chance that he got. I always left them beside one of the doors, but he insisted on placing them in the stairwell to the basement on an old black shelf. Every time I looked for them, even after taking them off five minutes prior, he had already moved them. He was like some phantom, swooping in and moving the shoes. That was the beginning of my irritation. I reminded him, "Please, don't move my shoes." And then, "David, you did it again. Don't move my shoes please." He was already out of sight and I was left to mumble to the black shelf, "I don't want my shoes on you." I thought that he was purposefully trying to aggravate me.

And, that certainly didn't help with my worries. I wondered about murders from the past. War in the present. Thought of an imaginary future that failed to offer anything other than scenes of torturous retribution, disconnection from my husband, and a continuation of escape. Retreating to the trails and ghosts of Shawnee runners and hunters shifting along a lost path from the shadows, I realized that I no longer felt equipped to fix any more of David's experiences. I was allowing him to take my experiences away by being unhappy. I couldn't use the computer, watch the television, adjust the volume, leave Maggie with him, or even prepare a meal without his interference at almost every turn. He lacked humor or enthusiasm. He lacked buoyancy. I pressed my palms against my breasts and folded into myself sometimes simply to feel the embrace of a compassionate adult, even if it was my own recognition. Why was it so easy for other military families to have it all together, to seem so cool and polished, unfazed?

"I feel like I'm dying," I whispered or thought often. "He is suffocating me. He's dense."

When I purchased the incorrect brand of razor blades, he stomped and called me "stupid." That was a first in our relationship. The thick and permanent tension had climaxed.

"What is happening here? Did you just call me stupid?" I asked. Maggie was watching a movie in the living room. I was making a salad in the kitchen. I remember that in particular because I twisted the lettuce and listened to the crisp turn and felt so little and insignificant, so disconnected. I wasn't scouting any terrorists out of caves or climbing the steep terrain of Afghanistan, wasn't trying to calm a friend and soldier, wasn't discovering former Al Qaeda camps. I had never heard of the cities where David resided most of the year and didn't understand that it was laughable to think of those places as cities. And I had always felt educated. I felt ashamed of how unconcerned I had been. How I didn't know about the work they were doing—some units built temporary, small water treatment facilities for Afghan villages because they had no water treatment plants. And, I was devastated that instead of sharing his experience and teaching me all that he had learned and seen, he was judging me for failing to get it. I was ready for a confrontation.

I followed him down into the basement. "You're only angry because I don't automatically get what you've experienced. I don't understand it or have any idea about it, and you think that because I don't get it, that it's okay to make me feel stupid and to belittle me and to push me out of the way. Like you don't even have to pay attention to me right now, right? I'm just some bitchy little spoiled wife whose got it all and doesn't understand what her husband does for their family and millions of other Americans and people all over the world, right?" And he looked at me then like I was mocking him, like I didn't respect him. So, I continued, "For instance, you think that I'm being disrespectful right now, but I'm not. No, you've got it all wrong. I want to understand and I want to learn about it because I do respect you and I'm only raising my voice because you are the one who's not giving me enough credit to get it, not trusting me to talk to me and help me to feel smarter about the war and to feel even more proud of you because I know what you're about. So just think about that," I said, my finger pointed, and turned around swiftly to catch my breath. I was so proud of myself and really felt like I had articulated my feelings well.

As I went through the doorway, he said, "I asked for one thing, and you can't even get that right."

"One thing?" I was ready, whirling around. "No, you ask for me to cook dinner, wash and dry your clothes, care for our daughter, buy everything that we need, pay our bills, and pretty much wipe your ass when you're here. You ask for a lot and don't you forget it!" I said. "And, stop moving my damn shoes! I'm gonna end up getting bit by a spider!"

"Yeah well, you're not in a war and you get a lot of money to do whatever you want without having to work for it. Who cares about your shoes? You should keep them picked up and out of the way so no one trips every time they want to go in and out of the doors."

"I do work. What are you talking about? Have you lost your mind? Where is the person that I married who agreed with me that teaching and caring for our child and household is work? I still farm this property! I think you've forgotten what goes into this place."

"You farm?" He smirked. "What farming do you do?"

"I sell the peonies every spring. About five hundred of them. Did you just wipe that out of your memory?"

"You mean you hire some guys to help you cut peonies that grow naturally, on their own, no ritual planting, every year and you truck them into the florists in town."

"And to Nashville. I have to coordinate the whole thing. I have to maintain it."

"I would hardly call that farming."

"I suppose my teaching at a university isn't really teaching either?"

"Well, it's not like you're in an inner city school with troubled youth. That's what I might as well be doing. These new teenage kids still have mothers at home that were making their beds, and now they've got to decide to shoot an eight-year old boy who points a gun in their direction. Why? Because he might blow all of our heads off in the next instant. Why? Because he believes that he'll go to heaven and be remembered as a martyr. Because that's what his parents believe, and he gets to watch torture videos every night before he falls asleep. You don't know the first thing about difficulty, so no, I don't think what you do is too much, not at all. And yes, I do expect the correct razor blades."

"So, I'm your servant! How's that any different than how those men treat their women? Yes, sir, I'll make sure to have the diapers and pay the mortgage and get those five-bladed razors and brush my own fucking teeth which I haven't even had time to do today. I've been doing this by myself here—" I screamed and shook and was so angry that I couldn't speak in complete sentences.

"You're crazy," he said. "Just look at you. What are you even talking about? I don't stop you from brushing your teeth. This is stupid. I'll be happy to leave again."

"No, you're an asshole! And I'm talking about how you don't do anything around here, not for Maggie or me. You don't even act like you have a daughter. She's terrified of you and for good reason, who can blame her? You're a stranger. I can't do this anymore. I don't even know who you are, but I know that I don't like you."

"Well, I don't like you either."

"What are you, a fifth grader? You just repeat what I say instead of taking any responsibility for your own actions? In nine days, you'll be gone and that's just fine with me."

"Bitch," he said, shaking his head like it was a matter of fact. It's better when someone says it like a dare or with a lot of angry force. He seemed amused.

I couldn't believe it. This was not my college boyfriend; clearly this man was someone else. I followed him into the kitchen and slapped his face quickly while I continued to shout. I can't even remember what I was saying, but I had decided that I wouldn't be afraid of him. His face hardened and his arm shot up from his side and he grasped my throat and pushed me into a kitchen chair that was in the corner. "Shut up! Shut up! Shut up, Ellen!" he said through clenched teeth while shoving my neck into the back of the chair. I kicked and hit his knee. I struggled to move his wrist with both of my hands. Maggie stood in the doorway screaming and crying. The look of terror shook Maggie's entire body. She extended a hand and screamed, "Mommy, No! Mommy, No!" She pointed her tiny, toddler hand at David and screamed, "No!" David backed away and strode into the living room.

I followed him. "It's over now!" I screamed. "Over! You have totally ruined everything!"

"Please, just shut up, Ellen. Just shut up," and he ran out the front door. I heard gravel pop under his tires on the driveway.

Maggie shook and cried and screamed, "No! Mommy!" over and over. I tried to comfort her.

"I'm so sorry, baby. So sorry."

I turned a few circles while holding Maggie, cradling the back of her head. I saw the backpack carrier slumped into the corner of the room. We hadn't hiked as much since David returned. I called Jordan and left a message when I was en route to Cumberland. Maggie sniffled and said, "Hiking."

The foliage was becoming dense, and the summer solstice hadn't happened yet. I thought about the past weeks while he was at home. I had been spending my time reading some of Granna's old books and sorting through her lists and notebooks in the attic. I didn't want to talk to David and felt uncomfortable in the same room with him, so I went to the attic when he used the computer. Otherwise, my life operated through the computer where I could chat with old friends, snoop, watch videos, download music, find recipes, and post pictures in order to pretend that life was relatively happy and normal. Since David returned from Afghanistan, he spent several evenings a week playing World of Warcraft and other games on the computer. When we argued about computer time, David said that my communication with old college friends on social networks was just a computer game as well.

"That's ridiculous. I don't blow up and gun down my friends on the computer," I said, but wished it could be erased when I saw the hardened glaze in his eyes.

His shoulders sagged, then he took a deep breath and straightened up as tall as possible and clenched his jaw, changed his tone, "We'll divide up the time on the computer, period. I couldn't care less whether you regard your flirtations and bragging rights as games. I'll take Monday, Wednesday, Friday, and Sunday. You take the rest, are we clear?"

When I had walked away that evening, I told myself that I'd purchase a new computer the following day in order to remedy the situation and teach him a lesson. I'd one-up him as a way of showing that we were crystal clear.

Walking with Maggie on the trails at Cumberland underneath the young green leaves, I thought about that incident and wondered why I'd forgotten to purchase the computer. Why did I automatically give in to his demands and allow him to play computer games on the nights that he had ordered, when I retreated to the attic to prowl through the boxes of Granna's possessions? I had told myself that he gave me a reason to finally sort through the boxes. I found a way to change the situation into something positive, as if he created a good situation for me without even knowing it himself, as if he knew best in some higher scheme of life that I was only just beginning to understand.

I hated my weakness, to be a peacemaker, to give in to his hardened requests, and I pulled a strand of my hair as hard as possible until tears swelled. Maggie walked along the path, collecting rocks in her little fists, then throwing them at the low branches of the trees that we passed. Each time she threw the rocks, Maggie let out a roar, "Rrrerrr!" and then laughed. We rounded the top of a hill and neared one of the rustic, wooden benches that were placed close to each mile marker along the trail.

I scooted Maggie to the opposite side of the trail so that she wouldn't throw rocks at the woman who was seated on the bench. Maggie's fists were full of rocks, and she dropped several as we passed by the woman who used it as an opportunity to talk.

I replied with the standard, "Good, thanks. How are you?"

"Help you," Maggie said. "Help you. Help you."

"Okay, I'll help you," I said and squatted to pick up the rocks that kept popping out of Maggie's fingers when she tried to curl them around the extras.

"How old is she, about three-and-a-half?" she asked.

I nodded, trying to avoid specificities.

"I have a granddaughter that age. Don't get to see her very often usually, but lately I've been able to spend some time with her."

"That's nice. Kids are great," I said automatically with no thought to my responses. I wanted Maggie to hurry up and said, "I'll carry these for you and we can throw them in the water when we get there. Come on, let's keep going so that we can make it around to the water."

"My favorite time in life was when my kids were little," she said. "My husband is dying now, and I don't know what to do." Her shaggy, frizzy hair bounced on her head. She had large, dark eyes that didn't want to be saddened by the events in her life but that also seemed honest about the truth of it, not trying to avoid it by making useless chitchat. If she was going to talk, she was going to get somewhere.

"I'm so sorry," I said. "That's terrible."

She removed her thick-framed glasses and her eyes seemed even larger and beneath them wet freckles lit up in the sun.

I'm not the type of person to confess my personal life to strangers. Even on long flights out of the country, I would angle myself into a corner, face the window if I didn't have headphones, and send the signal that I didn't enjoy communication with strangers. The harder I worked to avoid it, the more people positioned themselves to reveal their secrets and problems to me. Jefferson's manuscript was one extreme example of that thread in my life.

Her shoulders vibrated slightly as she cleared her throat and shifted uncomfortably. She was in her early fifties, wearing hiking shorts, boots, and a khaki t-shirt over her slightly bulging waist. Otherwise, she was a fit woman adorned with a few tattoos. She cleared her throat again and said, "I wish that I had spent more time with my kids when they were little, but it doesn't always happen that way for a soldier, especially during war times," she said. "I was a medic and was just really messed up a lot of the time. My kids were young and wanted to play and be boys and I was so lost and like I said, messed up. I lost a lot of time that I wish I could have back. It's not the same once they're grown. I didn't figure all this out until I met up with some Indians," she laughed and shrugged, "but that's another story and I really don't know why I'm wasting your time when you've got to make it to the water, don't you little one?" she turned and asked Maggie with a broad smile. "Sounds sort of silly when I say it all out like that anyway."

"Yes," Maggie said and started down the trail. "C'mon," she waved, "to the water. C'mon."

"I think she wants you to follow her," I said and pointed to Maggie.

"Bye," she called to Maggie and waved.

"You mean a Native American tribe?" I asked, changing my previous mindset about avoiding her, and instead hoping for a conversation.

"Yes," she said and stood to follow us but hesitated. "They have a ritual for their warriors when they return from battle, and I went through that ritual—"

I gestured that she should accompany us on the trail.

"I'm sorry," she said. "I didn't mean to tell all of my problems to you. I don't usually tell people my personal business, but today was a tough day. My husband has been having radiation treatments for cancer and he's been terribly sick. So sick." She shook her head and cleared her throat.

I didn't understand and allowed the silence to take up some space, then asked, "Can you tell me about that ritual?"

We followed Maggie while she talked. The three of us threw rocks into the water until the sun created a golden crescent in the corner.

"The process of welcoming a warrior back from battle, that's what I did. All native tribes have rites of passage. They train the young children, both boys and girls, concerning rites of pass-" She paused and smiled as three helicopters passed overhead and covered her voice.

Maggie pointed into the sky, said, "Helicopter." I clapped, proud of her pronunciation.

After the helicopters were over the tree line, the woman continued, "Rites of passage. The preparation for the rites of passage is itself a step along the path. Their rites of passage include hunting, sexual union, marriage, children, combat...those types of activities. One of their traditions is to offer a ceremony to warriors who have returned from battle."

Maggie picked up a stick and struck it against the tree trunks. Some of the leaves shredded on the ends. A few flitted toward the ground. Suddenly, she screamed, "Water!" Maggie ran down the bank toward the lake. I chased her. Maggie screamed louder and stomped as she wiggled her wrist beneath my fingers. "Stop it! Go to water! Water!" she shouted over and over.

The woman stopped herself, "I'm sorry—I'm probably keeping you from time with her."

"It's okay," I said, looking around for a way to distract Maggie. "I've heard about these re-entry rites but never met anyone who had been through one. I would like to hear more about it."

She continued while I showed Maggie how to chase after a spider with a stick and catch one of its threads then move it to a new location. "These men and women are not allowed to re-enter the tribe until they complete the ceremony," she said. "The tribe feels that the warrior needs to discuss his or her joys and sorrows about the battle. We must talk about the experience of war. Tell the story and not gloss over it. The tribe has a council, many of them women, who listen to the stories of the returned warriors. The council doesn't judge the warrior. They offer what's needed. And, it's a sacred contract between the warrior and the council. It's a time of listening and healing. The purpose is to heal and to cleanse the warrior's vision so that he can rejoin his people without sadness and destruction on his heart or without dominance and pride in his head. Every warrior is different and has a unique experience. Some need one night to tell their story and others need one week."

I learned that soldiers like David are often unable to merge their beliefs with the reality of war because they haven't been given the proper mental reasoning to do so. The soldiers return from combat with hostility to television advertisements and headlines that pretty much ignore what's been happening in their reality. Most of them don't know how to make that change back into civilian life without some validation from the society that sent them to war. And if that society shouts at them, tells them they're evil for making mistakes, makes a woman in New Hampshire feel as if she can't exit her own home while wearing her uniform, then our society has sent a mixed message, a message that the soldier should hide her deeds, should cloak her training, should whisper and plot and plan and go off mission, should become someone to be feared instead of trusted and solid enough to hold our safety within a protective embrace. "I should have known this," I said to her, with a sinking sorrow in my stomach, draining my face. "Shouldn't I have just got it?" I asked.

"Oh, no, how could you?" she said with a questioning smile and looked around, "From thin air? Just realize aha, warrior culture is x and civilian culture is y?" The woman told me that tribal councils helped with those transitions, "Many tribes acknowledge the realities of combat and war where the rules of survival are not the same as the civilian world."

"My name's Fran, by the way," she said smiling, "Maybe I'll see you around here again sometime."

*****

Just behind my ears, close to my hairline, were small purple bruises from David's fingertips. A serious communication break in a relationship is just stubborn. Outmoded, sullen, and mean. We each kept our end of the stubbornness. I repeated these adjectives under my breath for a week. I'd been stacking the anxiety and extra weight into my shoulders and knees, into all of my joints. I didn't want to carry it anymore. Mumbling was my way of putting it out there, but he wheeled around corners and doorways with his shoulder pushed forward. We didn't speak directly for over a week.

I arrived home from a run one afternoon and found that David had packed the canoe on top of the Jeep and loaded it with camping supplies. I sighed irritably, but then considered that we may be able to fix our relationship if we could only sweat together. In my mind, a connection was that simple.

David knew that the loud music often annoyed me, so he turned down the volume on the drive. He opened the door and gave me a cup of coffee and a chocolate bar when we stopped at a rest area. He tilted his head and smiled. "You're pretty," he said.

I distrusted his sudden kindness but Maggie was happy in the backseat, saying, "Camping all together with Daddy. With you and me and Mommy." She smiled.

We arrived at the camping spot at dusk and still had to find wood for a fire. David pitched the tent in the shadows while I unloaded our bags and supplies. He rearranged the fire pit while Maggie and I grabbed the small fallen tree limbs that were close by. He splintered those quickly and built a little pile that tapped out tiny audible flames. David disappeared into the expanding shadows of the forest. I wrapped a blanket around Maggie and gave her some snacks. She was satisfied, curled in a chair close to the dissipating fire. My anxiety was beginning to loosen and swirl into something wispy but tangible, when David returned with his arms and hands loaded with all shapes of wood; even his neck was carrying a tree branch. His teeth held one of his gloves. I grabbed it free and some of the wood.

"Thanks. Let's get this fire going," he said smiling toward Maggie. "First, you need a little kindling fire like that. Then, you position your mother log close to the center. The mother is the best log you have. Next is the father.

Keep a little space between the mother and the father, but make sure they touch." He selected and placed the wood on the fire as he said all of these things. "We must make sparks fly between them and they have to last for a long time, so we stuff the space in the middle with more little branches and a few leaves. You can use newspaper," he explained to Maggie. He pulled a small hatchet from the back of the Jeep and began chopping the wood that he stacked according to diameter. As he chopped and stacked, he continued telling Maggie how to build a fire. "You want to protect the fire of the mother and father log so you take these long thinner pieces and encircle the fire with them, like a teepee. Make a couple of layers if you can and then stuff the inside with more kindling. Always be sure to set aside another mother and father log in case you stay longer than expected."

He started cooking for us on a nearby grill. "I'll make the rest of our meals over the fire, but I didn't think the fire would get hot enough quick enough so I brought charcoal for this first meal. Should be okay."

I was baffled by why we should be disappointed about using a grill that was welded to the camping site for all campers to use. "What's wrong with using the grill?" I asked, imagining that they must be contaminated and not healthy for people to use.

"Nothing," he said, "I want to really camp. That's why I didn't want to stay at our place. You'll see. I'll make you a cobbler for dessert tomorrow night," he smiled and it felt so good that it was painful to see him again, to like him again. I wanted to hate him and tried to remain angry. I turned my face away suddenly. I answered with short statements, acted uninterested in his ideas and his skills. I watched the flames flicker toward the stars. I jumped at noises from the woods over my shoulder and imagined other campers abducting us, killing David, taking us away to a life of sex slavery. I had watched television programs based on real crimes and heard an NPR story about the thousands of children and women forced into slavery every year. Maggie fell asleep in the chair with her head collapsed onto her chest as if her neck had disappeared. David moved her onto an air mattress in a little tent beside ours. I didn't think she would sleep alone in her own tent and argued with him about even putting it up, saying it was a waste of time.

"I told you that extra tent was a good idea," he said. "We can go stretch out in the other tent."

"Humph," I responded.

"We have to relax sometime, Ellen. I'm sorry." He knelt beside my chair, held my hands. They trembled and I withdrew them. "Are you scared of me?" he asked.

"Sometimes."

He put his head in my lap. "It was the wrong reaction," he said, "what I did, but I'm begging you to trust me." I sensed he wanted to touch me, but he didn't. He waited, showing me that he had more to tell me. "There are so many things to bring us fear, to make us afraid, but this is me, Ellen, this is us, and we love the stars. We dance with them and the wind, remember?"

One of our best memories was dancing under the stars with the wind blowing. We drifted apart in our dance on the edge of an autumn field and David shouted to me, his voice rising on the wind and being swallowed by it at other times, but he repeated it while spinning and rocking, "I can love you more. I can love you much more. For a lifetime, much more." That was it. I was with him without a chance for rescue. No one intervened with the ability to compete.

In the tent, I watched the shadows of the tree branches cross and sway. David didn't speak. First, he traced his fingertip along my arm. Then, with all of his fingers relaxed in a loose curl, he moved his knuckles back and forth along my arm. "What's it like for you when I'm away?"

"Lonely," I said. "But sometimes I get used to it and it's more like a productive solitude. I guess that's what we have to do. What about you?"

"It's different," he said. "I have the job and all those soldiers. Too busy to think and then it becomes a zone. Just go into it, get the job done so I can come home. That's as far as I get. If I get further, then I worry you could find somebody else or have an affair or just get sick of it and divorce me while I'm over there."

"I do get sick of it, but I wouldn't have an affair or send you divorce papers in the mail."

"It happens to so many soldiers. You don't understand what it's like—"

"Yes, I do understand," I said pushing his hand aside. "I'm living it exactly the same as you. I'm living it too, okay!"

"Hey, hey," he whispered, "That's not what I meant. Yes, you live it too." He tried pushing my hair aside, but I inched further away from him. "Ellen, I'm sorry," he said. "I just want to be close to you."

"So now you want to be close to me?" I asked. "After everything else? After all this time?"

I stiffened. "I'm sorry that I've hurt you," he said. He touched my back and kissed the top of my head then unzipped the tent and went out by the fire. He added another teepee layer. I watched him peek in and check on Maggie. I watched the firelight move across his face until I fell asleep.

The next morning, he and Maggie were cooking breakfast. They had already been fishing early that morning. When I awoke after ten, Maggie was laughing, "That fish was so funny like this," she said and moved her little arms side to side with her body while her head lolled and her tongue hung out the side of her mouth. "It was funny, Daddy."

Four days later, he left for training again and I sagged back to the Cumberland trails. Maybe he came back home before being deployed again, but I can't remember. They became so mixed up, the arrivals into departures, until drifting away was the constant. With letters and Skype, we tried to maintain regular contact. He mailed a vase. I sent boxes of cookies, the fade away mints, packs of gum, crackers, baby wipes, new blankets and pillows. I don't mean to skip these details. They just feel so standard to military life. You start packing them up before the other one is mailed. You buy extra at the grocery as a matter of habit. All of it stuffed into a flat rate box until you're in line with all the other military wives and can't remember what's in the box when you're asked by the postal worker to write it on the label. You learn to write standard items: chips, crackers, shirt, candy. You and your daughter stroll out into the sunlight, make plans right over Father's Day weekend without even noticing until you go out to a restaurant for a change on Sunday and see all the dads and kids. There's a fear that it will sink into your daughter's mind, that even though she's a pre-schooler, she'll notice in a few moments that all the kids are with their dads. She's so excited to be at a restaurant in that kid-having-an-adventure way that you can't leave. You wait, and she notices, but with a distant knowing, one that will take a

112

year, hopefully more, you think with a wince, to become fully conscious.

I saw Fran again and she asked, "I saw you crossing the street last week, but I was going somewhere. Do you live around here?"

I told her about the farm.

"Yeah," she said in a slow high smile, relaxed and easy, "I thought you might be from there. Don't you all sell the peonies?"

"Yeah, that's us."

"Great. Those are beautiful and the colors are fantastic. Wow, how great is that? How long has your family been doing that anyway?"

"Oh, I don't know. Decades." We walked up a hill with quick strides.

"Did they ever log it? I bet there are some great trees at your place. I noticed the one on the corner, the big grandmamma."

"Corner?"

"Of the intersection," she pointed and then cocked her head, considered her direction, turned in a little laugh and pointed through the forest again, "of that intersection."

"Yeah, yeah, I think I know the one. No, it wasn't logged," I said.

"How long's it been in your family, at least a hundred years? Is it a century farm?"

"What's that?"

"You're an historian and you don't know what it is. That's just wrong," she said slapping my arm lightly, "and I don't mean that as a criticism toward you, I mean that as how backward our system is that most people don't even know and no one has notified you, but I bet people have offered to buy it from you, huh?"

"Well, what is it?"

"A century farm is one that's been farmed by the same family for at least a hundred years. It offers protection for your land." She touched my shoulder. "Hon, I'm sorry. I shouldn't be so forthcoming with my opinion because I really don't intend it in a critical way toward you, honestly, but it does seem that way to you or anyone else and I need to stop that. You've only just met me. Please forgive me for prying into your business."

"It's okay," I said. "I think my Granna would appreciate this discussion. She loved talking about her plants and the farm and nature in general."

"Seems like I would like that woman. What was your Granna's favorite plant?" she asked. We were both sweating in a fast stride parallel to the street, having veered from the trail to walk on the brown needles in the shade of the pines.

"Tiger lilies," I said, trying to wipe the sweat away from my neck, the gnats clinging to my face and flicking themselves into my eyes.

"What about you?" I asked. "Are you from here?"

"No, I'm originally from Arizona," Fran said. "But I've moved all over the place and I've been here about ten years."

She worked in the hospital on post for a while, but lately she was pursuing a hobby as a career and taking nature photos for websites. That's why she liked Cumberland. Sometimes, she set up her tripod to eye the blue heron, belted kingfishers, and the great horned owl.

She asked again about the peonies at the farm and if she could photograph them sometime. They created a sea around the house. About five hundred of them. I had a memory flicker forward, and move through my head like a motion picture: those spring months in the greenhouses, cutting the peonies and riding in the trucks into town and sometimes Nashville, I felt full—open to a soft edge from the butterflies and bees and the fragrance of moist, moving vegetation that swarmed us with an unbearable pressure of succulence, of an overpowering ripening, to the point of becoming thick and muddy with sweet, pulpy, infectious petals. And then, the truck's doors swung open and warmth billowed through, waving it out, airing it with a penetration into the neighborhood that brought the ladies and gentlemen out to purchase all that spring ruffle and oversexed vegetation.

Spring ripened into summer months in the greenhouses and Aunt Darcy had long fingers with smooth nails that scooped tiny shovels of dirt as she filled more plastic containers with a combination of leaf mold and sifted black dirt, then turned the mixture with her hands until it was fine for the fragile threads of the roots. Thunder announced an approaching storm with flickering sprinkles against the glass. The room turned a dismal yellow with the combination of fluorescent plant lights lingering above the one aisle in the greenhouse and the cloudy sunlight filtering through the windows. Aunt Darcy plucked up the baby ferns silently and became lost in the depth of their tiny ever-expanding world. Ferns bordered her house and were the plants that created an obsession in Aunt Darcy's mind. Granna's philosophy was that one plant grew in the minds of most people, even if that meant the cut roses at the grocery store. The fertile hollow, where Darcy's house was located, created the perfect environment for the ferns.

In the greenhouse, I smacked my hands together suddenly. Aunt Darcy jumped as a shower of dirt speckled her face and the counter. It rained upon the ferns, and out of Darcy's fingertips, a wad of wet fluorescent green fern life flew into the aisle and splattered onto the concrete.

She didn't wear an apron and gave an indifferent shrug. She misted the transplanted ferns with water, and I followed behind with lids to cover them. We slipped along the shaded, slick floor of the greenhouse. The fluorescents above our heads swayed in response to the thunder, and the metal around the windows rattled slightly.

We placed the sealed fern containers on a high shelf in the corner. Darcy patted the tops of the containers with her palm and sang to the plants, urging them to grow quickly. It wasn't long after my dad died, I don't think, and Mother probably hadn't met Darryl yet, or wasn't serious. It just seems relevant to me because it was the last time I can remember Tyler being at my Granna's house. That must be weird for him. Completely severed from our dad's family. Maybe it isn't. I just can't imagine, but then, I'm almost completely severed from our mother. So that's weird too.

Darcy helped Granna with the little floral business she kept going. That's why she sold the peonies as a cash crop as well. There were enough peonies to fund many of Granna's projects, which included donating arrangements to art shows and events.

We were making some arrangements that morning for Granna, and I followed Darcy into an adjacent room with large windows. In the greenhouse, misting pipes rattled and fanned water over ferns of all ages that washed the shelves with their dark fountains of green leaves and fronds.

A small cart rested at our feet. Buckets on the cart overflowed with zinnias, lavender, rosemary, dahlias, and a variety of bedazzling garden blooms. Folds wilted with raindrops and dripped to a shine. As they dried and warmed, their fragrances stuck to our breath, and with every inhalation, we sucked in the aroma of lavender and roses. A few bumblebees, weighted with water, wiped their matted furry legs and buzzed toward the windows, where the rain began to splatter. Lightning flickered outside, revealing the frantically approaching rain. The lights faltered in the room before thunder trembled the door from the greenhouse. The rain continued to speckle the windows with fat drops, but the thunder tiptoed all around the distance.

Suddenly, the doors whipped open as Tyler and Jordan thrashed the wet blustering wind through the greenhouse. Lightning yellowed the gray sky and tinted it a glowing antique green. The boys sweated in a wide-eyed gallop. They jumped and waved swords that were actually gardening scissors, gleaming flashes of silver. They chanted, "Victory is ours!" around us and down the aisles. Darcy began marching along with them, playing their game, and then waved at me to join in.

"We have succeeded in slaying the tigers!" one of them shouted.

"They're all dead!"

"Yay! We've beheaded them all!"

"Let's go to the kingdom we've overtaken!"

"Hooray, let's go!"

"Down with the tigers! Victory is ours! Victory is ours!"

The clouds swept in thick rolls of white on the horizon and the yellow charge lured the line of us outside, where we found devastation. Hundreds of our family's heirloom tiger lilies, the tall ones, were decapitated, strewn about helplessly, their black speckled orange tongues rolled away from their faces. The two boys continued to chant and march, but Darcy just covered her mouth, then turned, and ran toward the greenhouse.

"What did you do?" I asked them, shaking my head. "Granna will be so mad, so sad!" I shouted.

I ran behind Darcy and found her removing wet foam blocks from a bucket. Pieces of green foam slipped between her fingers and the blade. She cut the foam and squished it into china bowls, vases, and teapots waiting in front of her, waiting for an art opening or book club meeting or church altar.

I threw some buckets onto a cart and filled them with water. I wheeled into the yard and scooped up the strong-arching stems of the tiger lilies. Thunder was under my feet. The flash and snap was in my bones, and then the rain fled from the sky in pandemonium as I filled the cart. I marveled at how flat the ground suddenly appeared without the tall tiger lilies filling the space. The ground rolled out small hills in other places where I had never realized there were hills. I rounded one of the potting sheds and scooped a handful of tiger lilies into my fists.

Tyler screamed something about a traitor from behind me and pointed the scissors at my neck. I was startled and dropped the flowers. Jordan pushed me from the other side and I slid into the mud.

"Traitor!" they continued to yell and laugh. "Prisoner!"

One of them tried to grab me, but I slipped and wiggled away as they fell into the mud. I ran and grabbed the handle of the cart. The storm engulfed them and me. I don't know how I made it into the greenhouse. I was prepared to burst through the doors and tell on them, but Aunt Darcy said so matter-of-factly as if there wasn't a furious storm outside, "Looks like you slipped up in the mud," she arched her eyebrow, "And, you have a large cockroach on your shirt."

I screamed, and flicked it onto the floor, waving my hands in a stomping frenzy. Tears sped down my cheeks.

Aunt Darcy turned back to the arrangements and said, "You know eggs could be on the bottom of your shoe now. If a cockroach is pregnant and you smash it, the eggs can attach to your shoe or whatever you crush it with. They're also the number one thing ear doctors remove from people's ears."

"Stop talking about them," I said. "They're disgusting."

"Cockroaches aren't worth your tears," she said. "You pranced around with that butterfly on your shoulder yesterday in the cutting garden."

"I like butterflies. They drink nectar."

"And dog shit," she said and flicked rosemary leaves at me. "Since you're so scared of roaches, you may want to remember that rosemary repels them."

If she had made eye contact with me, I wouldn't have been equipped to hide it. She didn't, so I learned how to forget, suppress and feel threatened. For a while, I forgot about the tiger lilies and that she never reprimanded the boys for chopping them down. Did Granna? I don't know. Forgetting is so much easier than remembering.

*****

Jordan and I reminisced about Granna one afternoon during a hike.

"Sometimes I find myself singing like her, 'Precious memories how they linger. How they ever flood my soul. In the stillness of the midnight, precious sacred scenes unfold,'" I sang to Jordan.

"I haven't thought about that song in a long time," he said. "My mom hummed it too, if she wasn't singing it."

"I didn't know it was a church hymn for a long time. Where do you suppose they learned a church hymn? I don't remember that they attended one."

"Yeah, Granna and my mom went to that one downtown sometimes," Jordan said. "Granna's parents were super religious, I think. That's what my mom told me once, and that's the reason they didn't visit because she married someone that they considered a bootlegger, even though that really wasn't the same thing." He changed the subject suddenly, as will happen when it has been practiced for such a long time that you forget this is the real moment of asking. "Why did you move in with Granna anyway? And why did your mom send Tyler away to school? Why don't you ever talk about him?" he asked.

I pointed to a bent tree at a crossroads. "Did you notice how all of the trees are twisted around in here today like it stormed this week? But, it didn't storm this week, did it?"

"I would like to jog through here in the rain," Jordan said. He looked into the tops of the trees as if they could tell the sky to produce rain and only needed him to say that he wanted it to happen. Just then, I thought that I saw the Native boy, the one that I had seen as a child, the one I followed into the forest, who laughed at me with the fish on the end of his line. I jogged ahead of Jordan, looking for the boy.

He had become a teenager with me, had lured me off the path and into the bluff enclosure that was sealed into the hollow on the backside of the cave entrance. I had taken the flask that I'd found in my Papa's desk and tried to induce the boy's apparition. I had taken Papa's notebooks about the distillery, but no one cared. They weren't wanted papers, just tossed aside instructions from a long-ago time and tradition. I had baggy pockets on the shins of my pants and kept the flask there, where Granna wasn't likely to press against it during a hug, and where it wouldn't bulge when I sat down, where it wouldn't bump against anything and announce my secret with a deep metal ring. The scent was all the announcement that my Granna needed, and she monitored my time after that, especially when I had a week of nightmares after the flask disappeared. I wanted that boy to be real, someone like me, wandering the trails alone, soft shouldered and dealing with the forces of nature that fall from ledges or get caught on the end of a line. I had my turtle, and he had his fish, and if he were real, I would have known that he lived in Cumberland Cave after his mother died, after she taught him about the attack, about the death of his father and the warriors, the shaman passing into the Warioto, after she taught him how to fish and hunt, to kill and hide, to grind roots and heat water, after she taught him how to live alone without a tribe. But, he wasn't there, not when I grew up, not when I became an adult.

A few minutes later when Jordan caught up with me and we passed a large maple that had split and splintered across part of the path when it fell, Jordan said, "Like you, I've noticed that the wind makes a dramatic appearance in this area. I really would like to be in here during a storm, just to see what happens."

A week later, Mother and Darryl visited and kept Maggie so that I could have some free time to myself for a few hours. Mother and Darryl lived six hours away and worked incessantly, so they were only available to visit two or three times a year. They glowered with disapproval when I announced my engagement to David, though both of them now use his military service as a way of bragging to their friends and entering into discussions about conservative politics.

When I revealed that my degree was in history, they had cleared their throats and gazed at one another with stiff, serious eyes until they threw up their hands in a what-did-we-expect-anyway gesture. David's military salute and Maggie's early cesarean birth continued to breed the idea that I needed to be rescued from my life time and time again. They tried to forget the time that they failed to rescue me, so much so that I had forgotten it. They wanted my amnesia too, so they sent me to Granna. And it had worked. I forgot to ask for money before it arrived.

I met up with Jordan at Cumberland Cave after they arrived for their visit. In the late afternoon, we entered the forest and jogged slowly, as if we were both waiting to say something but didn't know how to begin. There was an unsteady pressure between us and we bumped into one another on the trail during the first half-mile. I stumbled over a tree root and rolled my ankle, quickly hobbling and continuing. After the first mile, thunder rumbled over the landscape, trembling the ground and announcing the path it would travel under our feet. "So, I've been thinking about the last time we were here and you never told me why you came to live with Granna? And, I've always wanted to know," Jordan said after five minutes of silence and another half mile had passed between us.

"I just liked it there and Mother and Darryl were always so busy with work. They traveled to Darryl's lectures, too."

"Was Tyler always at school or did he actually go with them to lectures? Where was he?" Jordan asked.

"It's so humid," I said.

"I'm sorry, do you not want to talk about Tyler?" Jordan asked. "I didn't mean to pressure you if that's a sore spot, but I've honestly always wanted to know what happened. Since we were kids, I've wondered if your mom just dumped you at Granna's after Uncle Jake died."

"It's okay," I said and my voice cracked and trembled. No one had said my dad's name in a long time. I was surprised by the sound of it seeming so familiar coming out of Jordan's mouth. The sound of my own voice allowed the emotion of the past to take shape. Rain started to drop through the tree canopy. The birds quieted. Clouds rolled out heavy blankets of pressurized moisture that flickered energetically while we ran up the last big hill on the path. We moved faster, bouncing along the edges and winding on the path into the wild grasses. And then, I couldn't stop my voice from describing how alienated I felt after Dad died. It was like my child's voice finally spoke aloud. Mother and Tyler bonded and that felt like a betrayal when Darryl came along. "I didn't belong with them. I wanted to remember my dad, and they just wanted to forget. She said that Tyler never wanted me as a sister. He was a go-getter and I was different."

Jordan and I ran and then climbed a small bank beside the path and sat underneath a birch tree while the storm arrived and swirled the tops of the trees with wind. Sticks and leaves rattled to the ground. The earth trembled underneath us while Jordan listened. I tried not to cry.

"How does it feel when they visit you?" Jordan asked.

Rain dripped down my face. I rocked gently back and forth with my knees under my chin and rhythmically pulled a strand of my hair over and over. Jordan reached out his hand and my back rested against it.

"I don't think about it since I only see them two times a year, maybe three. We talk about Maggie or David and the war or something like that. We've never talked about Dad."

"I know she's your mom," Jordan said, "but she's just evil for telling you that about Tyler, for creating a wedge between the two of you. You didn't deserve her criticism. You were just a kid who didn't know what was going on."

The shock of sympathy caused me to stop rocking, and I put my head on Jordan's shoulder, sobbing until the storm passed.

7 FILL FLASH

Maggie and I waited at a picnic table. I was anxious to talk to Jordan after the weekend. Mother and Darryl were gone and I rushed them to leave early. I couldn't believe that I pushed my own Mother out the door, waving my hands, with her purse dangling from one of my wrists.

I said, "I need for you to leave, Mother. You and Darryl are upsetting me and I need to be alone. I'll call you in a few days."

She argued, saying that I was being irrational. "You're frightening me, Ellen. And I don't know if I should trust you with Maggie," she said when I insisted that she leave.

"Mother, I'm asking you to leave my home earlier than you had anticipated. That's all. Whatever else you're trying to insinuate is about yourself, not me." I waited for her to argue, but she didn't. Darryl packed his suitcase and walked out the front door.

"This is terribly rude," she said. "We don't deserve this."

I didn't say anything, but waved her through the door and placed her purse in the driver's seat.

When Jordan arrived Monday morning with newly picked blackberries, warm and plump, I needed someone to tell me that I was right and vindication was a forward step. I also needed for someone to answer the big question, why hadn't I ever confronted her about my dad's death and why she pushed me away from my brother? The idea of confrontation wasn't a possibility until that afternoon in the storm when I talked to Jordan. My mind whirled with the notion that the experience of being rejected by my Mother and Tyler had been petrified there all along, and I had tried to avoid discovering its slumber. Juice dripped from the tips of some of the blackberries. One berry on top had a mushy side, slightly gray. Jordan said, "That's a sick one. I had a bunch of those. Better throw them out for the ants and flies." He plucked it from the basket and started to sling it to the ground.

"You can use those to make smoothies or put on ice cream or something like that," I said. "They're just a little mushy. Granna used them for preserves, even cobblers."

"You can have them if you want, but not me," Jordan said, dropping it back into the basket. "The outside is a reflection of the inside." He pursed his lips and looked slightly to the side of me. Once when I was pruning the trees around our house, Jordan commented on how to correctly remove some branches by cutting out the crossing ones. Similar details spring to mind like the number of months until the expiration of paint, how to store an iron skillet, the proper water temperature on the hot water heater, and how to prevent grass molds by watering during the morning instead of the evening.

I didn't comment about the mushy blackberry again, but Jordan wanted to win. "I really believe that's true," he said intensely. "The outside always reflects the inner state."

"Okay," I said. "I just don't think that's absolutely true all of the time for everything and every person in existence. Sure, it's often the case, but sometimes appearances can be deceiving and we should never judge a book by its cover."

Jordan pointed at me with a forced smile that softened as he spoke, "You can follow that old adage if you want to. I just see it differently. Anyway, I came by to give you some of these blackberries and let you know that I can't walk today. I've got a doctor's appointment in an hour, and I don't want to be hot and sweaty."

"Are you okay?" I asked.

"I'm just in a hurry," he said and stretched his leg against the curb. "I'll call you next week or something."

"I meant are you sick or hurt? The doctor?"

"It's just my knee. I'll be fine after I get some damn medication." Jordan hugged me quickly, kissed Maggie on the head, and waved while walking to his car.

"I hope you feel better," I called. I knew that Jordan was lying in order to leave. Next week? We had been running and walking almost every day. Jordan moved in a lot of social circles. Sometimes, I didn't feel important enough in my isolated hermitage of Cumberland and home. My only travel destinations were the school, grocery store, post office, and gas station.

The morning of the mushy blackberry, Maggie wanted to walk down the rocky path to the lake. I tried to convince her to get into the backpack for a hike. She wiggled away from me. I didn't know what to do with the baskets of berries on the picnic table. Of course, I ran after Maggie who fell just before I grabbed her. Maggie screamed repeatedly, "Let me walk!" While I carried her toward the picnic table and inspected the scrape on her shin and forehead, Maggie struggled to free herself. She flung her arms up and turned into a heavy plank. I passed the picnic table and tried to place Maggie in the backpack carrier, but she kicked and knocked over the carrier. I righted it and tried again, but Maggie's kicks scraped my face. I couldn't still Maggie's legs long enough to get them into the holes in the carrier. It fell to the side again. Maggie screamed louder, "No! Let me walk!" She arched her back, flinging her arms and kicking her legs. I quietly and forcefully tried to place her in the carrier but it fell again.

Then, I remembered the picnic table with the half dozen containers of warm blackberries drawing gnats and a few flies. I flamed into furiousness when I thought about Jordan trying to show kindness by bringing berries but leaving them while knowing that I had planned to hike with a toddler. Why wouldn't he have brought them over to my house? I picked up Maggie who screamed, but I tucked her under my arm. Then, I picked up the cartons, not even bothering to wave the gnats away. I stacked them on top of one another. The cardboard smashed into the top berries. The little tower leaned in my other arm and two baskets tipped onto the pavement beside me as I made my way to the side of the street. I squished a couple of berries under my feet. When I finally made it across the street with Maggie's legs kicking my side and her high-pitched scream winding down, I looked back and noticed that I had left the backpack carrier and the other blackberry baskets both turned on their sides at the picnic table. Cursing at Jordan for his gifts, I boiled the berries into a few small jars of jam.

The following day, Jordan called. "You want to walk?"

"What about your knee?" I asked.

"Cortisone shot and it's fine," he said.

I met him at Cumberland. Maggie cooperated and walked one of the trails. She pulled a stick along behind her in the path, marking our way in the dust, defining her freedom. We wound our way through the trails. It felt like we were spinning a web. My hair caught in the branch of a dead cedar tree.

"The cedar trees are like totems, the spirits of the Indians. Don't you see them too?" Jordan asked dreamily as we passed a section of the forest with about forty dead cedars lining the path for a half-mile.

"The trees or the tribe?" I asked.

"Both," said Jordan. "They're one and the same."

The silence lingered while we climbed a hill and a rock rolled underneath my shoe, but I caught myself.

"Please, don't think I'm crazy," Jordan said. "As a child, I always imagined Indians along that bluff. And one afternoon when I was walking through here, the dead cedars looked like people, almost like Guthrie's statues," he said.

"This doesn't seem possible, but as a child I always imagined the same thing," I said and struggled with my hair tangled in a low hanging tree limb. "Ahhrrrr," I growled irritably and put my hair up in a ponytail on the front of my head.

"I want a ponytail," Maggie said and I pulled a fountain of her hair into an elastic band.

"It looks like you have a horn on your head," Jordan said. When we finished the hike and said our goodbyes in the path between our houses, I offered Jordan a jar of jam that he declined with the remark, "Nah, those berries just didn't look that good to me," as if he hadn't picked them in the first place.

*****

I faded in and out of consciousness by my distractions. I didn't interact with Maggie and David, Jordan, Mother, or the past as much as I tiptoed around them with superficial interest. That's how I could run and hike around the murder location. I needed to repair the shadow world and how it functioned within my life. Phantoms of the past were no longer staying away. They were confrontational when I least expected.

Jefferson was in the news, his lawyers saying he was not competent to stand trial. I was cooking; steam rose up from the pots on the stove and behind it Jefferson's mug shot drifted like a hologram. The news anchor discussed his mental illness and his family's involvement in the case, saying the family believed he was not guilty by reason of insanity. They detailed his criminal record prior to the murder charges, his obsessions with a government plot to play mind games with him—a test subject for ideas like telepathic communication and programming the human mind to carry out abductions and crimes without question. I was in disbelief and chuckled. Maggie pushed the remote control and turned off the television. The quick silence that emerged from that accidental click made me aware of my laughter about a murderer, and I felt repulsed by my reaction. How could I still be so insensitive, especially with my husband in a war zone? That laughter was a sign of my distance. The metal lid on the chicken stock shook, and more steam escaped with a wet signal on top of the stove, a sizzling under the surface. What should I do with that manuscript? Give it to someone? Tell someone... who could be the wrong person? I stood over the sink, next to the picked bones of a chicken carcass, with overwhelming nausea. Maggie giggled and pointed the remote control toward the ceiling, then the radio, the door, at me, while pushing all of the buttons. She ran toward the television and pointed the remote. Click. Click. Click. The screen flickered on and off and a voice blared out one syllable each time.

That helped me regain focus while I dumped the chicken bones into a plastic bag then walked outside, straight back through the trees, following my well-worn path, hoping that Nuance would be lured back into our home. His disappearance saddened me, though I scolded myself, knowing I should have expected it. Looking up into the treetops as an automatic response to the sound of helicopters passing overhead, I marveled at how interested people are in the criminal but not the victims. The media reported on every detail of Jefferson's life that they could uncover: his childhood in Georgia, why he had moved, and his presence on campus. Apparently, he never knew Kate, Leslie, and Jay. Maybe he had watched them at the Grille. The trial would bring out all of the information. Books would be written about him. He and countless other criminals, the criminal mind in general, the animal brain, the hunter captivating everyone's attention. The fight taking precedence over the family, the feasts, the everyday stretch and tug, scratch and yawn.

My view of murder in our society wasn't specific. I saw murder rates generally, and tended to group big cities into categories and smaller town crime into another category and so was convinced that most people involved in the process, from the criminals and media to the attorneys and shrinks, needed victims. And thus, they needed destruction as it ensured their way of life but they didn't want to lay claim to a death propagation. Those victims often included people wrongfully accused and convicted. They added another ingredient to the consumption. Not only did the lives of the victims end—their physical bodies were often violated and sometimes unrecognizable. The more tragic the story of the victim, the more interest in the case. The victims were often used as a way to define a certain brand of people, especially serial murderers, by the people who studied and counseled them. I thought all serial murderers were narcissistic and that the system played into the idea that criminals have more power than the system that seeks to punish them. I wanted to know how to focus on the victims without a further violation.

Around this time, I started to search stories about victims. Very little information was available for reasons of protecting the privacy of the victim's personal life and their families. In the end, the silence seemed only to memorialize the victim by a brutal death and not by her accomplishments in life.

I asked Jordan if he planned to attend the trial.

"Why?" he asked. We were walking quickly before starting our run. He stretched his arms overhead. "That's why we have reporters."

"Would you go with me?" I asked and began to run.

"I don't think it would be wise for you to delve into this any deeper," he said. "You need to let the justice system take care of things and try to move on. He isn't your student anymore. He was only in one introductory course, so why are you worried about going to the trial? Plus, I heard that it'll be on TV."

I didn't want to tell him about the manuscript for fear that he'd want to turn it over to the police immediately, and I wasn't ready for that attention. I didn't want the questions, the newspapers, and the suspicion. For what? Just because someone placed a stack of paper under my door? I didn't know him and hadn't interacted with him beyond class lectures and returning essays and exams.

Jordan interrupted the silence that emerged after his question. "You have enough to worry about," he said. "We're all okay. He's going to trial and it'll be over soon enough." He patted me and ran ahead. Motioning for me to follow, "Come on, get your ass moving," he called over his shoulder. "You'll feel better."

I stayed at Cumberland more than my own land. I hadn't cared for our property. The place was wild and not only fecund, but it cackled with a raspy wildness on certain edges of the land. Jordan tried to maintain the greenhouses and stopped complaining about my lack of care. He called me "lazy" more than a few times, but now he shrugged and called them his greenhouses.

"I have plans for them," he said. "You're going to be in there potting up cuttings before you know it. I'll lure you in there." He laughed. His legs left me, barely touching the trail as he moved through the forest. I ran behind him. We met three times a week for a run together while Maggie was in pre-school. I had finally worked up to a pace that allowed me to stay within sight of Jordan, but it took all of my concentration and desire. Wanting to catch him caused me to run faster than I could have imagined when running on my own. I didn't have the same motivation when I was alone, no matter how much my internal coach tried to push.

Jordan and I played chase and switched up the roles, though I took an advance. He could catch up with me too quickly. I knew that Jordan wanted to play this game with the woman he was seeing, but he couldn't. She was a secret, but I wasn't sure why and, unlike most people, I allow others to keep their secrets quietly. I suspected she was married. Jordan probably already knew I had seen the two of them together, but though I combed the property and Cumberland every day, I remained unobtrusive.

I couldn't walk the trails at Cumberland without my eyes playing tricks. No longer content with the backpack carrier, Maggie insisted on walking the miles of trail with me almost every day. At the end, I carried her and crossed the road and reached our home, where she usually slept on the couch. On the trails, she ran ahead of me and picked up rocks to toss into ditches, ravines, and sinkholes. Her black hair curled in the back around her neck and flipped out as she marched up the hills and sat down once she was halfway up the hill. I kept Maggie focused on the path ahead, reminding her that ducks and geese were at the finish line, where the trail met the water. Lost in thought, I followed Maggie over a mile, and redirected when she tried to venture into the woods or along a deer path instead of the wider trail. Maggie said, "Hi" to the few people that we passed, a young woman with a headset wired to her sunhat, two more women in tank tops and shorts, a soldier wearing a rucksack for training, and later a bald man with a boy and a dog. As we neared a turn in the trail, Maggie said, "Hi!" enthusiastically, in the same way that she greeted the other hikers. I looked up and turned my glance from the rocks under my feet but saw no one. Maggie continued to say, "Hi!" as if someone was in front of her. Then, she laughed as if someone were playing with her. She bent at the waist and bowed. I stood still and watched Maggie in what seemed to be a dance with form and movement, during which Maggie laughed and seemed to be looking at someone taller. She bowed again and walked to one side of the narrow trail, picked up a triangle-shaped rock, then crossed to the other side of the trail and picked up another triangle rock. She returned to the center of the trail, sat the rocks on either side of her feet, and walked between them. She bowed and laughed as with a favorite playmate. I scanned the woods in a complete circle. No one was in sight. A tiny tremor moved across my skin and I stepped toward Maggie, placing my feet carefully between the rocks.

"I'm with her," I said into the space around us.

Maggie continued walking ahead and I followed and didn't say anything else. When we were about fifteen feet from the triangle rocks, Maggie turned back and said, "Bye." She waved enthusiastically above her head and laughed. "Bye," she said a couple more times.

When she approached the next hill, Maggie sat in the path. She refused to continue walking and said, "I want my friend to come back. I want my friend, not just Maggie to play."

Her legs were tired, and she reached her hands out toward me. Before I curved toward the lake, Maggie's head knocked against my shoulder and she slept for the remainder of the walk to our house.

*****

When we were kids, Jordan and I entered the cave through the park entrance once and explored the cave. It has been closed for years, since they almost snuffed out the bat population when a big fire erupted in one of the rooms during the early '60s. I heard the history from Granna while I was growing up, though it sounds unbelievable. When it was privately owned, the cave was briefly used as a fallout shelter and was full of ammunition and other flammable supplies. Many decades later, it caught fire one evening until it raged out of control. The unbelievable part is that the fire department arrived with large sheets of metal they thought would smother the fire. But those glaring bright hot metal sheets were successful in achieving just the opposite—stoking the fire, as air currents traveled into the cave through multiple pores, not simply one big mouth.

The bats were trapped in the cave and couldn't fly out the mouth since the metal had blockaded it. I imagined the frantic flapping of bats as they suffocated and burned. Granna helped an environmental group fight for protection of the few surviving bats and the cave has been closed for touring and spelunking since that time, before I was born. Only researchers and geology students were permitted to explore its corridors.

With our family's property connected above and below the surface, Jordan and I found an opportunity to break the rules when we were teenagers. Brand new teens with an itch to trespass. We were at the park, wandering up the ramp as a group of college students unlocked the gate. "The cave's closed. How are y'all going inside?" Jordan asked. I watched the young college guide finish unlocking the chain on the large metal gates. He motioned for us. He wore a t-shirt that had Cumberland Park embroidered on the right. The metal rang out together under the sunset. Water dripped underneath the overhanging ledge and ran in a green slimy trail toward the sunlight until it baked into a brown streak.

"Shhh. Shut up, kid," he said and cocked his head to the side. Maybe he was thinking that we would run away and tell on him, so he made a bargain, "If you'll shut up, you can go with us. Just be quiet. Come on," he motioned hurriedly. He was breathless, telling us to hurry through the gate, so that no one would see us. He looped the chain around the gate but left it unlocked, placing the lock in his jacket pocket. We followed him into the darkness. The guide, a geology student at the University, was working at the cave through the summer. He bragged about how he had stolen the key to the cave after telling the ranger that he would lock up the office for the evening.

Four of his friends were also on the impromptu cave tour, and they carried huge hand-held spotlights. Someone handed me a weak flashlight. I was almost thirteen and carried a small, wooden bear statue in my pocket. As soon as we entered the twilight zone of the cave, I could no longer hear the birds or any other outside sounds. I heard something soft and heavy but couldn't have identified it. Then, more dripping water became audible. The student guide started talking about the different life forms found inside the cave.

Jordan and I were the perfect pupils, as were the two shivering skinny-legged eighteen-year old girls that he and his friends were trying to impress and thrill so close to Halloween. Our guide pointed out the shimmering mold on the cave ceiling, rusty salamanders on the ledges and in the crevices, and fuzzy bats resting on the cold stone. The ceiling suddenly pushed up and away from the twilight zone into a cavernous room and tunnel. A gray glowing river wound along the sides like a vein underneath the surface of the skin, along the edge of bone.

In the curve of the tunnel leading deeper underneath the outside trails that I had walked with Granna and my cousins, the guide revealed cave paintings and mud glyphs created by Paleo-Indians, whom he said were the predecessors of the Shawnee Indian tribe. I recalled my dreams, my visions, and felt validated that I already knew them, but something bothered me about being there, with this group from the college. *Betrayal*. The word whispered violently into my ears, crossing across the front of my skull. I shook it off and listened to the student guide. He described the first set of drawings as a compass shaped like a sun, signifying the North. Beside it was another round object with a tail attached. With burnt river cane torches, the images were drawn in black that had faded to gray in some areas. Drawn with fire. The guide expressed uncertainty regarding the second object in the series. "Carbon dating determined that the drawings were completed around 1350," the guide said. "And many similar drawings and images were created around that same time all over the world, so a lot of archeologists believe that there may have been a comet or meteor or something like that significant in the sky." I imagined the tribe running over the hill, trying to chase down the comet; I saw it dancing over the treetops.

"He's really smart," one of the girls whispered.

"What's your majors anyway?" the other girl asked his friends. I don't recall their answers.

"What are majors?" I asked Jordan, now knowing what they were talking about. The girls snickered at me, but the boys didn't notice me at all. Jordan said, "What their jobs will be after they finish college."

The guide illumined a second set of images on the cave wall by shining special lights. My eyes led me closer to the images until my hand reached toward them. He pushed my hand away and instructed us to refrain from touching the walls and using our spotlights and flashlights in order to preserve the drawings. The second set of images revealed river cane glyphs with different sizes and types of concentric circles in rows along the wall of the cave. The guide said, "There are many layers of Indian spirituality that we don't understand, so this is obviously some type of spiritual message. They had medicine men that went into altered states to communicate with the spirit world and then they drew designs about that. We don't really know what they represent."

And medicine women, I thought.

"I've got something to put you in an altered state," the friend wearing a Mets ball cap said and waved his fingers around like he was smoking a cigarette.

"Just call him the medicine man," his other friend in a white button down shirt said and chuckled. The one in the white shirt kept whispering to the tallest girl and she giggled constantly at him. I had no idea what he was saying most of the time. Like him, Jordan was completely enraptured, but by the shorter girl; he couldn't stop staring at her legs and her toes. I noticed that he looked at her feet a lot.

The third drawing was another image created with ash from river cane torches, like the first set of images. The drawing was of a warrior lying down on his back. The guide said, "Any ideas about what's on his head?"

The two girls crossed their arms, puzzled. Then the whispering friend obviously said something funny because both girls laughed. The guide chuckled.

"What?" asked Mets. White button down tapped Mets on the shoulder, "Pass me that, will you medicine man?" Then, he turned to me, "You want some?" and smiled. I didn't want to smoke pot. I knew about it because Jordan had told me about the time that he smoked it and puked. I was hoping that he wouldn't take it either.

But the guide asked at the same time in a rather stern voice, "No ideas about what's on the warrior's head?" We stiffened by his sudden authoritativeness. No one had an answer.

"That's a blade," the guide said. "Like a hatchet." His eyes shimmered at us. He smiled. "These tribal people wore blades on their heads and would go running wildly toward their enemies in order to frighten them away. You see that other thing on his head?" He chuckled. "That's a fashionable, front ponytail."

"Did you say a front ponytail? What's that?" Mets ball cap asked.

"Exactly what I said it was, a ponytail on the front of his head," he said. "We think these guys wore front ponytails in order to camouflage themselves. They would hide in tall grasses, try to look like certain animals, blend into vines and lines in the rock bluffs."

"Weird," the short girl said. She twisted her hair in her hands and pushed it in front of her face. "Don't mind me," she said in an exaggerated Southern voice, "I'm just a spray of wild grass." Everyone laughed, even the student guide.

"Did you notice his legs and feet?" he asked. "They're bear legs and feet."

I saw the claws on the drawing and the thick, hairy legs. The guide continued, "They may have drawn a bear's legs and feet to represent strength since a bear was bigger than they were. Why do you think that the hatchet on his head is pointed back into the cave?" No one answered. They were coughing and giggling, or staring and gesticulating at the two girls. "Well, we think that's because the darkness is back there," the guide said, looking at me, and pointing deeper into the cave. "Like I said, these Indians had a lot of different ideas about the spirit world and they wanted to stay away from evil. We think that the hatchet means that they wanted to keep the evil back there and they thought that the drawing offered protection to them. It kept the evil back there. Now, guess where we're going?"

His friends made ghost noises and laughed as if they were Dracula.

"We're going back there," the guide pointed and laughed, "toward the evil." He motioned for us to go ahead and he smoked and coughed behind us and then hurried forward.

"Do you think that's true?" I whispered to Jordan.

He shrugged, and stared at the floor of the cave to secure his footing and also at the shorter girl's brown toes with red painted toenails. I thought about the shaman in my dream, the one who lived in the cave. She had loved the cave. I didn't agree with the student at all. The tribe feared the dangers of the cave. It might have been dark but that didn't mean it was evil.

As our group ventured farther into the cave, I saw the shapes of alligator and crocodile come to life in the stone, a wooly mammoth column along the edge of a dark ravine into the earth's bowels. Cave popcorn created a show along the passageways. Stalactites and stalagmites had merged and enveloped one another in a slow continuous expansion of water and stone. "You know how long it takes for one inch of stalactite or stalagmite to form?" the student asked. His friends laughed up answers of fifteen years, twenty-five, and two hundred billion.

"One hundred years," he said. "So, it might blow your already blown minds to consider the age of that column." He had already defined a column as a stalactite and a stalagmite that had grown together over time, stretching and reaching until becoming one entity. The column that the guide pointed to was as large as my bedroom and taller than Granna's house. "Millions of years," I said to myself. "Ancient." Luckily, it was dark inside the cave because I couldn't hold back my sudden tears. Maybe fear caused them or just an awareness of age or the embarrassment of my naiveté or the sexual energy of the girls, the boys tangled in their hormones and information and having fun.

My impulse was to lie down on the floor of the part of the cave known as the "Ballroom." The guide said that room was known more formally as the "constant temperature zone." I wanted to curl into a small circle and sleep for months. In that room, the temperature never changed from fifty-eight degrees. Even if the temperature fell to ten degrees outside the cave, it never wavered in the ballroom from fifty-eight. The room was massive. Hundreds of people could sleep and find comfort inside that one room of the cave. A bear might be inclined to hibernate there. I considered the drawing of the warrior lying down. Perhaps it was a directional marker to this room in the cave that would be a wise shelter for all sorts of times during the year—a room of counsel and comfort for the warriors who trained here. Maybe it was first the home of a bear that was defeated by a warrior. Granna said that the bear lived in this region, as it was an area hospitable to them, offering a number of caves, bluffs, and streams.

After I recalled the memory, I wanted to ask Jordan if he remembered that cave tour. He and Maggie walked toward the cemetery with me. He said, "I wonder if our names are still spray painted on the ceiling? Must be since it has always been closed." I felt a pain in my chest when forced to remember that I was the one they pressured to paint our names in the cave, but I still don't remember the names of the students. They had all shouted up to me and joked that they'd drop me if I didn't spell everything correctly.

Jordan laughed suddenly, saying, "What a wild group. You know they must have had an orgy that night."

I was confused. "What are you talking about?" I asked.

"You don't remember how they were already making out, about three of them, when we decided to leave?" He laughed. "I've thought about that a few times and wondered what in the hell was in that joint to make them all suddenly start a heavy make-out session. It was like one minute that park ranger guy was lecturing and the next thing I know, he has his hand down one of the girl's pants and she's kissing her friend. I thought it was amazing, but you were crying and started to freak out, so we left them there. But wow, yeah," he said with a disappointed smile.

I had forgotten something else. And then I heard myself saying something that surprised me, "What if those girls didn't want to have an orgy, but they felt like they had to? There were three teenage guys and only two girls, not counting us, and we were kids. I clearly felt uneasy and yes, part of that had to be about my own immaturity," I said uncomfortably, "but the girls couldn't have been attracted to all three men and yet all three must have expected something. They swarmed them like bees. It's almost like we were just there to make the girls feel more comfortable initially, like they expected us to go away or get lost anyway."

"I wouldn't assume that," Jordan said. "You make it sound like they premeditated practically drugging the girls to have sex with them. You can't say the girls were girls and the boys were men. That's not fair. They were peers, and I just thought they were college students having a good time, experimenting with drugs and sex—"

143

"Maybe they did premeditate making the girls feel obligated or forced into the situation," I said.

"It didn't seem like it to me. Why would they have let us go with them if they had some kind of sinister plan?" he asked and looked at me with a wounded expression. "Damn it, Ellen, you just ruined one of my favorite memories." He tried to shake loose of the disappointment for the remainder of our walk.

*****

Traveling along the back entrance through the cave was a different experience. I remember Granna leading me across the field, climbing down the bluff and turning on her headlamp. I followed behind her with a flashlight. As a thirteen-year-old, I tried to pretend the tension between us didn't exist.

Unlike the entrance through the park, my family's entrance wasn't reached with ease, but there were no restrictions, no gates, chains or locks, nothing to keep out animals, so Granna stood outside the entrance and shouted into the interior. She banged on a rusted metal chair that had been left there long ago. Three other broken-down chairs and a table lay in old weeds along the limestone bluff.

She wanted to show me some things, teach me why I couldn't be going into the cave and spray painting, why it was a bunch of trouble to disrupt the earth. "You can't tell anyone about this," she said before we went into our side of the cave. "They'll be crossing all over our land and trying to bring a bunch of people in and out of here. And the park rangers don't care enough to crawl through the part of the cave that meets up with ours. You can crawl it though. Takes a little while and some scooting."

I must have looked concerned. She continued, "We're not crawling through to the other side today. I just want to show you this."

"How far is it?" I asked.

"You'll see," she said and motioned for me to follow her.

The cave walkway was narrow after the first small room, and we went down a steep incline that looked like someone had scraped along part of it to make a path.

"Must be what they did," was her only answer to my inquiries. The top opened up suddenly and I had to stop to look up, afraid that I'd lose my footing and there'd be a hole, descending into the darkness. I lost my equilibrium and squatted in the path. Waiting for the vertigo to pass, she simply stopped ahead of me, only looking back one time. She waited and started telling me about the columns and how they formed. Saying almost the same thing as the student guide.

I asked questions, maybe to distract myself from the vertigo, and the nervous stomach that reminded me I was down in the cave because of the trespassing I had participated in. I was in trouble and being in the dark, in the mouth of a cave and descending further into its watery throat caused a catch in mine. She didn't answer most of my questions, and I stood and continued.

"This reminds me of a Dr. Seuss drawing," I said. Rounded columns layered the room, all around us, a winding cave village, and it was as if we'd stepped into a cartoon. Never mind the ballooning shadows that stretched into a sinister king or a lion. All of the walls moved in and out, dancing in their own wondrous cast of absurd faces—the dog at the feet of a hunter, a giant rat, and a whale bounding through a false wall above the river that uncoiled into the view. I was mesmerized, and stopped everywhere to move my light over the carnival. A tiny beetle form came to life on the column beside me. "Papa's family must have been wary of outsiders," I said. "How could you keep a place so beautiful such a secret?"

"This place isn't very accessible," she said and shrugged as we passed under an archway in the path, and the stones narrowed in on us.

"One thing I do know about the Masters is that they used to come down here and cool off in the summer. They had some wooden steps built down the bluff. And, Papa said his father named this column, The Sphinx, 'cause it's so big. And tell me if it doesn't look like a cat's face on part of it?"

We turned a corner in the cave and she turned on a large flashlight and shined it across a column that stretched to the ceiling of the cave and was as wide as our house.

"That's bigger than anything in the main entrance," I said. "It's Goliath. No boys could knock this one down."

"That's probably a better description," she said. "You see," she turned her lamp in my face like an interrogator, "You see?" I felt her finger point into my breastbone, "Why you can't go in and destroy, make a mess, paint on the walls?" I was stunned and afraid.

"But I told you about it," I said. "I didn't lie." I wanted to cry.

"Do. You. See?" she asked again tapping my breastbone with the tip of her fingernail with every word in the question. I couldn't say why I was crying then, but I couldn't stop and my shame was unbearable. I lay my face against the moist column, felt the cold stone that was alive and forming. She snapped her fingers, "Don't touch it," she said. "You harm it just by touching it." I jumped back, looking at the column with awe and fear. "It's not here to comfort you," she said. "It's not here to comfort anyone. Now, you know." I felt defeated, and wanted to be soothed by anything. But, she didn't speak to me until we made it back home.

8 LATENT IMAGE

Certainly, I heard the hardwood floors shift under the weight of someone's feet. I felt confident in my auditory ability to track the intruder from the laundry, through the kitchen, and into the living room. I held a tall, sharpened pair of fabric scissors behind my back. It was about one a.m. and I'd been working on Maggie's quilt, made from Granna's fabric collection along with the scraps from one of David's uniforms and a few of my favorite maternity dresses. I stood in the doorway to the kitchen and confidently sensed the energy of another physical body. I closed my eyes and decided that I wouldn't wait for someone to hunt me down any further. I couldn't stop sweating. I stepped out with a racing heart to confront the psychopath. And no one was there. The living room was empty, along with the laundry room, basement, bathroom, guest room, all of the closets and showers, the storage space in the attic, between the dresses in the wardrobe, under the kitchen sink—all empty. I slumped against the counter, baffled.

When Maggie and I arrived home after grocery shopping or playing at the park, I expected a man to lunge at me when I opened the coat closet. Three men might be in the living room waiting for us. Would I scream if they pointed a gun at Maggie or me? Should I try to play a mind game with them? What sort of mind game would I spin? Could I even think of games if I were under real life-and-death pressure? Would I simply go crazy like a wild animal, kicking and screaming, biting and pulling with all my might? Maybe a stalker followed me in secret and slid around the house, under the desk, behind the bathroom door, in the pantry or linen closet, down the back stairway to the tiny wine room connected to the deck. The house had too many small spaces and passageways in which someone could slither and hide. The house was old, but I tried not to think about all of those souls who rose and fell within its walls.

Think about something else, I scolded myself. I was on a roundabout, back to the war. I sat in front of the fireplace, stared at the flickering, wondered how David survived out there, joking about MREs and actually having to eat HOOAH! bars, stretching his eyelids in training maneuvers, cracking his busted knuckles, smelling the dusty metallic sweat.

I read from my teenage journal. I found the notebooks in the attic, the stories about tribal warriors who had smelled a similar opponent, had trained their eyelids and limbs, and slept in a stoop during battle. After the scouting, the attack, and bloodshed, after the looting and returning, native warriors sat in the center of a circle of women and men. The man talked, describing the scent, the heat, the ferocity and fear. The women nodded as he talked about the face that dangled into the earth from a corpse, as he described his own shame in celebrating the death of his enemy's child, as he detailed his courage when a fellow warrior was being surrounded, as he discussed thoughts of stealing from his comrade's bag of food in the middle of the night

149

when he was hungry, as he admitted his doubts about the shaman's predictions, as he swore at his leader's boastful story-telling during a gathering, as he challenged his desire to remain outside the tribe and in a perpetual state of fighting. Leaders were held responsible for their mistakes during a battle. Leaders stepped forward to claim their mistakes without having to be nudged. They had to answer to the council more than the younger braves. I thought about many of the typical issues of warfare, and these thoughts were centered in my attention at a young age without any knowing of why. I was just imagining, but I was already entrenched in an awareness of violent warfare as an adolescent.

The parade of the warrior's story into their ears and throats and how they held it in their breasts and wombs. They nursed the stories until the brave was ready to experience a rebirth and be loosened from the death hunt. Until the brave completed the process, he could not return to his tribal home. First, he told his story to the circle. Fran was a soldier who told her story to the circle, and since that time, every year, she sat as one of the listeners.

I wanted this circle for David and so many other soldiers. I became obsessed with the history of warfare and how to cure the beasts it birthed into the world and how to make it most beneficial when it was necessary to destroy an order. Native warriors had fought brutal, hand-to-hand combat against one another. They weren't accustomed to large armies of men, killing at a distance. In wars like Vietnam, Iraq, and Afghanistan, the Special Forces and first strike units were often isolated initially and fought door-to-door, village-to-village, and checkpoint-to-checkpoint.

From a distance, the war was happening at the same time. Airstrikes crumbled mosques and apartment buildings, businesses, and libraries. Little villages might be wiped out in the night. That was different than the smells on the street.

I wanted to gather it all. I started yearning for my husband and the only way to get close to him was to find the stories. Going through the gate with my card, blending in on post, and thinking one of those men could be my husband. Same uniform, same haircut, same boots and hat. I told myself that I knew his form so well that I'd never miss him or mistake someone else as him, not in a moment. I longed to bump into him when I was on post, as if being there might bring him back to me. I'd find activities that gave me an excuse to drive thirty minutes to post. When the University opened an education center there, I signed up for classes and left the main campus. I shopped at the commissary and PX and took water aerobics at the fitness center. My obsession grew until I faced twenty students for a world history class.

Teaching had never felt exciting or intensely thoughtful to me. I did it as an automatic response—a matter of course for my research interests and leisure time after acquiring a lengthy education. That's it. I entered the classroom, shared the information, gave the quizzes and tests, administered the grade, and started it over again. I was not interested in sharing my personal anecdotes, becoming chums and drinking pints at the bar, or entertaining any of their commentary about what they thought they knew about history. They were taking the class for information and I was assigned to give it.

The classes on post were different than main campus and my approach to teaching changed. I wanted to listen when they shared stories.

The sergeant was young and enthusiastic, and she talked after class with several other students. I listened while turning off the overhead projector. She was saying that her life was not for the squeamish—she was out there on a nonlinear battlefield, across the wire, sleeping in a truck in the desert, digging a hole and shitting in it, getting very close to her men. They were crude and she'd heard it all—fine ass, long legs wrapped and stacked up with round well-ripened melons—but she wasn't taking any shit, just making the boys run if they got into any trouble, telling them to turn their attention to someone else because she was only interested in doing her job.

"I'm serious," she said and turned when someone snickered from the back row.

"I agree," he said quickly, glancing up from his phone. "I work with a lot of lazy guys, only thinking 'bout one thing. Sure haven't been thinking about doing their jobs properly. Hitting the mark and all that." He chuckled and looked down at his phone again and started typing a text.

I shut down the computer since no other classes were meeting in the room that evening. She continued about how she'd been shooting her weapon on the mark since she was seven. Tracking, scouting, building fires, pitching tents, planting, climbing—she liked all of those activities and that's why she joined the Army. She pushed back her blonde hair with a quick hand, and said, "There are sexist battles, but they're no longer tolerated by the upper command."

She told a story about a fellow soldier who was going to rape her one night so she slumped in the driver seat with a 9 mm ready to kill her friend, someone like a brother to her, if he broke the window. She covered the window in a brown t-shirt, taped it to the interior ceiling of the truck. The Army had taught her how to defend herself in times of need and complete the proper paperwork to conduct an investigation on her former friend.

Another woman nodded. One leaned forward on her elbows, looking at me intently. Were they all wondering what I thought about her story?

She kept talking, saying that he was *a friend* who had repeatedly tried to pry open her door, *some friend*. When his attempted rape didn't work, he started to slander her to the other men in the unit. Those guys, they knew if she said "no", she meant it, and that he was just hard up and lonely and full of it, but they waited to get back home to nail him with the paperwork side of it.

"Y'all know it," she said. "The desert in Iraq doesn't need a carpet to sweep anything under. People know, but they don't care too much that everybody figured it out—Abu Ghraib, Jessica Lynch, Shoshana Johnson, not to mention the lack of equipment, weapons jamming, stolen armor, up-armoring weak vehicles, Saddam's invisible weapons of mass destruction, his trial and execution." A couple of students put their heads in their hands. "Oh great," a woman muttered and fished in her purse for her keys. A man cleared his throat. "Y'all know all that and more," she said. She looked at me, "Do you need for us to leave this classroom? We're just waiting in here until our class starts in an hour across the hall. There's a professor in there with some students right now."

"Just turn out the light when you leave," I said and locked the cabinet doors on the desk. I placed my notebook and materials in my bag.

She looked at her peers, "I bet y'all can't name any famous female soldiers?" The room fell silent, and she turned to me, "Professor, please, don't help them."

"Athena," the man said from the back row.

"Okay, she's a warfare icon," she said. "What about a real person?"

"Joan of Arc," a woman said.

"Okay," she said. "Yes, but what about American soldiers or famous generals?" The silence lingered too long. "Deborah Samson," she said. "She disguised herself as a soldier during the Revolutionary War."

"Great," I said, surprised by that answer to her own question.

Turning to face the students in the back row, she said, "You probably never heard of Annie Fox, the first woman to receive a Purple Heart? Or first Lt. Cornelia Cook, the first woman to be awarded a bronze star? You know, there are men who stay at home with children so that their wives can fight in these wars?" The man on the back row nodded with emphasis.

"Show off," one of the women said. They laughed.

For an intense moment on the drive home, I wanted to strip myself of everything military. I had viewed families in other places who seemed completely disconnected from warfare. It didn't factor into their lives except as a part of history or a part of television broadcasts. I envied their distance.

In the classes on post, I also wanted to answer when they asked a question about me. Share some part of my life with them, show that I understood their way of life, even if I was learning more from them. And though I didn't want to admit it to myself, I deeply desired a date, drinking and talking, but I suppressed it by swallowing bitter black coffee and keeping my eyes averted as often as possible. I could just fool my eyes and tell myself that the men didn't resemble David.

Invisible energy carries those tiny forces of nature, the quicker pulse that you sense when a man approaches the desk and asks about your comment on his paper. His energy is the same as your husband's, your husband who has been gone for so long that you ache at the idea and salivate when a man's scent rushes toward you. I was often lost in the company of so many men, and not in a weak way. From intensity, like I was running solid, in mile five, hitting my stride and excited at the feeling, swept up in a euphoria of energy and movement, but I didn't know where I was going. I missed the companionship, the conversations, and the meals we cooked together. I missed just staring at him, sitting in silence and staring at him, but tried not to think about what I missed about him because it was too much like he was dead and that was even more difficult to consider. What if I never stared at him again? What if he returned with injuries, paralyzed, and the "what ifs" always crept up on me. They'd invade my thoughts and reduce me to weeping if I started down the path of the weary soldier.

Students—soldiers, those on active duty, and those who retained training in their stance, their posture, their direct gaze, they reminded me of him so much that I realized that David's features weren't defined to me anymore. Was he white or black? Jew or Arab? Was he so mixed up? After years of David being deployed more months than not, I was circling, trying to sketch in a solid nose for him that wasn't based on some photograph. I was gazing at these men, seeking his face, and sometimes they obliged my imagination unknowingly.

9 RETICULATION

Jordan invited us to his house for dinner. Aunt Darcy was visiting and she wanted to see us. He was trying to distract me from thinking about the trial, which was one of the reasons for her visit. She hadn't returned home in years and wanted to check on us. He said, "You need to see the wisteria blooming. It's beautiful. Mom can't stop talking about meeting Maggie." He talked so much that I almost broke my silence to ask about the trial or his girlfriend. I felt compelled to mention all the topics that were usually off-limits between us.

I couldn't accurately picture what it would be like to have other women in my life. I had been without an aunt or a mother figure or sister stand-in, so I wasn't prepared for how Darcy's presence would make me territorial. She phoned to say she would rent a car and drive in from Nashville. It was two a.m. when she finally arrived, after her flight was delayed and grounded in St. Louis for half the day.

Maggie fell asleep effortlessly in front of the television, without rocking, reading a book or singing lullabies. I carried her to the spare bedroom and decided to spend the night. I'd wait with Jordan for Darcy to arrive. Maggie's curls fell in damp black ringlets along her neck and across her cheek. Every person begins in a similar state. Break down, distribution, growth. A leaf formed in my mind as I traced an imaginary fingertip across its veins. Granna once traced my fingertip across the scratchy swell of a leaf's vein and the soft, wiggling vulnerability of one of Granna's great blue veins that wound as a blue racer along the tops of her hands and climbed her forearms. I imagined the snake coming to life and rising above the surface, breaking through Granna's skin as if it lived there, a perpetual undulating inhabitant and I was meeting it face-to-face for the first time. When I first moved in with Granna, there was a snake that climbed the rafters of our house and slinked underneath the sofa from the corner of my eyes. Then, it was gone and not because Granna banished it. She said that the mouse family was all gone, so the snake must be moving on as well. That's when I told Granna about the turtle that I placed in the lake to drown, my face hot with shame. "You had the correct reaction," she said. "We shouldn't make other living things suffer. We do enough of that to one another. Just remember, every living being doesn't receive the same interaction. If you face a bear in the wild, you shout and make yourself big to earn its respect. If you find a suffering turtle with a crushed shell next to a lake, you take away the pain. If you see a skunk in the forest or rattling through your trash, you quietly move in the opposite direction. And, we let the snake eat the mice hiding in our home."

Jordan startled me by knocking on the door to ask if everything was okay. We stood over the bed, looking at Maggie. He put his arm around my shoulder. "She's the continuation of our family. Of this place. We have to protect that," he said. "Granna would want you to."

We walked out to the kitchen and I told him about the daydream of the vein as a snake and the little animal statue Granna gave me. She gave me a coiled lapis lazuli snake about a half an inch high. It was the first piece of my miniature animal collection. A wooden turtle was next, and then a brass rabbit, a limestone fish, and an amethyst pig—each time we experienced an encounter with an animal, bird, fish, amphibian, or reptile, Granna tried to find a representation.

"Those are totems," a voice said from the doorway and she moved forward as if she'd been a seamless presence in our lives. Aunt Darcy continued, "Granna was like a modern shaman." She laughed, but those two words caused a sudden motion in my memory. Little passages from past conversations with Granna drifted into my thoughts, and she described the meanings of the animals and birds. She had instructed me to learn the animals' paths and to respect those areas that they travel, and I had forgotten all of the lessons associated with those statues because they didn't seem like lessons, just time spent with Granna. Aunt Darcy was wearing a navy blue dress that lilted against the doorframe but was practically uncreased except at the waist with a few tight ripples on the edge. She smiled, a large bright unflexed and happy stare at the two of us. It was one of those truly grand memories bereft of pain, containing only the pure joy of reunion. This was one of very few ever to occur in my life.

"How could I have forgotten all of those lessons from Granna? It wasn't so long ago. How can that happen to a person?" I asked Aunt Darcy as we talked and tried to play catch up for the distance of my entire life. My body rocked back and forth. "Am I seriously messed up?" I asked, trying to make a joke about my bad memory.

"I really believe that you have PTSD," Jordan said, switching suddenly to a serious diagnosis. He noticed the shock on my face and the embarrassment in front of his mother and quickly added, "It's good to have your memories flood back and to also notice that your mind is messing with you."

"Are you saying that I have a psychological disorder?" I asked defensively. I didn't want him to tell me that I was a crazy schizophrenic.

Conveniently, an interruption does often allow people to assume they have license to speak what they wouldn't have mentioned if it weren't for the opportunity of intrusion. Jordan's PTSD diagnosis was the hard smack of an acronym that fit my neurosis. I couldn't shift that quickly. All those transparencies were on the blip, faltering, and filmy. If my visions were a psychological disorder, how would I have motivation to run and continue without the natives? What would help me with the fear of the unknown answers in life? What if one of the answers was that I couldn't remember what was real and what wasn't and that some of the real wasn't good to remember?

"Listen, this is just a temporary condition brought on by a traumatic event," Jordan said with ease, as if he'd been practicing, something that he'd said so often to other friends and relatives that it felt as though he'd said it to me half a dozen times already. "It's not a psychological disorder so much, in that it can be changed, especially once you're aware of the issues concerning memories."

"What do you mean traumatic event?" I asked, my knees shaking. I denied the need to grab my daughter and run. I would have left if Maggie hadn't been sleeping. I wouldn't have endured the summation of what felt vile for someone who'd never spoken about any of the pain until very recently.

"It can be anything, like war, physical abuse by a parent, a near death experience—"

"Nothing like that has happened to me," I said calmly, shaking my head. "No. I thought PTSD was a condition that mainly affects soldiers."

Jordan was quiet and pressed his palms onto the counter top. He hesitated. Aunt Darcy took the opportunity to leave the kitchen, placing her suitcase in her bedroom. The silence stayed and stayed and swelled like it did with David, but it grew to an awkward nausea since this was supposed to be a homecoming for Aunt Darcy. My face was hot. I felt trapped.

"Just tell me!" I shouted and tried to recover, "Is this a damn game to you, Jordan!"

"You discovered your dad's dead body. Then, your mom treated you like you were a problem. That's definitely traumatic to a child. Not to mention, she put your brother on a pedestal and gave you to Granna without even trying to help you reintegrate into your own family unit. At the same time, you must have sensed Granna's underlying pain left over from the wreck and Papa's paralysis and—"

"What wreck?" I asked. Aunt Darcy walked back into the room and sat beside me at a barstool.

Jordan looked for distractions. He brought out salsa and mashed avocados while Darcy explained that my dad and Papa had been in a wreck and hit a tree head-on when they were returning from a buying trip out west. They were only a few hours from home. I had always known about the wreck, but Granna never said that my dad was driving and had fallen asleep at the wheel, or that was the speculation since neither Dad nor Papa could remember anything from the morning of the wreck.

"Jake was so haunted by that," Aunt Darcy said. "He always had a pained expression after that, like he was pursuing the impossible. I know he longed to unlock that blank spot. I'll never forget what his friend who gave the eulogy at his funeral said, 'Captain Masters was locked on his goals, always persistent in his belief that he could accomplish a mission with every piece of equipment and every man intact.' It really showed me how much he tried to be precise. And, he probably blamed himself for the accident, even though no one can be certain that it was his fault or that he fell asleep. A deer may have jumped out in front of them or another vehicle may have been present, who knows. They did know that the truck rolled and seemed to right itself and keep on going before hitting the tree."

She leaned her head back, recalling with a smile, "We called your mom, Bee. A nickname your dad gave to her." She reached for the bread that Jordan served and said, "She tried everything to help him. Hypnosis. Talk therapy. Chanting. Whirling. Returning to the site. Damn, he loved your mom. It was almost sickening how much in love he was with her, looking and longing and spellbound by that Bee, but who wasn't? Your mother was a gorgeous honey. She loved flowers and was always busy and that was that as far as nicknames were concerned."

Who was that woman she was describing? I couldn't imagine it. How could a person change so dramatically into someone else without a trace? Flowers? Bee?

"I can't talk about her right now," I said. "I'm wondering why Granna never told me that Dad was driving during the wreck?"

"She didn't think it mattered," Aunt Darcy said. "She always told Jake he had to move on, go forward in life." She looked into my eyes with a sharp stare. "Speaking of, let's get back to you. What's going on with these hallucinations of tribes and nightmares and people creeping around your house at night? Don't you think that you may need to talk to someone about all that's stored up in there?" She asked. I averted my eyes and narrowed in on Jordan who bit his lip. Aunt Darcy tried again to look into my eyes, which stayed focused on the counter. She patted my leg while I bounced my feet on the stool.

"Are you two going to tell me that I need medication?" I asked and hastily scooped green sauce onto the bread. I took a few more so that I didn't have to say anything, and mentally strained to keep my dialogue internal. *Talk about anything else. Say something, Jordan, I wish you would say anything else. Talk about running. Anything. Don't corner me anymore. Don't intervene. No more interventions. Stop. Stop. Stop. I can't take anymore. Why can't David be here, for God's sake? This is lonely and sad without him. I miss him. I want him. I need David. I feel sick. I haven't had sex. How can they do this? This. This attack and cornering. God, did Jordan plan this? He probably planned this. Well, of course he did. It's obvious. So sickeningly obvious. Goddamn, Jordan. I don't have anyone else. What can I do? I can't just dump him. Scream and rant and run away. Leave him here with her. Who the fuck is she anyway? What does she know about me? Probably everything that Jordan has told her. AH! This madness has to stop. Maybe I am mad and crazy and seeing tribes, the past, but they've been around more than her. Her! She hasn't been here for...* Finally, Jordan spoke, trying to change the direction. "No, just a beer," he winked and poured two beers into tall glasses that were foggy from cold at first, but soon sweated into the heat.

"Beer?" I asked defensively.

"It's the drink of choice by runners," He raised the glass and smiled. "And warriors. Come on, Ellen. Cheers! To a new beginning."

"Not for me," Aunt Darcy said. "You have any good stuff?" she asked Jordan.

"Sorry sweetie," she said to me, "I hadn't thought about my Jake in a long time."

Her Jake. Yeah, he was more her Jake than my dad, and that's just sad. It makes me so sad. But I would rather have him for a dad for that short, short time than have her, her, uh, her for a mother. She's just as bad as mine. Oh, please, please, don't let me be like them. So selfish and absent. Selfish.

Jordan turned and poured her a scotch.

She doesn't deserve you, Jordan. She's a sloppy lush. I can sense it and she doesn't deserve you. How did you do it without decent parenting? How did we do it? Well, I had Granna. And you didn't for very long. Maybe that's why you ran and escaped. That's it. To forget these fools.

I gulped half of the drink away and said, "You know what, Jordan? I feel like running at Cumberland is training me for something. Have I told you that already?"

Jordan shook his head and eyed his mother who stared at the scotch, "Yeah, a marathon?" he asked.

I continued. "Which goes along with the idea that's been building in my mind since I started to run there. And the warrior in the cave painting also coincides with it. So, if Cumberland were a place of vision quest where the tribe trained the warriors for battle... that makes sense to me. You can't really farm the area because it's too wooded, but it's close to rolling meadows and the river. Though I keep envisioning women, who worked with the braves who were training, and retained the lines of communication with the tribe. I see other women, spiritual seers or something like that. The first woman I saw, she's the one who discovered the bodies of the dead warriors after the attack."

"What attack?" Jordan asked. "Did the student guide mention that in the tour?"

Darcy swirled her glass and sighed, then motioned for the bottle from Jordan.

"No, he didn't mention it," I said. "I've had a repetitious dream that there was an attack by a rival tribe, and they killed many of the warriors as well as their medicine woman. As a child, I thought that the spirits of those warriors were telling me that the other tribe didn't fight fair. That was their sacred place, not a battlefield."

"Wouldn't every place have been considered a battlefield?" Darcy asked.

"Probably depended on the tribe," I said. "But it was commonly agreed that some places were considered communal hunting territory shared by several tribes."

"As far as I know, they've never discovered a grave site there, or anywhere close by," Jordan said.

"In my version of the story that I created as a child," I said with emphasis, so we could skip the "she's crazy" undertone to Aunt Darcy's expressions. I continued, "The woman who discovered the bodies dragged them away from that area. I used to imagine that was why all of the small trees and vines in that area look like something dragged across them. They were always pushed down." After an awkward pause, I added, "Perhaps the childhood mind needs an escape."

"So, are you saying you think there's a curse in place?" Aunt Darcy asked and swirled her wrist and opened her hand to the ceiling as if to say, *Hand over the information and make it more tangible. It should be able to fit on my palm.*

I shrugged. Aunt Darcy stared at a distant wall and looked like she was sorting the files in her brain. She turned her head slowly and said with precision, "That would explain why everyone who has tried to use the cave for monetary purposes has lost all of their money. It explains all of the vandalism. The brutal murders," she continued.

"Don't you think those are simply coincidences?" I asked, looking perplexed. *Huh? Who said anything about a curse?* Even if my life felt that way, I thought everyone's existence must include the hidden atrocities of abuse and discomfort, avoidance, and pain.

"No, I believe in synchronicity, not coincidence in the form of random chance," she said. "I've been thinking about this so much, trying to put it together, but I haven't talked to anyone about it until now." Jordan filled my glass again with beer and cleared his throat with a soft groan on the end, as if to say, yes she has talked about it and you're going to need this to make it through the impending conversation. He turned to the opposite counter and prepared a salad along with a plate full of sliced chicken and roast beef. Even though she never reached a point about the cave or curses, the scotch had uncorked Darcy's resistance to explanations, and she revealed her childhood with Granna and Papa.

*****

Darcy's knees shook as she stood on a chair, staring at her dad's second face. She must have been in elementary school. A crooked scar ripped across his bumpy skull. His head seemed to be smaller on one side now. Darcy wondered if part of his brain was missing. He gave her the camera and asked her to take a picture of the smiley face that had been drawn on the top of his head. A gap in his front teeth, his smile caught you in a grin. Darcy just wanted to smile back at him without speaking, without asking when he would be coming home from the Army hospital, without questioning all of the new changes that would transform their home into his world.

She could smell the cut grass after her brother mowed, as she watched her dad walk back and forth across the lawn. He was a tall, thin man, and looked out of place in their garden. The lilacs pointed pale, purple blooms in front of peony flocks. Heavy, sweating scent of wisteria drifted with dandelion pollen across the small lawn and into the peonies that were allowed to form a ruffle just before the cut, then the twirling white dandelion seeds wafted farther into the woods. With his left hand, he sort of threw the cane out in front of him, stepped with his left foot forward, and dragged the right leg behind him. His right arm rested in a sling like a limp, soggy dishrag thinned from over-use. Even though his skin had tarnished to a chalky gray with a pale, blue pulse illumined underneath, his regal complexion and profile remained. A black hat covered his weedy hair that grew at odd angles even after reconstructive surgery. His right arm and leg never functioned properly again. After a few warm-up laps, he would motion for Darcy to accompany him. They walked around and around, and then back and forth, in patterns across the lawn and into the garden while she memorized song after song, strengthening her voice. When she tried to use her hands while singing, he held the cane under his arm and slapped them with his left palm. She said that he was quicker at that motion than one might expect.

"We're working on the words now. The voice," he said as if tasting the word. "The gestures, the directions of movement, will be developed later. We must feel the song in your voice first. It begins here." He pointed to his lips. "Shh." He took her fingers and held them with his left hand. "First, listen to yourself," he said looking at her hands. Music had been his obsession, though he joined the Army as an eighteen-year old and jumped out of a plane over Normandy, but it was falling off the back of a Jeep onto hard concrete while drunk that caused the brain injury much later than that.

Darcy's momma sat on the screened porch, stringing green beans, peeling parboiled tomatoes, slicing up peaches, and otherwise fanning herself between cooking and hanging out clothes.

From her dad, Darcy learned music, a love of trees, and to be proud of her bravado, which included crude language and excessive scotch and brandy drinking.

She, her momma, and brother Jake made a sacrifice for him. He wanted the land and as few people as possible, away from it all—that noise of the world. He needed to plant and live and teach his daughter music.

Maybe it was all of the projects. Her parents relied on constant projects to propel them into the future and to make decisions for them in the now. Her momma canned every year. The first month after they moved into the house, her momma painted and tiled the kitchen, adding a backsplash behind the stove. She could move a saw with a skill and efficiency that deemed a carpenter unnecessary for much of the work on the Masters' house and property, where her dad's great-great grandfather had planted the first of the plum trees. They moved Little Gran, her dad's mother, out to the cottage in the woods, the one that Darcy lived in later, and the same place where Jordan lived. Her dad stayed busy as well. Darcy thought her momma avoided conversation by performing tasks, while her dad numbed his thoughts any way possible, especially making brandy, cultivating trees and escaping to hear music whenever possible. He wrote lyrics behind his cigarettes and practiced with Darcy. He planned another garden. Then, he might set himself to organizing the gardening shed, or "God forbid," she said, "worrying about old Guthrie and cursing his nonsensical existence, even if the old devil did buy up the brandy and bring people driving through to crane their necks at those bulky statues." Her dad couldn't understand why someone like Guthrie, who obviously had some skills and time, would want to live in a shack that was little more than a tree house and erect random statues on the roadside.

At sixteen, she didn't drive. Darcy's dad had promised to buy her a new car if she waited to drive until she was eighteen. He read the statistics from the newspaper in order to show her the death rates from driving. While standing over his shoulder, she could see the pulse quickly vibrating the soft, slumped portion of his head. He shifted under the weight of her stare—maybe it reminded them both of his close brush with death, which he never talked about. He cleared his throat and reached for the black hat that rested on his kneecap. She was frustrated and understanding, angry and grateful, but she agreed to wait for the car.

Her dad sat with his legs spread out in a V on the ground. His left hand gripped the spade and he dug out a trench between his legs. Then, he scooted back and dug the trench closer to himself again, and kept on scooting. Veins and sun defined his left arm—as if perfectly molded for a marble statue, while the right arm was smooth and supple, pale and overly ripe in a sunken and soft numbness. The fingers were long and pointed, and contained a stillness that almost suggested they had never been alive in the first place. On the left hand, his fingers were always moving, busy, and full of the rhythm of tasks. If no task was necessary, as when he watched television and the popcorn bowl was suddenly empty, then he moved his fingers back and forth as if perpetually calculating a sum.

Ironically, Jake was the one who crashed his Dad's car. Darcy knew that Jake was tormented after the wreck. His view was that his dad lived through a war and then a brain injury, but had a fool son. When her dad died after the wreck, Darcy slept at the end of her momma's bed every night. She couldn't go back on stage. She had the lead with a band but exited, parked the car her dad had bought for her at the end of the row he had been digging. A convertible. They had laughed on the first drive and he never stopped smiling, even when his favorite black hat flew off. She left the car at the end of the row that spring when he died; weeds sprang up around it. The bean plants climbed up the antenna and dangled thin pods. Before they could plump themselves full of beans, Darcy's momma pushed her out of the house with a spade in one hand and the car keys in the other. It was over, and her momma made the demand—prune this place and get it cleaned up. The car started on the first turn. It moved away and the ground seemed relieved.

Darcy's momma dug at the other end of the garden, as Darcy moved the car. She stooped and tugged at the earth, forcing the grass, earthworms, and dandelions out. She stood again and gazed at Darcy, who had never paid attention to her momma. The wind flung something into the sunlight that Darcy thought were spider webs whirling around her momma's face, but they were tiny streams of sweat flying into the light. That was the first time Darcy realized how strong Granna was and how beautiful.

She said, matter-of-factly, "After that, I started singing again and was pretty good, playing some places in Nashville. But, I got knocked up and fell in love, kept having babies until…you know, the rest is this."

*****

"I've never been drawn to the cave," Aunt Darcy said to me, interrupting her story and leaning into the curve of her elbow. "I was always most distracted and free in the orchard, the rows of the greenhouses were also a perfect line of stage, and bright with flowers of all sorts. The distillery had a cloak and dagger feeling to it. The smell of barrels, the wet darkness of fermentation," She smiled and waved her hand. "The cave," she said, pushing her mouth into a soured pucker and shuddering, "it's so sinister and always has seemed that way to me."

I realized how different Aunt Darcy and I were. I watched her cross the room to grab a blanket lying on the opposite couch. She was trim, dark gray hair, neckline sneaking into her push-up bra, manicure with pedicure, and most probably a minor cosmetic enhancement or two like tattooed eyeliner and liposuction.

My thin, blonde hair was lilting in a ponytail, a short wagging tail, ever so eager to agree. My loose button-up white cotton shirt looked like the sheltering of a small picket fence hiding any semblance of breasts that may have graced my body. It hung down over my brown pants with their precise, ironed creases and pockets on the sides of the knees. I wore cargo pants with flip-flops, even when teaching, though I did try to reserve my naked feet for summer classes. I shuddered at having to reveal my toes with French tips as if they'd been dipped in White Out— that seemed so unnatural.

"Where was Uncle Jake while you were memorizing songs with Papa?" Jordan asked his mom. "Were you the favorite?"

"No, there wasn't a favorite," Aunt Darcy said. "They were very fair parents, surprisingly so. Jake wasn't a musician, but he was social in a different way, a constant buzzing worker. He sold brandy all over town for Daddy. Even as a little boy, he seemed like a quiet hustler, going over to the cave and selling from our stash of brandy." She stared into her glass, swirled the ice. "He even repaired the greenhouses. He built the big garden shed. Well, he renovated this house for me. After Little Gran died, this house had to be connected to the sewer and a modern bathroom had to be installed." She stopped as if it were the first time she realized the significance of that. "He also did most of the modern updates on your house, Ellen, the Masters' house, that's what we always called it. And, this one is so efficient, even now. So cozy."

Darcy and women like her stretched and arched their bare feet and flared their white tipped toes over and over with ease. They'd taper out a leg, maybe with a palm flat against their shin or gently cupping the back of their thigh, reaching for an itch and then the foot is raised, arched, toes flared and pointed for emphasis, held taut, again and again, while they stare at their own toes and talk and look back to the table, the dinner rolls, their drink, my button-up shirt, the people on the television behind my head, but over and over the foot flares and arches, then points for emphasis. What a remarkable workout Aunt Darcy got in the two hours that we talked. I considered adding the practice to my own regimen in order to strengthen my leg workout and perhaps make my toes appear more edible. But for whom?

"Someone gave me a written statement by Philip Jefferson about the murders," I interrupted Darcy and blurted out. "He wrote it from jail. So far, I haven't found anything in it that proves that he shouldn't have been arrested. But looking at the manuscript and all of the court documents attached with it, more questions may need to be asked, maybe. I'm just not sure why someone would leave it for me."

"Who gave it to you?" she asked.

Jordan had left the room, but I found myself whispering and wondered why I would share the information with Aunt Darcy and not with Jordan. "Someone just left it underneath my office door at the school."

"What did the police say about it?"

"I know that you might think I'm crazy at this point, but I didn't tell anyone about it."

"How do you mean?" she asked.

"In my mind," I said. "It cannot be a coincidence that I received the manuscript, and I live about a mile from Cumberland Cave. I'm terrified. I don't want to be hurt. I'm not an investigator, and I don't trust anyone."

Aunt Darcy had drunk so much that she looked like she wasn't sure what I was referring to.

"I just think that people are numb to exploitation and brutality," I said, relieved to speak about all of my ideas without Jordan telling me to "let it go." I continued, "They're numb to it on a large scale, like the war. That's why war headlines are like the fifth or sixth headlines down on the page. They aren't the top stories unless a woman wades into a group and blows herself up. Even filming a decapitation doesn't faze most people. It's as if war has become boring. Using a dull knife as a weapon in modern warfare and broadcasting that is ironic.

"Maybe it will become so dull that eventually humanity won't care about violence. Since abuse, torture, violence, and killing have happened in every way imaginable at this point in history, perhaps there's no uncharted territory and it will gradually fade out of our way of life by virtue of evolution. Most people learn history in relation to wars, battles, generals, and the treaties made and broken. I can name more battlefields, cemeteries, jails, and places of execution than museums, parks, and centers of growth and life. People know our city by those murders, and that's awful. I really hope that new chapters in history exist for us in the future. Maybe we'll move away from violence if we see the deep scar it causes to people and to the places of the earth. Cumberland Cave is just one example of that to me."

We talked until three a.m. when Aunt Darcy's speech slurred and I sank into the chair. Somehow, I dragged my feet along to Jordan's guest room and quickly fell asleep. It seemed like hours had passed when I awoke suddenly.

"Ellen! Ellen!" I heard the screams several times before I fully opened my eyes and realized the shouts were coming from outside the sleep world. I couldn't remember where I was for a moment. I stretched my eyelids very wide for an instant and thought maybe I imagined someone shouting my name.

"Ellen! Ellen!" Jordan shouted from down the hallway.

I pushed the blankets aside. I ran on my toes into the darkness, which he suddenly opened up with a light switch.

"Are you okay?" I whispered, shielding my eyes from the sudden brightness.

He gasped and shook his head. "I think I just had a terrible dream and you were in it," he said. He was trying to regain his awareness. "I'm sorry for shouting," he said. "So sorry for waking you."

Maggie called from the other room. I snuggled close to her and slept late into the morning. I smelled coffee and pancakes when Maggie giggled in my face. She smiled beside me. "What did you dream about, Mommy?" she asked.

"You and Daddy, and we were on the beach building a boat," I said.

She smiled when I mentioned her fascination with boats.

"Did we catch fish?" she asked. I nodded, but she was already asking, "How many?"

"Too many to count," I said.

"I would ride the waves over and over to pick up my daddy and he could eat pancakes with me today."

Her eyes brightened. Sometimes I didn't know what to say. Go along with the imaginings as I did so often. Change the subject in a fake perky tone as my own mother had done. Cry, as I felt like doing most of the time. That day, I could respond with a positive truth, "He'll be here tomorrow so you'll have a lot of mornings to make pancakes with him." Jordan knocked on the door.

"And to go fishing," she said with a smile.

"I know that I disturbed your sleep," Jordan said, "so I wanted to make it up by having pancakes for breakfast. I know how much you both love them."

Maggie clapped and jumped out of bed. She poured half a pitcher of syrup onto her plate before we arrived. The pancakes were saturated and suctioned to the plate. I marveled at how comfortable she felt there. She turned on the television and moved her soggy, syrupy pancakes to the small corner table for an easier view of the cartoons.

Jordan handed me a cup of coffee. He looked satisfied, as if Maggie filled an empty place in his life. He had been trapped in a relationship with a married woman for years. Who could know how many years exactly? I didn't know her name, as he acted like he was dating multiple women but just renamed her in order to receive advice on the rare occasion that he might seek it. I caught glimpses of her occasionally, both of them on the property. I eased away from their naked bodies on the horizon of a hill during the afternoon; at least three times it had happened. They never knew their silhouettes had interrupted my run and I turned and traveled in the opposite direction. He never said so, but she was definitely married. I knew it for certain when I saw the child seat in the back of her Volvo and the post stickers on the corner of the windshield and that meant she was military. I wasn't sure if she was a soldier or the wife of one or both.

While he stared at Maggie, I sensed that he was thinking about her that morning, about wanting a family of his own, but how could I discuss someone I wasn't supposed to know about?

"I didn't remember your mom being so interesting," I said.

He smirked. "I guess if you think alcoholics are interesting."

"Oh great," I said.

"She's a scotch-drinking female Rip Van fucking Winkle or something like that," he said. "Unavailable except for some theorizing and sentimental soliloquies."

"Whose mom is a sowiwokwe?" Maggie asked while dragging her finger through the syrup.

"Mine," Jordan said to Maggie. "I'd have you meet her but no doubt she'll sleep until noon and drag herself out of a hangover by two, just in time for dinner and a soak in the tub before topping off her second scotch in the afternoon sunset."

"Jordan! I can hear her moving around in her room now," I said. "So, maybe—"

"She's vomiting," he said.

I started to laugh and he looked like he might throw me out if I made that chuckle audible. So, I asked him to tell me about the dream he had in the night. It suddenly rebounded into my mind. At first, he said he didn't remember it, then he shuddered and said it was the most vivid dream he'd ever had.

"I thought you couldn't remember it."

"I don't want to tell you because it's really horrifying."

I could hear the bathroom shower in Darcy's room.

"Did something happen to Maggie?" I asked. He motioned for me to be quiet as Maggie started to become distracted by us. A commercial for something glittery caught her eye again and I hushed my tone, "Now I'm going to wonder all kinds of things," I said, irritated, and spilled coffee on my leg. "Damn it!" I said reaching for a dishtowel. Jordan sighed, and he dumped the weight of the dream and its repercussions onto me.

"Someone had broken into your house," he whispered and hesitated, then added quickly, "and they stabbed you repeatedly in your bed." He paused, and added in another hurried whisper, "Over and over. And David was there, just lying there in your bed, and he didn't do anything about it. Your screams were terrifying, and it seemed so real," he stared at the opposite wall as if he were watching the movie projection of his dream happen there. His forehead began to sweat. "I could hear the sound of the knife pounding…" I backed away from him.

"Jordan!" Aunt Darcy said from the doorway, "That's enough, you two." She looked at us, then between us and smiled.

Maggie was staring at Jordan as if she understood everything. "Who's going to hurt my mommy?" Her lip puckered and she looked frightened. "Where's my daddy?" she asked me.

"Mommy's okay. Daddy's okay. No one's going to hurt us," I said.

"Where's my daddy?" she asked again.

"Maggie. It's okay. He's on his way home from Afghanistan," I said. "He's okay—"

"Hi, sweet one, I'm Aunt Darcy," she said, "and you must be Maggie. I've heard so much about you. I bet that you love makeup and purses."

Maggie buried her face behind my leg.

"I brought this eye shadow for you," Aunt Darcy said. Her hair was wrapped in a towel, and her age showed without makeup.

Maggie peeked around my leg and smiled. "Sometimes I take Mommy's lipstick out of her purse," she said and smiled.

"This is Jordan's mom," I said.

"I'm your Aunt Darcy. Come on," Aunt Darcy said, "And I'll show you all my makeup."

Jordan looked at me with an astute intensity, "That's the scariest dream I've ever had. I'm sorry that I woke you and that I just told you the dream."

"Shh!" both Aunt Darcy and I scolded him at the same time.

After Maggie followed Aunt Darcy to look at makeup cakes and wands and portfolios with mirrors, I hurriedly dressed and got into the woods where I ran and ran, trying to escape my fears and uncertainties.

I was enraged with David. While I ran, I imagined punching him. I landed a hard right hook on his jaw. So broken and angry, I uppercut and hit him in the flabby side of the gut. I slammed my knuckles into his left temple. I watched his spit fly. He didn't fight. I just allowed myself to punch freely. As my body jarred down the hill toward the hollow, I ran crying and I sobbed and hated my own self. I imagined punching myself twice, and then I couldn't do it anymore. I could only see myself in an embrace alone. The lonely embrace locked. Even though he was coming home the next day, I told myself to accept my isolation.

10 RELOAD

The day that David returned home for almost a year was the same day that the murder trial of Philip Jefferson began. When I suggested that I should go to the trial and that I would see David later, Jordan grabbed my shoulders and shook me. "You have to go pick up your husband! Wake up to your own life!"

I don't know why I mistook his gesture as anything other than a friendly jostle in the right direction, but I reacted with anger. I pushed him and he shoved me back. I stumbled backward, "Jordan!" I yelled.

"Why do you care about this so much?" he asked.

"Because, it could have been me. He's a psychopath, and he could have just randomly chosen anyone who went over there, and I'm there all the time. I could've been one of those victims," I trembled. "I should have known there was something weird about him. Someone could have done something to change it."

"No, no, Ellen. You didn't know and there's nothing you could have done. This isn't your burden to carry."

"It's everyone's burden," I said. "This is happening here, in our society, for no reason. Why are people murdered for no reason? It's not a war zone. There are no enemies. I just can't understand the senseless brutality."

I went round and round with Jordan about why I should care, and maybe I could figure out something more, but I didn't know what that might be when he questioned me about my statements. Finally, he was frustrated with the ideas I continued to spin about murder.

"You have to stop obsessing about this and go deal with your life," he pointed his finger in my face.

I was also frenzied at that point, emotionally stirred up, so I shouted, "Get out!" enraged and overwhelmed. "Just get out! And leave me alone!"

He walked to the door, but turned after closing his eyes with a sigh. "You must be afraid to pick up David," he said. "But he wrote a remarkable letter and if it's all like he said, then he's on the right track. It will be okay, Ellen."

The letter arrived before Aunt Darcy's visit. And, it wasn't a letter. Instead, David had mailed a notebook filled with his missives, his apologies, his hopes for me and Maggie, and what he noticed around him—tales from his fellow soldiers, little anecdotes about someone's daughter, a good laugh with the natives in a village, something random and surprising, a memory, a desire, a drawing of a landscape, a mountain peak, a face, different angles of the camera, lenses, squares, shaded triangles, and circles. He wrote that he had been calling Phil and talking when he could and his dad suggested the notebook as a place to work out his issues. His dad said, "Just burn it if you ever get worried about what you've written." David wrote in the notebook that he decided to write it to me because I was the most important person to him. Phil had asked him, "Son, what's the most important relationship in your life?" In the notebook, David wrote to me that he thought Phil was expecting David to respond with "Jesus" or "God" or some Deity along those lines, or Phil himself. When David was quiet and didn't give an answer, Phil had said, "We don't have a lot of time to play games or talk on the phone, so let me make this easy for you. You're a man. The most important relationship is with your wife. She's there at home with your child. That's the entity you should have in your mind by now. You've been doing this long enough that I shouldn't be calling to ask about your family and you respond that you haven't spoken to them in two weeks. That's a damn shame, son." He wrote to me that if Phil knew about our argument, he'd feel a greater shame toward his son. David wrote, *It's not like me at all. I have no idea. I have no excuse. I am ashamed that I pushed you and that I picked you up like that and acted harmfully. I hope that you will forgive me and know that I would change it.*

Along with the notebook, he included a photo album. Women in burqas with dark eyes looked out from a bright, cement doorway and two men stood in a small, cotton field. Another image showed a long, wooden kitchen table and bowls of food that I didn't recognize. A young man looked proudly into the camera from a storefront, his chest squared and his chin lifted. Stacks of porcelain goods on shelves surrounded him. Three women walked through a little, flat garden of red rose bushes. Some angular fruit trees stood in the distance, but the overwhelming color of the photograph was brown, as if David added a sepia filter, the sand casting a dull coating on so many of the outdoor images. Then, the mountains rose severely above a sunlit valley. Another photo showed rough, rocky points and snow dusting the edges. I considered the slippery beauty of the roads he traveled. A man wearing long, gray robes leaned heavily on his right foot in the foreground of the last image in the album. He seemed bored. The tan shaggy-haired bodies of his sheep blend into the earth, but their black spotted faces and legs stand out in contrast.

I told Jordan about the notebook and some of its contents, though I was too ashamed of our fight to reveal those parts to Jordan. I was embarrassed for David and wanted to protect us, but I also doubted our ability to make it in a long-term marriage. What if he wasn't interactive? What if he distanced himself again? What if I was full of anger?

When I left, Jordan stood underneath the maples. The leaves were bright green and they flattened themselves out into a lush wall. On the drive to the airport to pick up David, I bit all of my fingernails until they throbbed in a raw bulbous pain. Maggie wanted a sucker for herself and a rose to give to her daddy.

She smiled and bounced on her feet, "Can I watch cartoons with Daddy? I want to take Daddy to the playground. He can go fishing with me today." She went on listing the activities that they'd do together.

On the way to the airport, my impatience caused me to itch and break out with hives. We waited outside the security gates. *Where was he?* I started to panic as the time passed and we waited. Families traveling together moved by us. Maggie stared. I scratched at the hives and wished that we could experience the bigger homecoming ceremonies I had heard students talk about. Though, I recollected, they did complain about having to stand in formation and sing before hugging their families.

"I wouldn't want you to be gone, too," Maggie said, interrupting my thoughts and raising her arms for me to pick her up. She squeezed my shoulders.

"I'm not in the Army," I said. "So, Mommy will never go to Afghanistan. I'll always stay with you."

She tucked her head onto my shoulder. I closed my eyes and took a deep breath to steady myself. I felt lips on my cheek. David placed his forehead against mine as I opened my eyes.

"I missed you two," he said and circled his arms around us. Maggie giggled. I cried instantly, leaning into his body.

"Daddy, you wanna watch cartoons with me when we get home? You want to?" She nodded her head enthusiastically. Lately, she expressed a need to connect with her dad, especially after seeing her friends in pre-school being picked up by their dads. David mirrored her expression and we walked toward the baggage claim. "Welcome home!" a man said.

Maggie remembered her rose, "I got this for you, Daddy," she said pushing it under his nose.

"That's so nice," he said. "Thank you, both."

On the drive home, he talked nonstop about his plans to add new gravel to the driveway, clear the trails on our property, and sleep outside in the hammock. "I'm going to stand for as long as I want to on the bank at the lake and fish," he said. "You want to go fishing, Maggie?" They talked back and forth on the drive, listing all the activities they could think of, even outrageous plans to run faster than a spaceship. Maggie laughed and said, "It's a pink spaceship."

As soon as we shut the front door to our house, he picked me up and spun around and kissed me. He tasted my mouth and face and inhaled deeply against my neck.

"You guys," Maggie said. "Stop it right now. We don't have time for that. We have to watch a movie and go fishing."

"How did you grow up so fast?" David asked her. "What's happened?"

"I was planning to ask you the same thing about your behavior," I said.

"I love my life," he said and slumped onto the couch with Maggie.

"It's the middle of the day," I said. "Shouldn't we be outside?" I regretted my disruption of the mood just after I said it.

"No!" Maggie began to whine and cry. "You said I could watch cartoons with my daddy and I never ever get to watch TV with my daddy."

"It's okay," I said. "You can watch movies together. Forget I said anything else." I turned the corner into the kitchen and scolded myself for trying to tell them what to do, for breaking the reunion.

"Ellen!" he shouted from the couch, "You want to run together tomorrow?"

I shook with tears and slid down the wall into a squat. I tried to catch my breath so that I could answer him without the sounds of crying.

"Ellen?"

"Mommy?" Maggie called.

Finally, after a deep swell and steadying, I said, "Yes, I'm here. I would like that very much, David."

Later that night when we were lying on the hammock outside, after Maggie had gone to sleep, he told me that it felt out of place to hear me say his first name. He was so used to being called by his rank or his nickname, Bloodhound, and its shortened form, Hound.

After the apprehension of David's homecoming and the bewildering euphoria of his calm state, I had forgotten about Jordan and the trial until the next morning when I saw him emerge from the maple leaves along the footpath between our houses. Jordan knocked on the door, an act that prompted uneasiness since he usually just opened it and started talking or called for me to hurry up so that we could begin our runs.

"It's open!" I shouted. "It's always open, as you know."

"I didn't want to be rude," he said and began picking at the food on my breakfast plates once he reached the kitchen. "David just got home and I want to be respectful of your family time." He noticed the silence. "Where's David?" he asked. "And Maggie?"

"They went to the store for butter," I said. He looked wounded and confused, knowing that I never went out to the store for missing ingredients before calling to ask if he had what I needed.

"I didn't even have time to suggest asking you for it," I said, "because David was already out the door with Maggie and on the way to the store. They should be here anytime. Do you want your own plate?"

"Of course," he said. "After yesterday, I need to eat and then drink later tonight. I need something after yesterday."

"What happened yesterday?"

"We can both say that we have mentally incompetent mothers," he said. "Maybe it's her alcoholism that causes her to fall back into her old habits and means of cruelty." He spoke quickly and crammed a strip of bacon between his teeth.

"What?" I asked, not following any of it.

"Yeah," he said. "That's what I asked her, 'What the hell are you talking about?'" He strode across the kitchen to the coffeemaker and poured a mug. His hand shook as he dumped two big spoonfuls of sugar into the mug and stirred.

"She wants to sell the property," he said. "Just sell it. After all of this talk about family and connections to me." He dropped the spoon onto the counter with a loud, vibrating ring, and continued as he slurped at the hot coffee, "Can you believe that? She asks me to renovate and make repairs and tend to our side, and all along she's courting some contractor."

"I don't get it," I said. "Aunt Darcy has a boyfriend here?"

"That's not what I mean," he said. "She's been talking to a contractor about selling our, well her, part—" he said. David and Maggie returned with butter and a small bouquet of roadside daisies. David handed the flowers to me before addressing Jordan who stood when they came into the room.

Jordan stuck out his hand, "Good to have you back, man."

David patted Jordan on the back while they shook hands, "It's great to be home. And for almost a year. I didn't think this one would be over fast enough." He looked past us and out the window. He narrowed his eyes. "Who is—?" he was asking when Jordan interrupted.

"Oh great," Jordan said and put his forehead in his hand and squeezed his face before taking a deep breath and continuing, "I didn't want her to come over here this morning."

I strained to see through the window and noticed Aunt Darcy's dark gray hair glint in the sunshine as she crossed the lawn to the front door.

"That's my Aunt Darcy," I said to David. They had only met once, at Granna's funeral.

"He was lucky until now," Jordan said over his shoulder as he exited the room so that he could open the front door before Aunt Darcy made it onto the porch. "Mom, I thought that you were…" Jordan's voice trailed through the door and we heard it shut behind him. We heard their muffled argument and then Aunt Darcy's distinct demand echoed into the house, "I'm determined to ask them about it, Jordan, and I can't do anything about the bad timing. It's always going to be bad," she said loudly.

"Well, you've been warned!" he shouted. "She's not going to sell this place. I'm so tired of telling you, so go ahead!"

My face turned hot and little needlepoints electrified my spine and my head. My hands shook, but David grabbed them, "You wait right here, okay?"

"David, don't go out there and say anything to her. Let me…" but he was already leaving the room.

I listened to him open the door, "Hi, you must be Darcy," he said and the door closed behind him. I hurried across the room to listen in a position that offered more clarity. He introduced himself and cut straight to the point, "David Hart. Nice to see you again."

"Glad you made it home okay," Darcy said warily like she knew that his tone was already leading somewhere that wasn't agreeable with her. "I've heard—" she began to say weakly, but David kept on as if she hadn't spoken one word to him.

"I couldn't help but overhear your conversation and I think it would be best for me to tell you right now that there's no way we'll be selling this property to anyone for any amount of money."

I peered around the corner and could see Darcy's profile. She kept her arms folded across her chest and she shuddered a little waiting for him to finish his refusal. Jordan stood on the steps, just behind her. He had lifted his arms overhead and held onto the roof of the porch and smirked as David spoke to his mom. I couldn't see David at all.

"Well," Darcy said, "I've spoken to a contractor and you'd stand to make a lot of money if you sold it. Yes, they want to develop it, but after all of this murder and an orchard that doesn't produce decent fruit trees anymore, it's time to get out of Dodge and let all of this go. Move on. With the money you'd make from the sale, you could buy twice this amount of property in Elk Springs and that's only fifteen minutes from here."

"Sell your part if you want, but why do you care if we stay here?" David asked.

"I just didn't want to see you pass up a good business deal," she said. "And a good opportunity to keep your family safe."

"I don't need you to explain how I should keep my family safe. I'm equipped with that skill," he said and cleared his throat.

Darcy rubbed her arms quickly as if she were cold, but I knew it was a nervous reaction. She scratched her head. "I should at least be able to talk to my niece about this," she said.

"She doesn't want to talk to you about it," David said. His statement was true, but I felt like a coward with David and Jordan blockading her.

Maggie looked worried. "I don't want to move, Mommy," she said. "This is my house." Her lips pushed forward and her eyebrows narrowed. I had forgotten about her, sitting at the kitchen table in front of her breakfast plate when the interruption started. She stood behind me, quietly listening.

"We aren't moving," I said. "I'll go tell her. Stay right here, okay?"

She nodded, "You go tell her, okay, Mommy? Tell her this is my house." I reassured her and went to the front door where I could hear them arguing about why I wouldn't talk to Darcy. I opened it quickly and interrupted, "Aunt Darcy, I'm not going to sell this house. It's Maggie's house, and we won't sell it for any reason. There's no amount of money that could make me sign it over to a contractor."

"I know you promised Momma," she said, referring to Granna, "but she didn't want you to be out here alone and miserable, afraid of a murderer and imagining that you can see some lost Indian tribe."

"Aunt Darcy, go home," I said. "It won't matter how you insult me, I'm not going to sell, and we don't need this right now. For God's sake, David just got home from a deployment."

"I'm not trying to insult you or interrupt David's homecoming," she said.

"Yes, that's what you're doing," Jordan said.

"Regardless, just go home," I said. "Please, take no for an answer and go home."

"I wish you would at least think about it."

"Mommy," Maggie said as she opened the door. "Did you tell her this is my house?"

"We should go inside and finish our breakfast," I said. "Now the food's cold."

"Did you invite them to dinner?" Aunt Darcy asked Jordan.

"I didn't have time before you showed up," he said.

"I have to leave tomorrow morning to go back home, to Alaska," she said to David, "and we'd like for you all to have dinner with us somewhere tonight before I leave."

"As long as you don't talk about selling any property," David said.

"Fine, just let me know where we're going," she said to Jordan as she stepped off the porch and started across the lawn. We turned to go back inside. "I apologize for the interruption," she said quickly over her shoulder. We didn't respond.

"You want to eat?" I asked Jordan who was still in the same position on the steps, arms overhead, holding onto the roof of the porch.

"What I think," David said, "is that she's got a contractor who said he'll give her more money for her part if she could get us to sell too. Ours is the part that he really wants because most of hers is lower elevation and probably in a five hundred year flood plain, right? Am I right?" He looked at Jordan who shrugged. David went inside with Maggie.

"What am I going to do?" Jordan asked me. I knew that he meant where was he to live if his mom sold her part. "I'll figure it out," he said, his arms collapsing at his sides. "Go on and have breakfast with your family. I'll call you later." He turned to leave, but when I peeked out the window after going inside, I saw him sitting on the porch stairs with his chin resting in his hands.

*****

Later, David asked me to run a marathon with him. I was shocked, my mouth gaping with laughter. He sniffed, said, "It's okay if you don't want to," and turned to walk away.

"I do," I said. "Definitely, but I'm afraid that I wouldn't be the best partner."

"It'll be fun," he smiled.

I leveled my gaze and flattened my enthusiasm, "Seriously?"

"You've been training with Jordan."

"Yeah, but that's only for a half, and I feel like I can barely make my legs cover that distance."

"That's what training is for," he said. "You could at least try it."

"Why do you want me to do this with you?"

"Why not?" He gave me a questioning stare and strolled outside with a beer and a book.

"What are you reading?" I called after him.

"Just some science fiction book," he said.

"Since when did you start reading sci-fi?" I tagged after him onto the porch.

"Since college," he said, insinuating that I obviously hadn't been paying attention.

"In college?"

"Don't you remember hunting the aisles of Great Escape and all of those second hand bookstores with me? Come on, Ellen, you okay?"

"Oh yeah," I said. "I don't know what I was thinking. I kept thinking about vampires for some reason and not proper science fiction. I was thinking of wizards and fantasy-based fiction. It's so damn popular right now. It's taking over every genre, even history."

"Definitely not the same thing," he said. He laughed a little, "Remember that time we stayed out in the park all night, reading books by candlelight? And you caught that book on fire and started screaming. I thought the cops or those homeless guys were going to come over."

"I liked that book too," I said. "I was really into it, all hunched over the candle. It shouldn't have caught fire so quickly though. It's like someone had doused it with lighter fluid or something, the way it torched up like that."

"It was crazy," he laughed remembering our frenzy to put out the fire.

"Makes me miss college," I said sighing.

"Me too," he said. "You were so timid. I couldn't believe that you agreed to a date with me. You were so serious and smart, but I couldn't look at the back of your neck anymore in biology without wanting to kiss it."

"Really?"

"Yeah, you had this dainty but edible neck and back, and I wanted to photograph you right away. Remember that?"

"What a nightmare," I said. "I was so embarrassed. No one had ever pointed a camera at me and said that I was beautiful."

"I had pictures of you all over the darkroom at school. That really was a cool senior show, wasn't it?"

"It's difficult for me to be objective, but I think the concept was well received."

He sighed and looked distant, as if he might have been imagining what our lives could have been like if art was valued in a different way, if it had ruled and controlled our life in a way that offered us support, in a way that gave us financial security. Where would we have gone? Would we have moved out of the double-exposed photographs from his senior show—the series of ghostly homes and skeletal remains of barns, the mill overgrown with vines, the abandoned foundries, the crumbling places—he took those photos and overlaid them with faded images of me or other people, as if we were shadows left on those places. He snapped himself out of his daydream and shook his head, smiling at me, "Let's go take some photos tomorrow. All around the property," he said. "And start training for a full marathon, okay?"

"That's a tall order," I said and sat on the boards of the porch, feeling the weight of his request. "That's twenty-six miles, David. That's like running all the way to Nashville."

"But not alone, not on the interstate, not without water and support," he said. "You have to think of it one step at a time, one mile at a time, not the end result."

"Yeah, but it's still twenty-six miles no matter how you look at it."

"Alright, just forget it," he said. "Maybe Jordan will run it with me." He gulped down a quarter of his beer and flipped open his book open.

"Maybe that would be best since he's used to those long runs."

"Maybe so," he said. "Do you mind if I read for a little while?" he asked without looking away from the page. I stared out at the lawn, watched two cardinals chase one another and the hummingbirds joust around the feeders. I sat with our discomfort and refused to leave simply because David had dismissed my fears and my presence. I closed my eyes and listened to the summer hum of the afternoon, knowing that Maggie should be awake from her nap at any moment. The intensity bedazzled me internally, and I didn't want to prove my strength to David, but I did want to run. I bounced away from my place on the floor of the porch and up the stairs until I swept on a change of clothes and looked for my shoes at the front door, but they weren't there.

Already some of the same irritations were beginning to creep back into routine. Since his return, he'd put my shoes on the black shelf in the stairwell. A place smoky with cobwebs, the shelf carried the weight of rusty cans, clothespins, buckets, rope, a cup of nails and a cup of screws, an odd assortment of blades, the hammer and flashlights. I imagined spiders living close by. Like Granna, I had always left them, but tried to maintain my distance. I snatched the shoes and mumbled as I banged them against the railing of the porch and laced them quickly. He ignored my complaints about getting bitten and *why can't he just leave my shoes where I put them?* They couldn't possibly be in his way that much. I was leaving, had to run, instructing David over my shoulder to give Maggie a snack when she woke from her nap.

"Where are you going?" he asked, throwing up a hand, as if I'd been invisible while cleaning out my shoes.

"To run," I said. "I'll take over when I get back and you can go out for a run then if you want."

"So you're gonna do it?" he called after me.

I kept going and realized after a moment that he meant the marathon. I circled around to Jordan's house. I didn't want to knock on the door and get Darcy's attention, so I peeked in the windows until I caught a glimpse of Jordan sitting in front of the computer between the kitchen and living area. His renovations opened up the inside of the house, so that the office, kitchen, dining and living areas were all combined in a zigzagging open space in the center of the cottage. And it was a cottage with an inviting mystique— all ruffling foliage, ferns and rhododendrons on the outside.

 I tried to imagine my great grandmother, that little stern woman in photographs, living there alone, far away from neighbors. I always wondered what those relatives must have looked like if they were smiling. How did they laugh or slice tomatoes? Did I retain the tired stance of a great-great grandmother after picking plums in the orchard? Was my squat in the field to gaze around the landscape while sopping the sweat from my forehead with a handkerchief, a shared gesture with my dad? I wanted someone to tell me if I was like my dad or my great grandmother. People would understand me. In my old house, I felt angular and hard, and as a whole, it didn't seem as comforting as Jordan's cottage. I tapped on the window glass to get Jordan's attention. He looked at me with a startled squint and Aunt Darcy's waving arm caught the corner of my eye. She was standing in the kitchen and motioned for me to come around to the side entrance.

"What you doing sneaking around the side of the house behind the rhododendrons?" she asked with a suspicious grin on her face. "Were you trying to avoid me?"

"No, I was looking at the new rhododendron shoots coming up from underneath…" I sighed and continued, "growing underneath the other ones and I want to take some of those to plant on the other side of Granna's hou— my house," I pointed and breathed, trying to cover my naked attempt to avoid Aunt Darcy. I turned to Jordan, "May I take some of those rhododendrons?"

"Have you been running?" he asked.

"Not yet. You wanna come with me?"

"That'd be great," he said, and looking toward his mom, "We can go out to dinner after we get back and get showered, okay?" He was already sliding his feet into his shoes.

"Did you all decide where we're eating?" she asked me and continued. "I just want to go where everyone else does and go to a place that's agreeable," she laughed, trying to seem friendly instead of angry about the disagreement from the morning. "I just want us to spend time together and to talk as a family before I have to leave tomorrow morning. We don't get time together. I don't even know Maggie."

"Okay," Jordan said. "We'll be back shortly, Mom."

"Enjoy your run, your time together," she said as we hurried out the door.

I started to cry and question my decisions. "Maybe we should go back in there and spend time with her," I said. "She is leaving tomorrow and who knows when she'll be back."

"When she sells the property," he said. "No, better yet, she won't have a reason to come back then, so she'll just have her real estate agent fax over the documents for her signature. Don't be duped by her pity party and play on family togetherness. She's not interested in telling any bedtime stories or preserving our family. She's interested in money, period."

Jordan was running and talking so quickly that I tripped over a root and felt myself gliding above the ground, for so long that I thought about the landing, thought about my frustration with Aunt Darcy, Jordan and David, all of them with an agenda, never asking about my feelings, about the impact on me... and that's about the time that I landed with a breathless thud. I couldn't focus for a few moments and finally the deep movement in my lungs settled my focus on Jordan who waited for me to become aware before asking, "Can you move? You okay?"

I quickly stood, wiped the dirt away from my palms, tried to pick out the bits that were embedded in the fleshy cushions of my hands, and gingerly stretched my raw elbow and knee on my right side. "Just slow down," I said and began running again.

"Blood is streaming down your knee," Jordan said from behind me.

"It'll clot up in a minute," I said.

"Not if you keep running," he said. "Ellen, stop!"

"It's not that part of my knee," I said and turned around to show him. "Look, it's a scrape, and that's below where my knee bends. It'll stop in a minute, come on."

I didn't really know why I ran to Jordan and asked him to go with me until I said, "Why did you tell your mom so much personal information about me? Why did you tell her that I have visions and nightmares? Do you think I'm crazy, Jordan? Because I need for you to be honest with me."

He sniffed and spat on the ground. I thought that I would have to repeat myself if he didn't start speaking soon. He said, speaking quickly, "I'm sorry that I told her anything about any of us. She's a con and I need to remember how good she is at extracting secrets and then using them to her advantage. Look, she and I became close. We were talking on the phone every day and she was playing the concerned mother because of the murder trial. Speaking of the trial, not much happened, just opening statements. And, I didn't go downtown to get in the middle of that media frenzy. I watched it on TV. As far as my mom, I should've known that she wasn't sincere, not really. Her agenda was to sell the property and to find out as much about you as possible so that she could play on your fears and convince you to sell, too."

"Your mind has been busy with that," I said as we climbed the hill, panting through our anxiety, and at the top, we reached a release and loosened our way down the path, nestling into the beech trees.

"Let's just slip back to this pace a little," he said as he slowed and looked through the trees. He closed his eyes for a moment, "I don't think you're crazy, no more than anyone else, and we're all delusional when it comes to our desires and childhood fears. It takes a lifetime to heal. I'd just like to help you and to see you become aware of that, of healing yourself. And I can't begin to imagine what David has been through and he probably needs someone to talk to about that. I think you both have a lot to consider going forward, and I want you to know that you can count on me."

I started to cry. "Jordan, that's so nice, but you should know, I've always counted on you."

"Don't cry," he said. "Cause you'll make me get sentimental, and all I can say is we have to stick together, Ellen. And I need to find a real girlfriend, someone who can spend time with me out in the open."

"Is she married?" He nodded.

I felt my opportunity to press forward, "Is her husband a soldier?" He nodded.

I took the advantage that he was giving me, "Is she a soldier?" He nodded. "Do they have a child?" He flipped his hand back and forth. "Does she have a child with someone else?" He nodded. "She has joint custody?" He nodded.

His pace increased as I questioned his relationship and he passed me just before the final question. I stopped talking, just to keep up. "Let's not talk about this anymore for now," he said. We ran our fastest and hardest, until nothing was left in our legs or our lungs. We would have peeled back the skin in a windy flap and strode into the air, thinner into the vapor. But there was the old house staring back at us, windows reflecting our panting and our stiff-legged gait to the front door.

"Your aunt called and she's gone to dinner with an old friend tonight," David said as soon as we walked into the house. "She said that she'd like for us to have breakfast early in the morning before she leaves, and I told her to come over here and I'll cook up the breakfast. She tried arguing, but you're coming here." David said, pointing at Jordan. We grabbed water and went out the back door with a swinging, metal snap. It rattled the frame, and the porch shook under the weight of us. Jordan leaned against the railing and I sat down on the wooden boards and stuck my legs out, leaned back on my palms and wrists. "I'll see you later," David said as he walked off the porch. He smiled back to us, "Maggie wants pancakes. I want omelets for breakfast. Let me know what your Aunt wants in hers." He ran in the direction of the orchard, toward the river.

"So much for dinner and Mom's emphasis on family togetherness and not knowing Maggie," Jordan said.

When David returned about an hour later at sunset, he caught me off guard and jumped on the hammock as I was daydreaming. Maggie watched a movie with Jordan and I could hear them laughing at the dogs in the movie, imitating them, "Squirrel!" the dogs said and jerked their heads toward the high branches of a tree. Non sequitur.

David rubbed his sweaty face against my cheek and underneath my chin. I joked about pushing him away but he lifted my torso and slid beneath me, and the hammock threatened to topple us until it eventually slowed. David pushed his elbow into the netting and we rocked. "I ran above the river," he said, "but the grass is pretty tall and I had to circle back and take Bert's Road up to the statues. I need to clear that grass tomorrow. It's terrible. I wish

Jordan would take some initiative. I'll just have to ask him."

"It's a lot for one person to manage," I said.

"One person?" he laughed. "You make two people." The hammock began to slow and his body was trapping me with a stifling heat. It slid around me easily and pushed away the breeze from the hammock, and the sky's sunset fires that had cooled into ashes weren't wafting any wind my way.

David tilted the netting again and we bounded awkwardly until his hips directed a steady motion. I closed my eyes for comfort against the hammock's inability to maintain rhythm. "I was going to tell you that I thought about the first time you brought me here and we walked along the river after climbing down that bluff," David said. "I really wanted to run on the edge of the bluff but the grass got in my way. I wanted to see that bluff we climbed down. I just wondered if it would seem steep to me now. You were like a mountain goat dancing down to the river. I knew at that moment, I wanted to marry you. You weren't as timid as I thought, just quiet, at first. I remember thinking that you'd never shut up when we were alone. I couldn't read four pages into a book and you were already saying something about the one that you were reading." He rested his hand on my shoulder and continued. "I can't sell this place because I always think about you being here and I know that you're okay. Your ancestors will always protect you here, Ellen. I know that. I have my doubts on all sorts of stuff about God and heaven and hell, but I do know that this place is holy to your family and you've got to hold on to that. They'll always protect you and Maggie. I just know it." The sky deepened until the stars lit themselves and the outline of the leaves blended into the darkness.

Maggie and Jordan ran onto the deck, "Boo!" they shouted and walked to the hammock.

"You have to see this movie, Daddy," Maggie said. "It is so funny. They have a lot of dogs. I know. I have an idea. Maybe we could have just one dog. Like Nuance."

"I wish Nuance would come back," I said.

Jordan picked up Maggie and placed her in the hammock with us. He grabbed the edge of the hammock, pulled us up, and let it go. Maggie giggled as we swayed, "This is fun."

"I'll see you all tomorrow," Jordan said. "Have a good night."

"See you for breakfast," David said.

"I love you, Jordan," Maggie said. "Isn't Jordan the best?" she said to us. "I love you and Mommy and Maggie and Jordan," she said to David.

Suddenly, I was perplexed. I just couldn't shake it, why was he so calm? How was he so different? Had something happened? But I didn't want to ask, as if that might break the spell.

The next morning, breakfast was uneventful. Aunt Darcy was eager to leave again. Jordan was bouncing to get her out the door. David was completely entertained by the tension that everyone tried to pretend didn't exist. Maggie and Aunt Darcy tried on some plastic necklaces and rings while watching an early cartoon. Before leaving, Aunt Darcy tried to share an intense moment with me by cupping my face in her hands, telling me, "Momma would be so proud of you. Bring that little girl and come visit me sometime."

"Okay," I said, "thanks," and stepped back toward David and Maggie. I looked at the ground as she got into the car. She paused before closing the door and gave us a wary look.

The dust hadn't yet calmed from their exit when David said, "You should go for a run. You'll feel better." Again, he was making suggestions that looked out for my best interest, that weren't about what he wanted or his preoccupations with whatever had controlled his mind during the other breaks, between deployments. While it all seemed like a smooth transition, I didn't trust it, especially when I couldn't find my shoes beside the door again.

"Stop!" I shouted at him when we were back in the house and I'd retrieved my shoes from the shelf. "Stop putting my shoes out there! I mean it. Why are you trying to aggravate me?"

He turned away and started to wash the breakfast dishes.

"Don't do this again, David," I said. "Not on another break, we can't do this again. I can't take these head games and I'm not—"

"Ellen, she's standing there listening to you," he said without turning around but gesturing with the dishcloth toward the kitchen table.

"We have to talk about things regardless," I said. "I'm not going to be silenced and controlled all of the time."

"What are you talking about?" he asked. "I'm not silencing you. I'm not stopping you from saying whatever you want, but she's capable of repeating you now, of repeating all of this."

"Well, stop moving my shoes and controlling me, and we wouldn't have to deal with it."

"Okay," he said. "Whatever. This is crazy, already."

"I am not crazy, okay?" I shouted. "I will not feel like this in my own house again!"

"Then leave!" he turned and shouted back at me.

The forest allows people in to walk and travel. Cumberland didn't care which feet stirred the dust or tramped through the mud. As I moved downhill alongside the trunks, I saw my own fluidity. I saw the weight of my legs impacting the ground, when I pounded with abandon toward the goal, a rhythmic gallop and hurdle through the trees, and when I tiptoed my resistance to sound and pressure by withholding the motion, pushing up on the points of my toes. I ran to find some balance between forceful progression and poised fear.

When I got back home, Jordan was there and talking about Aunt Darcy, how he wouldn't be manipulated by her. He ranted to David about her ability to connive and I'd never heard Jordan complain so much. My stomach flipped thinking that Jordan was weaker than I had imagined. He'd always been the one with the answers, the ability to aid others and receive their patronage. People liked him and he was the social one between us, but this made me feel exhausted as I tossed aside my shoes and climbed the stairs.

The next morning, they were gone—all three of them, fishing at the river, and left me a note to enjoy the day. My first instinct was to go back to bed, but I fought it with the challenge of a marathon suggestion and convinced myself to go for a long run. I could use it as a sign to tell me if I was up for the real thing or not. I dressed and went looking for my shoes, which weren't by the door where I'd left them. Furious, I opened the door to the stairwell, but they weren't on the shelf. Their usual place was vacant. I left the stairwell door open and stomped across the kitchen to the back door, flung it open to the point that it stuck on a board of the deck. I spun in a circle in the center of the deck, but they weren't outside. Everything shook as I made my way back into the kitchen and there, sitting on the counter beside the coffee maker were my tennis shoes. Maggie had drawn a smiley face and David had placed it on top of my shoes. I stood against the counter, berating my level of anger and anxiety as I slid my feet into the tennis shoes.

As I glanced up, I noticed a dirt dauber hover along the floor, having just entered the house through the open screen door. Its black body shined in the sunlight and it traveled along the bottom of the counters and passed by my legs and went into the door to the stairwell. *Great, now I have to get it out of there or it'll die.* Like Granna, I couldn't consider killing it, even though I didn't want to waste any of my free time chasing it down and capturing it in order to let it go outside. Maggie and I often trapped insects in Tupperware containers and set them free in the backyard, so I grabbed the nearest plastic bowl and decided to trap the solitary wasp that didn't sting people, the dirt dauber.

Why did it come in here anyway, and why do I have to become so angry that I lose my temper? I make the door get stuck and in flies the wasp? I asked this irritably as I passed through the doorway. I only moved down two steps when I saw it flitting in a streak of sunlight. The dirt dauber was stuck and wriggling in an old cobweb on the black shelf, just beneath where David always placed my shoes. *This makes it easier*, I thought and moved closer in order to quickly enclose the dirt dauber in the plastic bowl.

I moved the lid into my left hand and bowl into my right, preparing for the capture when suddenly a spider emerged from beneath the lip of the shelf and parachuted down a line to the dirt dauber. They faced and locked legs. *I knew it! A spider! I should have listened to my intuition, not David. I knew it,* I thought and moved closer to the spider wondering, *what kind of spider is it?* The light illumined the spider's body as the dirt dauber's bottom point moved and contorted. *Is the spider anesthetizing it? A brown recluse? It is a brown recluse. Look at that perfect fiddle pointing and held so still with the dirt dauber. This is crazy. I'll have to kill it. I can't let it bite Maggie or have babies. I knew there was a spider. Should I let it wrap up the dirt dauber? Should I kill them now? What are they doing?* I tried to look from another angle, but it only seemed like a tangle of legs and abdomens. I was thinking quickly when the insects fell onto the step. *What're they doing now?*

I only had a moment to have that thought when the dirt dauber lifted off the step, black and shiny as a helicopter rising. I was startled and stood straight up, glancing quickly at the step but the brown recluse was gone. I stepped back as the dirt dauber rose to my eye level and I saw the body of the brown recluse held in the legs of the dirt dauber. I backed up the steps quickly, the hairs on my arms rising in awe. The dirt dauber was in the kitchen, swiftly flying at eye level, and leaving through the back door, through its entrance. I followed behind it, outside into the sunlight as it flew toward the trees. I was electrified, stunned, thinking that it couldn't have actually happened. How could a dirt dauber fly in and take away a spider…just like that?

The fact that nature didn't discriminate, and my admittance into the forest was up to my attempt, gave me the determination. I was going to run a marathon with

David in November, and I had about ten weeks to train up and double my distance. Covering twenty-six miles on Cumberland's rugged terrain didn't seem possible, so I needed to adjust my running habits. I couldn't train on the familiar trails the entire time. I chose a variety of locations. The street, the University track, a treadmill, and I vowed to start.

I exited the soft path and ran along the street, all the way to the intersection of the bypass; then I turned back until I reached Bert Road, the one that came to a dead end on the back of our property. I followed the soft, powdery dirt road with the tall, chicory's purple discs and white Queen Anne's lace lengthening toward the gnats and brown, crispy butterflies, the crackling legs of a grasshopper popping across the gravel. The smell of death lingered from a mouse crusted over with flies, their moving shimmer of black and green glinted against the sun that illumined my back and streaked it with whelps and moved me forward as if a fire snaked behind me in the dust.

The shoulders of a man rose up from the grass as I approached the No Faces statues. The one-horned bull looked toward the river. Two headless men shook hands, towering black and charcoal. Rust oozed from the wires revealed under the crumbled, busted concrete in the statue's foot, his elbow, his hand that looked like a noose, its exterior having been shattered off by a hard blow from a baseball bat, scattering the concrete and flinging bits out into the night. I imagined the boys in hats, giggling into their scrunched shoulders, one of them sticking his chest out and legs extended, "WOOOO-HOOOO" ing it into the moonlight, "YEAH!" "OWWWW!" the primal release and inhale. Maybe they heard about the statues around town, heard the rumors that Guthrie hid money in the statues. I imagined those boys' breath could be seen puffing from their mouths. Looking around, one of them probably scanned the landscape, quietly, intensely. When it was his turn, he picked up the bat as if it was a staff, held one end on his shoulder and charged straight for the chest with the handle of the bat. "Uuhhh!" he grunted as the handle of the bat thumped into the statue's pocket and stopped. It remained sticking straight out when he let go of the bat. They all laughed but they didn't know why. He wiggled the handle free, around and around, furiously flaking off bits of concrete and pulling some of the wires out of the chest.

"You think people are actually buried here?" one of them finally asked.

"Ain't no one buried here. Just some statues a crazy man built."

"I don't want to be cursed by no dead people," another said.

"Guthrie," the quiet guy said. "His name was Guthrie and he didn't put any fucking money in here, that's for sure." He spread the busted concrete around on the ground, and flipped the large pieces over, examining them for something, with a flashlight in his other hand. He shined the flashlights into their headless torsos, into the hole of the chest, into the wiry elbow and foot, but there was nothing except wires and concrete to be discovered.

I panted in front of the statues, imagining what happened to them, how they were created, and how they were believed to contain something more than they did. I wondered if the boys noticed the cemetery just behind the statues. Did they wander around the property at all or just go straight for the statues? I traced my hand across the sleeve of the soldier and shook his noose for a hand. I slipped my wrist between the space and closed my fingers around the wire. I traced my hand across the bull's horn and rested my forehead against his.

I squatted to pee before running the final leg back to my house and considered which way I should go, beside the cemetery and around by Jordan's, or toward the cedar grove and to the back door of my house. I felt a tickling against my leg and thought that I'd messed up in my squat. I heard the hum next and felt the needling tingle flash up my spine and across my scalp. I couldn't think fast enough and tried pulling up my shorts as fast as possible, but I was sure they were in there, in my shorts, stinging me. I felt the heat of my crotch, my back, and I tried swatting them, but more were coming, stinging so swiftly, I couldn't think. I tried to scream once, "Ahh! David!" but no one could hear me so far away. My mind raced with stings as I started walking and flicking the yellow jackets and they kept coming. *I peed on them. How did I pee on them? No one will find me. I never go this route. I'll die out here.* I could feel my body changing.

The yellow jackets needled me, and I ran, as fast as possible. The voice in my head was a prayer, an incantation, but directed toward my Granna and my dad, *This is a bad mistake, please help me, please carry me, just give me the strength to make it down the hill, through the grass, whipping me, I can't see through it. What if they're still fishing? I can't breathe, the suffocation, nothing but tall grasses in my view. Keep breathing, just keep breathing. I'll die. They won't find me. I hear it, the tractor, I hear it. He's there on the tractor, probably with Maggie. I can't believe that my mind can work so fast, but it can, it is, keep going, make my legs move, please! Reach my hands up to the sky, move, reach, damn it! Reach! David! He'll see my hands, he'll see me in the grass, there's the tree line, come on, the cut grass edge, the line, turn, he's there, oh please David! Wave, jump!* "Help!" I mouthed. I waved frantically and collapsed. He stopped and grabbed the first aid kit that was in the tractor with him. He had to tell all of this to me because I couldn't remember this part. He called Jordan on his cell while running over to me, and he could see the bees flitting up, he could see them trapped in my sweat where I had smacked them dead, stingers embedded. He stabbed me with the EpiPen and picked me up and ran with me. He told Maggie everything was okay, and Jordan would be here in a minute. Jordan swept up Maggie in two minutes and took her back to his house.

"Can't believe that I'm okay," I said to David in the emergency room, "and that we're so efficient as a family." I was more proud of us in that moment as a cooperative entity than at any other time. Maybe it was because my life was at stake that I realized it.

I cursed the yellow jacket stings, but I also thanked them the following day when the phone calls started. "Did David make it home okay?" "Just checking in to see when we can come visit." David glared at me when I bemoaned the messages. He said, "You make it seem so dramatic, all those phone calls. We've only received three, from your mom, my parents and my sister!"

"Your sister who's basically a stranger," I mumbled. "And the rest of them don't really care about my well-being."

I sulked up the stairs. He waited and then followed me. "They do care. They just live far away. Since when have you tried to reach out to them?"

Propped on the pillows, I clicked on the television to watch the Philip Jefferson trial, along with everyone else in the state.

David crossed the room and sat in the chair next to my side of the bed, "Ellen, what is it that's bothering you? Is it because your mom called and she wants to visit?"

"It's because everyone wants to visit and I don't feel good, obviously," I said.

"No one will be visiting tomorrow or even the end of this week. They just want to plan a visit and make sure that I'm alright. That we're alright. You know?"

"Just do whatever you want to do." I turned back to the television after the commercial ended.

"It's not about what I want to do!" he shouted and tried to recompose himself. "I'm so sick of this trial already." He waved an irritated hand toward the TV. "Our families want to see us, to visit for a weekend. And we can do that when you're feeling better."

"Just do whatever you all want then," I said, staring at the TV. "I'm tired, David. I just don't want to talk to anyone. I don't want to call my mom back, or your mom, or your sister, your daddy, or anybody else."

"Stop paying attention to that," he said and stood in front of the TV. "I'm calling all of them back," he said. "Don't worry about it. Just get some rest."

"I just can't. I can't believe this shit. Those yellow jackets and those damn statues. Right after you just got back, and this murder trial." I let it all tumble out and closed my eyes, not wanting to face his reaction. "And, Jordan's crazy mother wants to sell our land, and maybe we should, after this luck. I don't want to see my mother. I don't. Or Darryl. I don't want to deal with them. And I know you just got back. From war, again, and I'm just another thing to take care of, a joke, a mess. I can't handle anything.

You should have some relief, and some recognition. Seeing your parents. I just don't want to, honestly, but I know you do, and I hate saying that, but I feel like I need to tell someone how I feel, and it's terrible. I feel terrible, and like I think only negative things, like all scary bad things are going to happen to us, and I'll never get away from living like this inside myself. You know? Maybe you don't know and I just sound stupid… and crazy."

He didn't say anything. During another commercial break, the station advertised another medical, forensic investigations crime show. I sighed. "Whatever. Just go call your people back and I'll get some sleep. I'll deal with my mother sometime." I muttered, "Just accept it."

"I know how you feel," he said, turning off the TV. "Thinking too much about what could or might happen if… I know what that's like. Too much time to wonder. Too much idle worry and you just don't know. You just don't." He smiled. "That's why you've got to think about something else in your mind. Plan something. Create something. Set a goal in your mind. That'll help you. And even when those other people are around, because they sometimes have to be, and they really piss you off, you think about that goal in your mind, you focus on that, talk about it if you have to, and they'll stop bothering you so much, and your worries won't creep in as much. That's why I'm running that marathon."

"Oh, that's what this is about. Great," I said. "How can I run a marathon like this? I just got over one hundred bee stings! Over one hundred!"

"I know that, Ellen. And no, this is not about convincing you to do a marathon," he said. "I was just talking about myself. I wasn't even trying to go there. Never mind," he tossed up his hands. "I was trying to explain how to help your mind. I know that I'm trying to help my goddamn mind right now, and," he sighed deeply, "some times are better than others." He took some heavy breaths.

"Yeah, you have it all together this time, huh?" I asked. "You're capable and nonplussed, right? While I, I, have just been diagnosed with PTSD, what you should fucking have, by my counselor cousin! Yeah, don't look so shocked, like I haven't been traumatized by you and, and," I shuddered with rage.

"I can't fucking do this, Ellen!" he said between clenched teeth. "I can't go here again. I'm trying my best to hold it together this time. I have one more, one more, and I cannot do this the whole time in between. I will lose it, and that's not a threat. It's just a fact that I have to keep it together and focus on something so I don't..." he sighed, "get so pissed. I'm still struggling, whether you see it or not. And, let's get back on track before this goes bad," he stopped and closed his eyes, refocusing internally. "Look, I know you don't want to run a marathon, and that's okay. Just find something for yourself, Ellen. Something that will help you. That's all I meant." He began to leave the room.

"I was going to run it with you," I said. "That's why I went a different way yesterday, but how can I now? Like this?"

"They'll go away," he said, without looking at me. "And soon. As long as Doc says you're okay, you're okay."

"Really? Poof, just like that, I'll be sprinting like a fucking deer tomorrow, right?"

"Look, I've to get out of this room right now. But, no, not tomorrow. And yeah, as long as you get some rest, you'll be able to run as good as normal soon."

"It won't affect my running later? In any way?"

"I need to talk to you about this later," he said, his face becoming red. His right hand was balled into a fist. He took another deep breath. "No, the bee stings should help you."

"How?"

"You'll be careful about where you pee from now on." He smiled. "I'm going to return phone calls and cook something. Go to sleep." He turned off the light and left the room.

David called my mother first and told her that I was sick and she'd have to visit sometime next month. "She was playing nice and sweet," he informed me of their thirty-minute conversation, during which Darryl took the phone away from Mother and talked to David for about half the time. "I don't think the guy has ever said more than five words to me before now, but he told me all about their new house and his trip to Egypt, and that your brother has been doing some service work in Africa lately, for an organization that does reconstructive surgery in places that have experienced war for a long time. Lots of children are disfigured. Your brother's been back and forth over the past two years. Then, he was asking me about my time in the Middle East. Evidently, Darryl's mother was a Jewish immigrant? It was really interesting."

"Please, spare me," I said. "I should care about history, but I don't want to think about Mother and Darryl and least of all, my brother. I'm glad he's changed his pompous ways, but let's not talk about it."

"Okay, well, my sister just can't get the money together for a visit. She checked the plane tickets after leaving the message, and they're over five hundred bucks each. I told her not to worry, and she seems like she's doing great, running that little bakery…"

"So I guess this means no one's visiting us until Christmas," I said.

"My parents are coming," he said.

Phil and Linda caught the first plane the following Monday and planned to spend five days with us. Linda jumped in through the front door and took over the matronly position of the house. She cooked, scrubbed the toilets, changed the bedding, weeded the flowerbeds, and even sewed a dress for me while she was here. She'd take a plate of lunch onto the back deck and watch the trees sway in the wind, the bees tumble toward flowers, and birds thump into the windows daily. She and Maggie made fresh ginger lemonade and mint teas. Maggie scooted a chair up to the kitchen counter. They turned on the radio and rolled out a pie crust. Maggie moved the cheese up and down on the grater while they prepared fettuccini alfredo. Linda and Maggie plucked herbs and baked cakes and I was the first person they served for every meal and snack. Linda and I talked about plants, insects, the weather, Maggie and her antics. We skipped all conversations about war, politics, the murder trial, and our men. We prepared coffee for one another. I left a vase of cut flowers on the bedside table in the guest room for her.

The last night of their visit, I woke after midnight and David wasn't in bed. I went downstairs for a drink. I heard voices on the front porch and realized that David and Phil were talking. I drank a glass of water and turned off the light. They were quiet, so I tiptoed toward the front door but didn't go upstairs. I noticed Phil's cigarette burning a red end from the porch swing. It creaked lightly as he shifted his weight and cleared his throat. David was sitting in a chair against the wall. He said, "I think it was Ellen getting something to drink. Sounds like she's gone back upstairs now. I just don't know, Dad. Sometimes, I think it would have been better to be a mechanic or to take a different job, one with a different purpose, that means something different."

I didn't move but listened to their barely muffled conversation.

"Yeah, but the way I see it," Phil said, "Every man or woman in any branch of the service makes killing possible. If that's your dilemma, you'll have to become far removed from the military, but then you'll have to refuse to pay taxes too, because the tax money pays for military moves and strikes. Mechanics who work on planes, fix the planes that drop bombs or that drop troops with guns. We teach and we train other armies, but to our purpose. The killing isn't the point in the end, but it's a necessary part to handle resistance that wants to kill you or a regime that tries to avoid giving people equality."

"Yeah, but I just don't see the equality, Dad. I don't. Politicians betray us. We're not accepted by some parts of society. We're all looked at as grunts on some level, and it doesn't matter how smart, in control, in shape, or precise. We're machines at some point, numbers in motion, and I just can't think past that sometimes. I reconciled the killing part long ago, the physicality of it. The purpose beyond is what trips me up. These competing forces of control that I don't quite understand politically and why they have fence-straddling deals due to a lack of force and acceptance of force... I don't know. I'm probably not making any sense. Doesn't matter anyway. I'll do the rest of my years and retire. Finish this up."

"When do you think you'll get another promotion?"

"Been thinking about that."

"You don't have a lot of time to decide," Phil rocked back and forth in the swing. I heard the squeak stop, "That what you mean? You haven't made a decision about that offer yet?"

"Not yet," he said. "I just don't want to move them and I don't want to be stationed that far away. I'd have to be there, in the Middle East, you know? There's no remote flexibility."

"Gonna be a tough decision," Phil said. "What did Ellen say about it?" There was a pause. I imagined that David shrugged his shoulders because Phil asked, "You didn't tell her about it yet?" After another brief pause, he added, "Just tell her and you'll work it out. Maybe her cousin could manage this place and you keep it as a summer home or a retirement home eventually. Just don't live here permanently. 'Cause at this point, seems like you can either keep doing what you're doing or take the other position."

"Yeah, wish I could find something here like that."

"I know you do," Phil said. "No sense in worrying about it right now. You've got a little time and you just got back." He yawned. "Let's get some sleep. Your mom and I have an early flight and she'll have to put me in a wheelchair so I can make it through the airport if I don't go to sleep now."

The next day, after we dropped his parents at the airport, David told me about the new position, something to do with intelligence. He had decided not to take it and was determined to find a position here that didn't keep him deployed as often. "We're over thirty now. We should have more babies if we're going to," he said. "I can tell by the look on your face that you don't like that idea."

"It's that I don't want to do it by myself," I said. "Live in a house with our kids and you're in another country for years and years. Back and forth like that. With a baby again? As much as I might want to have another baby with you, I don't think the fairy tale is possible. It'll be a lonely pregnancy or post-pregnancy."

"We could try to do it differently," he said. "And something may come along. Another assignment. A better one. Let me check on some things."

Jordan had taken Maggie to the park so David and I could have some time without a child and without parents. It was our first run together since he got back from Afghanistan. He reminded me of that fact as we emerged from the cedar grove onto the end of Bert Road, by the greenhouses and the orchards. The grass was cut and baled. David sold a few loads, and little patches lingered along the side of the road. The trees had begun to deepen and brown, some of them already primed for the golden-tipped glow of autumn. I didn't even look at the statues as we passed by and continued along the road. I shuddered with the thought of bees, but we didn't speak. David and I were in silence and unison. Our breaths were quiet and our shoes crunched with gravel. "How do you feel?" he asked.

"Good. Strange to feel this good." I expected to wheeze or struggle.

"How far do you want to go?"

"Let's just run and see what happens."

As we approached the intersection, David signaled to turn around, and we went back toward the house again, then turned around at the end of the road close to the orchard paths, and up and down Bert Road again and again. Later, David said that he wanted a flat path but he also repeatedly passed the site of my bee stings because he wanted me to be comfortable there again and to see that I could run without fearing harm. When I suggested that I was cursed or the universe had conspired against me, perhaps I'd angered the gods or some ghost, or the God, David said, "It was an unfortunate coincidence. Nothing more."

"I guess you know everything," I said.

"What does that mean?" he asked as we sat against the greenhouse and watched rain clouds approach. He handed a bottle of water to me.

"I'm just not so sure that I wasn't cursed or that my family isn't cursed. Or, maybe we're just unbelievably unlucky."

"Why would you think that? You have a healthy daughter. You're healthy and you live out on this beautiful farm. You own it and even sell flowers every year. Flowers that you don't have to do anything to except cut down when they bloom and truck them into town. How lucky can you get?" He said, as if he were questioning the dark clouds moving along the horizon, on the other side of the river. "You have an education and you're a professor in your family's hometown. That just doesn't happen for people, Ellen. You're really lucky." He gave me a level gaze.

I approached it as a competition and countered, "So lucky that my family's all dead except for an aunt with ulterior motives. So lucky to deal with death. Finding my own dad. And then people get murdered across the street, and I'm scared to death because my husband is deployed for the sixth or seventh or whatever time, and I'm so lucky to hear about my great brother and his life of service to the poor, disfigured children, while he helped rob me of my childhood, while he helped push me out the goddamn door to live in solitude with an old woman. I'm so lucky that I have no friends except my cousin. That's wonderful and full of luck. Might find a pot o' gold somewhere around here any time now. Oh wait, that's right. Where the treasure's supposed to be, I got stung in the crotch and all over my body, over one hundred times, by bees! There's the luck! That's right, I almost forgot about it."

It thundered and David stood on cue.

"Okay, have it your way. Life sucks," he said. "But I'm running back to the house before that storm gets here and your family's curse or whatever you think it is strikes us with a lightning bolt."

"You never take me seriously," I said, but he was already running along the path toward our house. The first large raindrops began to drop in splashes. I walked in the rain and stripped my clothes off along the way. Peeling back my shirt, trying to slip out of my shorts and nearly tipping myself onto the ground, rolling down my socks, until I was naked in the rain, just walking. The thunder stalked behind me, but I made it to the house as the full storm nipped at my heels with flickering threats. Inside the house, David sat looking out the window.

The next day, I met Fran at Cumberland and walked the trails. I felt like I was getting back to a part of myself, the me that was separate from David, and I felt a familiar agitation, that he had robbed me of something by the nature of his arrivals and departures, but I couldn't verbalize it until that afternoon with Fran. I found myself explaining all that happened since he came home, saying, "But I can't get over feeling like he's a stranger again, but I don't want him to be. Do you think that's normal?"

"Yeah, of course it is," she said. "You also need to understand why he thinks that you're lucky. He has seen women who can't go outdoors unless a man accompanies them. He's seen women hiding, women as objects in the extreme, he's heard his own men talk about women like that, but he's not like that. You don't have to worry that your husband will rape you. You don't have to wear a burqa, covering your entire body, whenever you're in public. You can walk naked in the rain on your own property. I know that there are still injustices here, but it's not the same from his perspective."

"Yes, I can see that," I said, "but from my perspective, I want a husband who connects with me, or wants to know how I view my own life. He should be genuinely interested in that, right? In me? In how I feel and what I think about my own life, right?" She was silent. "I don't think that I'm crazy for expecting that or wanting that from a partner."

"Maybe," she laughed. "Sorry, it's just that sometimes I don't know if men are capable of going to that level with us. And then, I know that they must be. They can, but you do have to heal yourself on many levels. You can't count on someone else to see it your way. Seems like that's what you're using as an excuse to remain confused or in pain, what you're struggling with, it's your own choosing, a repetitive voice in your own head that says you're not good enough or you deserved everything bad that has happened to you and no one else understands you. All those thoughts that you're repeating, and only you can change those into more positive approaches. Everyone has pain and trauma. Challenges. Think of all the different kinds of pain, just right now, that you can imagine. Put yours into some perspective against that and feel comforted, then let go of the curse that you are repeating in your own head. It doesn't matter if other people put it there. Your mom. Your brother. David. Jordan. The murderer. An Indian tribe. It doesn't matter because you're the one repeating it now. Over and over. Telling yourself nothing good."

"You don't really know me, Fran," I said. "How can you assume that I never tell myself anything good? How can you act like it's so easy to size up my life?"

"Just hold on," she said touching my arm, "I'm not trying to act like I know everything about you. I'm just responding to your need. You want someone to talk to you, but you don't want to hear what they have to say about you, or you don't want my advice, maybe." She walked a few more paces. "I'm sorry if I hurt your feelings or if my comments seem insensitive. I don't intend to be so harsh."

"I just don't think there's anything wrong with saying that I want a partner. I want David to be that, to step up and be that. I'm tired of all this deployment and going alone at life. I didn't ask for this when I married him. He was supposed to be someone else. Do you get that at all? I don't think he gets that."

"No one gets that," Fran said. "In many ways, that's what every person in a relationship thinks. Surprise! I'm someone different, depending on the situation, and especially in a long-term relationship. Bring in more pain, war in your case, trauma, disease in my relationship and yeah, you're dealing with another person. Of course, you are. How could you be the same? How could he be the same? It's impossible. Just as impossible for me and my husband to ever be the same. He's got cancer, chemotherapy, vomiting, you name it, and I'm not the Fran I was when we met, that's for sure. Some days, I'm fucking pissed off at the world. I'll yell out at God, how could you let this happen? Other days, I'm laughing with him at some stupid commercial on television and I'm just happy he's alive. Sometimes, I feel the same old marital stuff, like I could kill him for not turning the shower handle all the way off and letting it drip like that for eight damn hours. After twenty years, you'd think he'd remember how to turn off the shower in our house. But I know he thinks the same things about stuff I do, like the fact that he hates, hates, how I cook bacon. Even if I try not to cook it too done, I can never make it like the Shoney's breakfast bar where the bacon is like a soggy, flexible strip of pink and brown marbled bacon. Some days I think he could scream at me for that. Yeah, it's that stupid, but that's how life works. That's what we're reduced to on certain days and I don't know why and how the shifts occur between that and thinking you've got it all, the world in the palm of your hand, if only for a second."

"I need to go home," I blurted out. I finally felt the depth of a friendship with someone outside of my family, and it overwhelmed me. "I do appreciate our talk even if it seems like I don't right now."

"Okay," she said. "Call me sometime and try to get some rest." She handed me a folded magazine out of her jacket pocket. "I flagged a page in there about the century farms. Consider checking into it to protect your place. You may be eligible for funding."

"Thanks," I said tucking the magazine under my arm. "I'm more grateful to you than I can express right now, but I'll talk to you later." I cut through the woods, following the deer trails until I met the row of pines along the road and crossed over to my driveway. I hurried away from Fran with a need to let it all sink inside me, to hold onto the awareness that I had reached the end of my fear, to savor the realization that I was going to be okay and I was losing my self-consciousness. When I made it to the hammock, I fell into the ropes and read about century farms while the hammock lightly dipped toward the dirt where ants busied themselves with transporting white grains, and the hammock rose away and back down again. I felt sleepy and satisfied.

When I woke, it was morning and the birds sang out in short, sharp sounds. They repeated themselves in the sunlight and I shivered in the blanket clinging with autumn dew. David must have brought the blanket, but my face was pressed into the ropes and I thought they may have broken through the skin and merged with my flesh if I had only gone by feeling and not looked in the mirror. Deep red creases lined my cheek and forehead, one across my left ear. I marched up the stairs and flung myself onto the bed in irritation. "Why did you leave me out there?" I demanded at six a.m. "Why did you leave me out there?"

He peeked out of one eye. "I tried to wake you up a few times." He cleared his throat. "You told me to leave you alone, but not that nicely, so I got the picture."

"I don't remember that," I said accusingly.

"Okay, whatever, but you did."

"Why didn't you pick me up and carry me inside after I went to sleep?"

"I was going to but I came in here to watch a movie for a little bit," he gestured toward the television which had a blank blue screen showing like a movie had ended and the television stayed on. He continued, "And I fell asleep watching it." He tossed the blankets aside and rummaged through his dresser for a t-shirt and shorts. "Get some sleep," he said.

"I can't believe that you just—"

But he cut me off, "Ellen, shut up. It's too early in the morning."

More than wanting to continue the conversation, I didn't like the command that he'd given me. "You can't just tell me to shut up like that!" I shouted.

He walked away and kept walking. I stood and started to snap at his heels, but he was gone, grabbing his shoes and jogging through the kitchen and out the back door. I ran up the stairs and watched him pass through the clearing and go toward Bert Road before resisting the struggle to follow him and keep arguing. Instead, I went to bed.

When I woke, I was resolved. I would run the marathon with David. No more going back and forth. Just moving straight ahead. I told him with conviction and we began at the University track, then on side-by-side treadmills at the gym. He added a bicycle seat for Maggie to his bike and we pedaled over the October leaves, watching the glow from windows through the neighborhoods pass by us. We explored the town. Helmet on, I puffed up the hills, pressing my toes into the pedals and coasting downhill with arms dangling by my sides while Maggie's stretched out wide and she laughed with her head thrown back.

I taught a full load that semester at the education center on post, but Dr. Hamilton talked me into taking one course on main campus. Jefferson was convicted on all counts, and I almost forgot about the manuscript. The summer motivated the students to forget about the murders. Amnesia relieved the administration. While I scrambled to finish grading quizzes before class, a student interrupted. "Hi, Dr. Masters," she said with her head peeking through the crack in the door.

"Can I help you?" I asked, failing to recognize her at first. She had been a student in my spring class, the same one Jefferson had attended, but she earned the highest grade in the course. "Oh, how have you been?" I asked.

"Great! I decided to major in history and wanted to thank you for teaching such an interesting and investigative course. It totally motivated me."

"I'm pleased to hear that," I said. After an awkward pause, I asked, "Is there something I can help you with?"

She looked behind herself, down the hallway, then came into the room and shut the door behind her. "You remember that I was in the same class with Philip Jefferson?"

I nodded.

"Well, I wanted to ask if you got the papers I left under your door last year?"

"You left those? Where did you get them?" I asked, trying to maintain my relief and my curiosity.

"Yeah, I got them from my aunt," she said in a whisper. "She's a guard at the prison where Jefferson was held when he was first arrested. She just thought his writings were interesting and there might be something in the papers."

"Okay?" I wanted to keep her talking, instead of seeming like an interrogator.

"She didn't want me to tell anybody where the papers came from, but it has been bugging me, like I needed to tell you."

"Why did you leave them here, in *my* office?"

"I don't know," she said. Her face turned pink and she looked down at the floor. "I just thought you might want it since he was in your class." She scratched at the bracelet

227

on her wrist. "I didn't know him or anything like that," she said.

"I didn't know him either," I said. "He barely attended the class."

"Please, don't tell anyone where it came from," she said.

"I won't. They're already gone, the papers," I said, "So, you don't need to worry about them anymore. He didn't write anything significant in there."

"Oh, good," she said, finally making eye contact with me and smiling. "That's a big relief to me."

"Me too," I smiled. "Just put it behind you and focus on your classes and enjoying the semester."

"Yeah, I will." She sat in the chair in front of my desk. "I also wanted to ask if you'd be my advisor?"

"Don't you already have an advisor?"

"I had a different major, and now I need a history advisor."

"Sure, just bring the advisor change form to me."

"I already have one."

We were both relieved, but not as we pretended about my new role as her advisor. We could stop carrying the burden and the mystery of Jefferson's papers. I knew where they had originated, and she knew that they had gone nowhere.

I slept, ran, and moved through my life with an ease that was previously unknown to me. David and I continued to train for the marathon, and my loss of anxiety allowed me to focus without the influence of fear. David and I ran alongside the river, the wind against our backs at lunchtime on Fridays, pressing us toward the goal. We reached twenty miles and that would be the farthest distance we would run during our training. The marathon would be my longest run, and David advised that keeping it as a goal in that way would help to motivate me during the final miles of the race. I wasn't so certain. When I ran the half marathon with Jordan, I knew that I could reach the end because I had already done it outside of the race. I felt confident in my abilities. For the full, I felt doubt and dreaded the possibility of letting myself down. What if I hit the wall after mile twenty? What if I fell? Legs unable to move. What if I dehydrated? What if there were unexpected hills? I wasn't running Cumberland as usual to prepare me for hills. In the half, there was a big hill at mile seven and Jordan and I were proud of ourselves for pushing over it. Like spinning webs, we stretched ourselves right up to the next point. I'll have to remember that, stretch along to twenty-six point two miles. Spider legs lengthening. Could that really help? Maybe, just move and stretch and lengthen. Breathe, and don't forget to relax my breathing. Easy in and out.

I was surprised by how quickly the time passed, and I faced the twenty-six miles on race morning. I felt sick but focused on coaching myself with headphones and numbing out the sounds in the corral around me. David bounced on his tiptoes in little bursts. His music already blasted into one ear, and the other earphone hung down his shoulder. He wore a brown t-shirt printed with red and black lettering on the back, *Master Hound,* and on mine, *Hound Master.* As a gift for me, he designed the t-shirts. On the front, he had created a silhouette drawing of a woman running with a dog.

"You have to do something to keep you motivated," he said. "And this way, if we get separated, we'll have matching shirts and can find one another."

The crowd stretched, bounced, swayed, made rubber bands of their legs and arched their elbows overhead, clapped, chewed gum, and gnawed at the energy, clawing into their minds to stretch and lean forward, hold the stride to perfection, reel in the mind and pump the heart, lube the machine with sweat. We were going, moving, trotting, going, bounding down the center of the street with a brisk wind at dawn, gray and threatening to be icy later, pinching in the clouds around the city and menacing us with a watery film of stillness. Legs pushed by me. Pumping breaths and spitting coughs. Streams of snot, and tendons leaning against the curve in the sidewalk. Water stations and thumbs up to David. Pulling away the headphone at mile ten to talk. David saying suddenly, "I'm glad you decided to do this with me."

"Me too, so far," I smiled. "I think it's gonna be okay. I think we're gonna be okay too, you know?"

"I'm glad to hear you say that because I thought you'd divorce me a couple of years ago, and you had good reason to."

"No, we're doing better. We're doing this. Hey, it's ten o'clock now. Jordan and Maggie should be on their way."

"I hope he gets a good spot," David said. "He's so damn proud of you for doing this. He'll probably have a megaphone out there to cheer for you."

We stopped talking again as we neared a turn-around that created a congested swirl of runners, as many were crowding around the water stations and into the race path. David and I kept going. "You want to stop?" he asked.

"Let's skip this one," I said.

"The next one is five more miles," he said. "You okay to keep going?"

I pointed and we moved around many of the racers, distancing ourselves from them and trying to create a space. I didn't feel invited as I did in the forests at Cumberland, as I did when David and I ran alongside the river. No breeze, no wide-open river or fields. In the gym, even on the treadmill, I could gaze out the window at the grass stretching out toward a tree beside the parking area. The marathon was road and sidewalk, concrete continuing and layered with runners. Little packs of people echoed by us, talking. One person might wheel by us as if their feet were pedaling an invisible machine. It looked so simple to glide forward like that.

"His gait looks painful," I said to David as we ran by a man whose legs looked bowed and pulled out at the knees, as if someone had kept his ankles tied together for so long that they'd almost become one solid piece at the bottom. They weren't connected but certainly gave the appearance of being barely snipped apart, so he ran with a short wobbling trot that looked as if the sharp points of his knees and the frail staff to his ankles would snap and splinter through the skin or pop apart like a grasshopper and allow him to fly when no one was looking, especially after we reached the water station at mile twenty and noticed him just behind us.

I became dizzy, but wiped the sweat away from my eyes and tried sucking down a gel with vitamins and sugar. My stomach began to turn and I slowed at mile twenty-two. David pulled out his headphones, "What's wrong?"

"I think I might be sick," I said. "You go on. I'll see you at the end."

"How are you sick?"

"Just go on," I waved him forward. "Please, go!" I shouted and put my earphones in. I scooted my feet in little sharp moves across the pavement and kept progressing. I knew that stopping would only prolong my chance to rest from the race. I had to make it to the end so that I could stop and rest. I was hitting the wall. This was it. My stomach bubbled and I noticed the portable toilets lined along the roadside about a half-mile ahead of me. I ran faster and was beside David when I veered into the darkness of the toilet. I barely made it before vomiting the sugary gel packet and water. I turned quickly and exited the stifling smell, sprinting toward the lettering on David's shirt. When I reached him, I tried to calm my breathing but it was loud and rhythmic. "You don't look so good," he said. "Maybe we should stop and sit down for a few minutes."

"I'm fine," I said. "Just shut up and keep going. I have to make it to the end so I can rest."

"We can rest right over there," he pointed toward the sidewalk where a few runners stood, drinking water, hands on hips. Another was stretching her shin against the lip of concrete.

"You're messing me up, David!" I shouted. "You're supposed to be coaching me, keeping me motivated, not telling me to quit."

"I didn't say that we should quit. I said that we could rest, but come on," he said. "We're at twenty-four, so let's finish this."

"You can go ahead of me," I said. "I know that you can run faster than this."

"You sure you're okay?"

I nodded.

"I'll see you at the end." He took a deep inhale and closed his eyes for a instant. His shoulders seemed to fall lower and he squared his arms, moving his legs faster and faster. I couldn't see him in the crowd after a minute. He turned into the stadium entrance. I pushed myself to go faster, to try to catch him, but I never saw him cross the finish line. I ran on until I was there, hearing my name over the speaker, and he was there with a drink and a washcloth. We were finished with a marathon and I was in shock. Turning in circles until I saw Jordan and Maggie with a bouquet of flowers, but my legs hurt and my body was tired. I felt beaten, not strong. I felt weakened, not accomplished. Jordan and Maggie took photos of us with our medals sticking to the sweat on our chests. David ate vanilla ice cream, but when I tried to drink my usual chocolate milk, I vomited in the nearest trashcan after two gulps. Even though David and Jordan recommended that I hydrate, I refused eating and drinking until late that night.

I couldn't walk down stairs normally for a week, and I didn't dare go down them the day after the marathon. David recuperated with few problems. After icing his legs that evening, he seemed as if he could run another one the next day. He did wait a week before running and then he only jogged two miles and rested again. I whined and wondered if my legs would ever be the same again. "Why didn't one of you forewarn me?" I asked David and Jordan as we ate dinner one evening a couple of weeks after the race. It was approaching the Christmas season, and we built a fire and drank soup out of coffee mugs.

"You wouldn't have done it," Jordan said. "Don't you even feel a little satisfied with yourself? With your body's ability?"

"No because it hurt so badly."

"It won't the next time," David said.

"Next time? Forget it," I said. "I'll be the one meeting you two at the finish line with Maggie." I felt peaceful, like I didn't need to prove anything. David was satisfied with himself, and I had been there to watch him run and allow him to teach me how to run that distance.

I wasn't plagued by the murder trial. Jefferson had received the death penalty and was scheduled for execution for the murders. I was almost finished with classes for the semester, lecturing on automatic pilot and administering grades as if they were timed medication.

Fran called and we walked regularly at Cumberland Park, and I accepted her guidance. Even if some topics could trigger tension between us, I finally had a friend.

Aunt Darcy put her part of the property on the market, but we didn't worry about anyone wanting to purchase it during a recession. Jordan worried, but I tried to alleviate his concerns by promising to build another residence on my part of the property if Aunt Darcy's part was sold. David said, "No one will buy her part without this part, so you two shouldn't be concerned."

Maggie played and wanted to start school. She sang and squealed at the bicycle Santa left on Christmas morning. Jordan bought a video game and we all played until our thumbs were numb and we wished for snow, but that didn't fall until January, when Jordan met a girlfriend.

That same month, David, Maggie and I drove halfway to meet Darryl and Mother at a restaurant for an afternoon of awkward tension. I knew with certainty that Mother and I would never recover. Some parts can't be wired back together, so crumbled that no one can fix them. Just as I knew that I'd never see my brother until our mother or

Darryl died and we had to manage their affairs, attend the funeral, make arrangements, and divide it all. There was no one else. I had searched for him on the computer after David told me he performed surgeries on disfigured children. He was there, his website and blog, photos of him, and it felt unreal, a tearing and a longing to have my family back, to recover, to have our dad. What would life have been like then? He was there, Dr. Tyler Masters, with the same kind eyes that our dad had in photos. The blonde hair that matched my own. He was rougher around the edges and more beatnik than I had expected. I vibrated like electricity inside and had to turn off the computer so I wouldn't scream. I couldn't look at him anymore, but still I shouted, "How could you just forget me? You were my brother? You betrayer! You could have called, all these years. You're intelligent enough to know!" I shook as a child who tightens her fists and clenches her teeth in a tantrum.

David stood in the doorway, and later he told me that he had been standing there the whole time, at first thinking that I was cybersexing with someone or looking up some man's profile, because I kept glancing up as if I were doing something secretive. Of course, it felt that way toward myself, as if I were betraying my child self for even caring about Tyler at all. My child self wanted to pretend that he was either dead or miserable or a complete asshole somewhere, and that he would be unhappy inside forever. But he wasn't most of those things. He was better than I wanted him to be. He seemed better than I, and I was overcome with fury.

David crossed the room and wrapped his arms around me quickly and squeezed me, just held me there against him in silence. I never experienced anyone hold me with such compassion and force at the same time.

11 OVEREXPOSURE

Honestly, hating one another had often been easier than loving one another. When we loved one another, the most intense pain emerged during our separations. Maybe we had created the hate after all, to be able to deal with what war had brought us. Or where war had taken us. The seventh deployment would be the last. David promised. He loved me again. His return home for almost a year gave us time, no training, just early morning breakfasts as a family. He and I ran together in the afternoons. I could never hear him breathing while we ran, and he, always slightly ahead of me, was a forward wingman. To see him there was an antidote; even if he was going away from me, I was going with him. We were traveling as an entity. That's when Nuance bounded back into my life too. The February cold caused him to need us, our warm home and the scraps from our meals. He finally slept inside, on the floor next to David's side of the bed. David even taught him how to fetch his running shoes.

After our runs, David picked Maggie up from kindergarten. When March warmed the landscape, I could often find them fishing at the lake, casting out and throwing the fish back in again. He made up stories with Maggie. Tickled her. Acted like a real dad.

Then, we knew the orders were coming... fast approaching, a surge of adrenaline to try to fit in everything. Go to all of our favorite places. Try something new. Run, run, run. Try to outrun it. But it came, the gym on post. The men, their pregnant wives, the women and their crying babies who would be living with Grandma while Momma is gone to war. That intense woman in a line of men, their medic. Those grandparents who wanted their soldier to smile in the photo. "Smile, Baby, in the picture with Daddy." Babies crying, wriggling away.

"How much longer is it going to be? Will the General speak?" *How much time do we have left before letting go?* David went to find out. He wanted to walk us out to the car. He didn't want us to wait in that line of people.

"Don't cry," he said. "Just please don't cry, this time." We stood outside and I fought with those reservoirs in my eyes. Maggie played with another child. The children all seemed to fade into a disconnection, a place of play and meeting friends that both relieved me and made me feel like a liar.

"I'll call you as soon as possible, all the time. We'll be on Skype. We'll be talking the entire time during this one. This one is different. Remember. Ellen, we can do it this time and it's the last time. I have a different job when I get back, okay?... Okay?"

"I know," I said, taking a deep breath, making up my mind to be strong, no victimization. I could help him by being strong. "Yes, you're right. We can do this. You'll call. You'll get one of those terrible Afghan cell phones. I know. I know." I leaned against him, would have collapsed if I could. "Just let me stay right here for five whole minutes, please."

He stood against the bricks of the building and I flattened myself against him. We were together and he held onto me. I guess we stayed that way for ten minutes before Maggie ran over and squeezed between our legs. She wrapped her arms around David's legs.

"We're all together," she said. "I'll miss you, Daddy."

"I'll miss you and Mommy, too. You gonna call me on the computer and tell me some stories? It's gonna be all right. Okay?"

He walked us to the car, buckled my seatbelt after putting Maggie in her car seat. He squeezed into my lap and kissed me. We laughed when his back pressed against the car horn and that made me long for him even more, but he waved us out of the parking space and pointed for us to go. In my rearview mirror, I saw him watch us drive away, the gun slung over his shoulder, one on his thigh. His uniform would be his skin for the next year. He waved. I put my hand out the window and waved back to him.

Ten minutes later, he called from the bus. I hadn't even made it home. "Did you turn on the radio yet?" he asked. I hadn't. "Turn it on, and I'll call you back when I get on the plane."

We learned to communicate through music, and it was sustenance when nothing else seemed to be. I could play a song over and over, the music goes round and round, as the old song said. I could lie to myself if I didn't know what to do and I could conjure David in my dreams. Yesterday seemed like a lifetime ago. I hardly knew how to proceed. I could sing along and the songs could wait on the calls with me. I could escape during the runs. Music had never been a requirement during my runs until the seventh deployment. I would run Cumberland Park, singing, and people thought I was crazy sometimes, especially Jordan. But he said, "You in love again?"

I worried and fought back the fears, the anxiety, tried to choose a goal and stay focused on it, like David had suggested. His plan was working most of the time. We both struggled, suddenly having to walk away in order to go deal with our anger, having a quick verbal outburst of rage, but they became shorter and shorter.

Jordan said to me after David left, "Well, he did it. He's saying, 'Mission Accomplished' right now." We sat underneath the carved tree at Cumberland and Jordan pressed the tip of his knife into the roots, rolling the bark in a brown, beveled swirl. He carved an "E" into the roots.

"What do you mean?" I asked, thinking that we'd passed the tree, met at the tree, sometimes called it the RIP tree and sometimes called it the Love Tree. Both were spoken for on the tree's trunk and branches, even its roots—the initials JP & FH alongside Blake Loves Holly, which was intertwined with R.I.P. Bobby 10/16/98. The beech tree's trunk was covered in tattooed carvings from many knives, for all sorts of endearments, but Jordan and I never carved into it, not in thirty years.

"I probably shouldn't tell you this, but I'm going to," Jordan said. "He's really having a hard time and has been trying to work on himself by helping you. See, if he's helping to heal you, then he's healing himself. It's so uncanny, but your anger is the same way he feels on the inside, too. He has the same anger. He has the same fears. Everything is the same. But, he made a conscious decision to… well, in a way, suppress his own recovery process in order to help you so that your family, his family, could be in a positive place. You see, soldiers feel responsible for their families' struggles at the same time that they're angry with the family for failing to see the soldier's struggle. The soldier is aware of both sides... sides of civilian and military, sides of life and death, sides of freedom and confinement. It's a huge burden that you can't understand unless you've lived it, and you only partially live it, and you're only partially traumatized by comparison, so that's why his anger was directed at you. Of all the people in his life, you should feel his burden the most... and you should sometimes lay aside your own burden in order to consider his... that's what a lot of soldiers think about their families and why they struggle so much with reintegration, why both sides struggle." Jordan had carved my name, ELLEN, into the tree root that ran through the moss in front of my feet.

"So, you two have been talking?" I asked. The beech tree contained the perfect stiff umbrella form for sitting under. It also had soft gray bark, speckled and dappled with tan patterns. The limbs were slightly knobby and thin and birthed scallop-edged green wedges of leaves.

"Yeah, when we ran together or went out for a beer," Jordan said.

"You said that he was saying 'mission accomplished.' What do you mean by that? 'Cause if there's something going on that I don't know about, you better tell me, Jordan!" I became anxious and started to stand. The tree lived above the path, on a shaded bank close to the lake, where moss grew as a cushion for those who needed to leave a mark on a place.

"No, it's not like that," Jordan said, continuing his carving, "I just told you what I meant. David told me that he was going to put off his own recovery process until after this deployment, and that in the meantime, he thought that helping you and learning how to really see the duality would keep him focused, and he could avoid alienating you. He pushed back his anger and defensiveness. He took it all as a learning experience and a challenge, trying to understand you, and I think it was a good distraction and pretty interesting for him after all."

"I don't get it," I said, completely bewildered by Jordan's confession of David's plan.

"You were his real life example of PTSD. You reflected his own self back to him, even though it was caused by different events. Many of the reactions are the same. Somehow, he started to realize." Jordan had finished the second word in his tree carving and was moving on to the next. Sweat created a steady drip from his nose and he sank the tip of his knife into the bark and peeled back a line for the next letter.

"How? How did he realize what to do?"

"I don't know," Jordan said. "He just did and we'd talk about it, like I said, when we ran or went to the pub… I'd like to believe that I did help him, by telling him that I thought it was a good idea since it seemed to be working for him."

"I still don't get it. How did he change the pattern of his mind?"

"Control," Jordan said. "Little by little. Just like quitting smoking. Just because you quit doesn't mean that your mind automatically stops nagging you and your body stops creating the chemical desire for a cigarette. The addiction, the pain, still exists, persists, even after you stop smoking, for a while after. I think PTSD is the same. You stop the reactive behavior, but the mind and body still try to trap you into that pattern." Sweat circled Jordan's face in a stream and cascaded onto the collar of his t-shirt. His green eyes looked bright as the leaves, looked soft as the moss, and he smiled. "I think the two of you will be okay," he said. "You've been through a lot and have dealt with it this year, so maybe that means you've cleared it, you know, you'll be able to move on and enjoy life. The marathon showed me that you can do it. You can move forward and push yourself to a new level of living a better life." He sighed and lifted the bottom of his t-shirt so that he could wipe his face. "There," he said pointing at his carving. ELLEN LOVES DAVID sank into the tree's root. I traced my palm over the rough edges of the letters and felt their smooth interiors with the tip of my finger.

I tried to guess David's locations when he called. Was he calling from Maine, during that second phone call? Then, Manas? A package arrived from there about two weeks later. He called from Kabul and gave me a cell phone number. I paid up the Skype and tried to connect. The call failed. On the second try, I could hear him but he couldn't understand my words. He kept saying, "I can hear your voice, Ellen, but I can't understand what you're saying. I don't know if you can hear me," he said. "So be quiet if you can hear me well." I was silent. "Just listen," he said. First, he whispered the sentences of our absent bodies. I closed my eyes. Then, he told me about the attacks from that day. He said, "It's intense here right now. We can't convoy out for the camp until things settle down for a couple of days. I'll call you later, okay? I'll let you know when we make it. I miss you. I love you, Ellen. Tell Maggie."

David called from the camp three days later. I wouldn't let him get a description in about his experience. "You'll never believe what Jordan and I ran into today on our run along the bluff," I said. "Just guess."

"A rattlesnake," he said.

"No." I laughed. "I still can't believe it." And I didn't allow any more guesses, but jumped straight into the details. "We decided to go all the way around, and instead of running down Bert Road, we followed the trails along the bluff since it's still early enough that the weeds haven't taken over. I was telling Jordan, 'I feel so energized and alive right now. So much better than when I trained last year.' And he tried to dare me to catch him, but I didn't want to race anyway. He took off ahead of me, down a dip in the trail, and I couldn't see him for a few minutes, but then he was coming back toward me with a serious look on his face. I didn't even have time to process it, and he passed right by me and said, 'Bear. There's a bear coming down the trail this way.'

"'Real funny!' I said. But he turned and grabbed my arm, and said, 'Seriously, there's a black bear walking down the trail. I'm not joking.'

"I could see the fear in his eyes, David, and I felt every part of my body vibrating. We were at the top of the dip. Well, I was at the top of the dip and Jordan was walking back down it in the opposite direction. He shouted, 'Come on, Ellen! There's a real bear coming this way.'

"I said, 'I see it. Holy shit!' And, Jordan started to run, and I yelled at him because the bear was moving in a trot, coming right at us, 'Don't run, Jordan! Don't run! It'll chase you!'"

David interrupted me, "Are you serious?"

"Yes, David. A bear! Just listen. I am so proud of myself because I just whirled around and faced the bear and started shouting, 'Go away, bear! Go on! Get out of here! Go away, bear!' over and over, and I stretched my arms over my head, and made them claw-like toward him while I screamed."

"How close was it to you?" David asked.

"About ten feet."

"How big was it?" he asked.

"Oh, about a three-hundred pound black bear."

"Did it stand up?"

"No, it just stayed down on all fours and slowed down. It stared at me, and I just kept shouting, 'Go away, bear!' Then, it went around us, took the high path over the dip, through the field. I shouted for a while, to make sure it would keep going."

"Where was Jordan?"

"He was down in the dip of the trail, just standing there, waiting and shouting, 'Where is it? Where did it go?'"

"You're serious?" David asked again.

"Yes, totally serious. I wish that one of us had a camera, but I don't think I would've remembered to use it. My instinct just kicked in, and I had a tiny flash of Granna telling me to make myself big if I ever saw a bear in the wild. I never expected it to happen in my life, much less on our property. Can you believe it?"

"That's amazing," he said. "Did you call TWRA?"

"Why do I need wildlife rescue? The bear didn't bother anybody. I don't think it will, and Granna wouldn't want me to report it. I had to convince Jordan that we should just leave it alone."

"You need to do a little more research," David said. "When did this happen?"

"This morning," I said.

"I think you should consider calling someone," he said, "just letting the county know that they have a bear population is probably a good idea. Bear haven't lived there in decades. Ellen, this is a big deal, to say the least."

"I know that, which is exactly why I don't want them tracking its possible hibernation to our side of the cave."

"Think about this seriously," he said. "Well, what was it like to stare into the eyes of a three-hundred pound bear?"

"Survival instinct. Powerful. I was definitely energized after that. And Jordan said that he was impressed."

"I bet he did," David said. "I am too, and I'm glad you're both okay."

David and I talked every day for two weeks, and he continued to ask me about the bear while I avoided notifying the county by saying that I forgot or didn't have time. The calls were a little clearer, and I wrote love letters, insisting that we had to maintain our postal fidelity. He liked the phrase and said that he was promoting postal fidelity to all of his men. About three weeks later, he called one day and sounded incredibly tense—a brief call, the line was crackling and fading in and out. He said that there was no privacy, tense situations all around, shady interpreter, and he had sent a package from Kabul. He emailed a day later that the phones had been shut down, but not the computers. There had been an attack at the camp. Two soldiers died on both sides. He would call as soon as possible.

He called four hours later. Generators sounded like helicopters in the background. His interpreter had shown up wearing all black that morning and had disappeared before the attack. He tried to save one of the soldiers but he couldn't. He asked about home, wanted me to talk about home more than anything. What was Maggie learning in kindergarten now? Was she excited about summer vacation? How was the garden? Had I seen that big buck while I was running? Did Jordan take the new job? Had he remembered to fill in the rut that had formed on the driveway? When did my classes finish? Was Nuance sticking around? Too many questions that we didn't want to ask or answer.

*****

The rivers rushed in after creeping up slowly over the course of a day. The creeks gushed and swelled after the rain continued. April drenched the peonies; water-logged and soggy, I didn't think we would sell them. In May, I ran in the rain showers, slipping in the mud. At first, I thought I was hallucinating again. The waters couldn't rise so fast without a proper warning from the Corps of Engineers. Certainly, they would have told us that the rivers were at capacity. Students said the sidewalks by the river were submerged, and the river lapped at the road. I noticed the deer had moved in closer to my house, bedding in the forest around me and eating down my early rosebuds. But I knew for certain it wasn't a hallucination when I saw the people who lived in a five-hundred-year flood plain trying to boat their baby beds, jewelry, and quilts down the street. Our house was safe on the hill overlooking the lake that had become a river, as it had been originally intended before they dammed it up not far from the mouth of Cumberland Cave.

The lake and river merged into a swampy, slow motion. The deer sought higher ground earlier in the week. Fawns were in our yard. I should have known something was going to happen. Part of me recognized it when I told myself that it represented a new beginning, adapting to a shifting landscape, only I hadn't realized how shifting that landscape would be. The homes across from Cumberland were down, underwater, under the hill across from the cave. I always considered the cave my own and sensed the transformations before they happened. Suddenly, this one surprised me. Then, the Corps made an announcement: the rivers hadn't yet crested, and we could expect major flooding. The losses to homes and properties were devastating. Some sportsmen were paddling kayaks down the streets. Jordan's house was flooded and that ruined any plans for Darcy to sell.

I was numb, angry and desperate. I dragged the canoe out of the basement. Maggie was eager and grasped the side and tried to pull it toward the water. She grabbed her wading boots out of the back corner of her closet and nearly tripped trying to quickly push her feet into them.

While tugging the canoe, she said, "I wish my daddy wouldn't be dead so that he could help us right now."

Gifts from David had continued to arrive in the mail after his death just after our last conversation. I didn't say any of the words I would have wanted him to hear if I had known, if I would have treated it as the last time he would hear my voice. Packages. Letters. At the post office. In the mailbox. Camel leather flip-flops. Lapis lazuli. Bells. Beads. The sheer black negligee. Wine glasses. Plans to take an assignment that allowed him to remain at home. Plans to make a baby during his eighteen days of leave that would arrive in two months. I piled all the gifts in the bottom of the canoe, clanging against the metal. Papers slid underneath my seat. I didn't have to drag the canoe very far until Nuance jumped inside, ready for the ride. I placed Maggie in, buckled her lifejacket, and started to paddle us away from our home and toward the widening rivers that had converged on the town. I didn't have an intended destination in mind. We were just moving with the current through the plum grove, toward the sunset.

Navigating through a swampy area of trees, I wondered if the current would become too strong and if I had made a mistake. The sun pushed away from a cloud, but stood behind a dark blot on the trees in front of me. I squinted until the dot came into focus and realized it was a plum on the family trees. Small red fruits grew on several trees. I tried to grab one as we passed underneath a branch and caused the canoe to rock. Nuance stood and barked out at the water and barked once up at me.

"I'm just trying to get a plum," I said to him.

"I want a plum," Maggie said.

I tried to steer through the current toward a tree with a branch so loaded with fruit that the tip dipped into the water. Little branches and leaves from last year, among other debris, were caught in the crook of the branch where it met the tree trunk. I made it just close enough to lean and pull the end of tree with a hard tug, grabbing hold of a plum at the same time. The river flowed more quickly and carried larger pieces of wood and trash. It licked at the trunks of tulip poplar trees and slopped its mouth toward the higher branches when possible. I saw the roofs of two old barns collapse into the brown gullet of the river. One of them had been Guthrie's. I thought of the river's feast, how it replenished the farmland and saturated the fields with its sediment, while the current grabbed at the edges of our canoe. I bit into the plum to see if it was ripe for

Maggie. "I want it," she said and pouted from her seat in the canoe.

"Yeah, it's quite good," I said, squishing my eyelids in a happy sensation. The joy I felt stirred up the pain. Any extreme feeling seemed like a betrayal, so I tried to remain unexposed. I leaned forward and passed the plum to Maggie while avoiding Nuance's attempt to quickly lick the exposed fruit as it passed over his head from my hand to Maggie's.

When we floated past the No Faces, I said, "Look Maggie, they have no heads and don't have to worry about keeping them above water." I dropped the wine glasses into the water. The first gulped under and the other one sunk in a wash of brown.

"They should have heads to see the water," Maggie said. "It's so much water. Everywhere." The flip-flops floated and chimed, before swirling and bobbing under the water.

Nuance whined and turned in a circle. Maggie wrapped her arm around his neck. "What's wrong, boy?" she asked.

The helicopters turned in the distance. Even though I couldn't see them yet, I could hear that they were low and loud. Nuance was afraid of the helicopters. At our house, he hid under the tables, and if he were outside, he crawled underneath the porch or the deck. I tried to paddle closer to the tree line just beyond the statues, while we were being pulled along.

I handed the lapis to Maggie and told her to aim at where the heads of the statues should have been. She didn't want to and stared at the blue stones in her palm.

"My daddy mailed these," she said. "I'll put them in my purse he sent to me." The helicopters moved swiftly in the direction of downtown, so they didn't cross us overhead.

Just after they passed, I heard shouts that caused Nuance to bark. He tried to move to the back of the canoe and caused us to rock haphazardly. "Stay!" I commanded. He tried to scoot his body underneath the seat. "Maggie," I said, "please pet Nuance under his chin so that he'll calm down. I don't want him to flip over the canoe." Maggie squatted next to Nuance and scratched his neck. She sucked on the plum, extracting every drop of juice from the fruit, while the extra dripped down her chin. I turned to see another canoe approaching from my right, and Jordan called out again for me to stop.

But so much had stopped and I didn't want to turn in a current again. I wanted to do something to propel me forward, out of the unexpected. Even my memories contained the shock of the unknown, and I wanted an action that was permanent and contained an expected outcome.

When Jordan reached us, he tied our canoes together. Nuance yelped happily and placed his head on the edge of the canoe, stretching to retrieve a few pats on the head from Jordan.

"What do you think about our plums, Maggie?" Jordan asked.

"Good," she smiled. "Really good."

"I'm so surprised," Jordan said to Maggie. "I never wanted to give up on them." Maggie laughed. Nuance whined and barked in a timid whimper. Maggie reassured him that everything was okay, especially since Jordan was there now.

"Ellen, you shouldn't be out here," Jordan said. "There's just too much water."

"Just let me do what I have to," I said and placed a stack of papers on my lap and Jordan watched as I folded them into boats. He paddled and guided us through the old cemetery and toward the tree line, out of the expanse. Maggie tipped the edges of the paper boats into the current and laughed as they floated and turned. I couldn't fold Jefferson's cursive words fast enough. I held a few boats and set the tops of them on fire with a lighter before placing them in the water myself.

"I want a fire boat," Maggie said.

"I'll help her put it in the water," Jordan said, insisting that I pass a paper boat on fire back to him. He glanced at the paper before quickly putting it into the water while allowing Maggie's fingertips to graze its quickly wilting edges.

"Don't," he said, "You'll regret it," when I passed him another one of David's letters, twisted and set on fire. I looked down at the remaining mail in my lap and read the letters IED written about another soldier, and I folded it down so small and burned myself trying to set it on fire. I saw Jordan wince from the corner of my eye. After I burned David's letters, Jefferson's confession, and the newspaper articles, Jordan turned us around to face the night's darkness and began paddling home.

ABOUT THE AUTHOR

Shana Thornton earned an M.A. with Honors from Austin Peay State University. She is the Assistant Director for the Institute of Arts and Social Engagement, as well as Editor-in-Chief of Her Circle Ezine, an online magazine featuring women's literature, arts and activism from around the globe. She lives with her husband, their children, and her dog Mojo. She currently has two more novels in-progress. To learn more about Shana and *Multiple Exposure*, visit http://www.thorncraftpublishing.com, her blog at http://www.shanathornton.blogspot.com and follow her on twitter @shanathornton.

www.ingramcontent.com/pod-product-compliance
Lightning Source LLC
Chambersburg PA
CBHW030404020726
47493CB00003B/932